THE DINNER

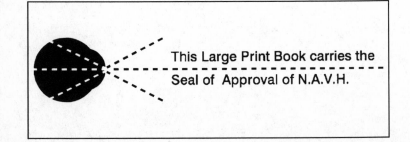

This Large Print Book carries the
Seal of Approval of N.A.V.H.

THE DINNER

HERMAN KOCH

*Translated from the Dutch
by Sam Garrett*

THORNDIKE PRESS
A part of Gale, Cengage Learning

GALE
CENGAGE Learning®

Detroit • New York • San Francisco • New Haven, Conn • Waterville, Maine • London

GALE
CENGAGE Learning®

LIBRARY OF CONGRESS CATALOGING-IN-PUBLICATION DATA

Koch, Herman, 1953–
  [Diner. English]
  The dinner / by Herman Koch ; translated from the Dutch by Sam Garrett.
      pages ; cm. — (Thorndike Press large print basic)
  ISBN-13: 978-1-4104-5929-9 (hardcover)
  ISBN-10: 1-4104-5929-2 (hardcover)
  1. Families—Netherlands—Fiction. 2. Amsterdam (Netherlands)—Fiction. 3. Large type books. I. Garrett, Sam. II. Title.
  PT5881.21.O25D56513 2013b
  839.31'364—dc23   2013006606

Published in 2013 by arrangement with Hogarth, an imprint of the Crown Publishing Group, a division of Random House, Inc.

Printed in Mexico
2 3 4 5 6 7 17 16 15 14 13

THE DINNER

■ ■ ■ ■

APERITIF

■ ■ ■ ■

1

We were going out to dinner. I won't say which restaurant, because next time it might be full of people who've come to see whether we're there. Serge made the reservation. He's always the one who arranges it, the reservation. This particular restaurant is one where you have to call three months in advance — or six, or eight, don't ask me. Personally, I'd never want to know three months in advance where I'm going to eat on any given evening, but apparently some people don't mind. A few centuries from now, when historians want to know what kind of crazies people were at the start of the twenty-first century, all they'll have to do is look at the computer files of the so-called "top" restaurants. That information is kept on file — I happen to know that. If Mr. L. was prepared to wait three months for a window seat last time, then this time he'll wait for five months for a table beside

9

the men's room — that's what restaurants call "customer relations management."

Serge never reserves a table three months in advance. Serge makes the reservation on the day itself — he says he thinks of it as a sport. You have restaurants that reserve a table for people like Serge Lohman, and this restaurant happens to be one of them. One of many, I should say. It makes you wonder whether there isn't one restaurant in the whole country where they don't go faint right away when they hear the name Serge Lohman on the phone. He doesn't make the call himself, of course; he lets his secretary or one of his assistants do that. "Don't worry about it," he told me when I talked to him a few days ago. "They know me there; I can get us a table." All I'd asked was whether it wasn't a good idea to call, in case they were full, and where we would go if they were. At the other end of the line, I thought I heard something like pity in his voice. I could almost see him shake his head. It was a sport.

There was one thing I didn't feel like that evening. I didn't feel like being there when the owner or on-duty manager greeted Serge Lohman as though he were an old friend. Like seeing how the waitress would lead him to the nicest table on the side facing the garden, or how Serge would act as though he had it all coming to him — that deep down he was still an ordinary guy, and that was why he felt entirely comfortable among other ordinary people.

Which was precisely why I'd told him we would meet in the restaurant itself and not, as he'd suggested, at the café around the corner. It was a café where a lot of ordinary people went. How Serge Lohman would walk in there like a regular guy, with a grin that said that all those ordinary people should above all go on talking and act as though he wasn't there — I didn't feel like that, either.

2

The restaurant is only a few blocks from our house, so we walked. That also brought us past the café where I hadn't wanted to meet Serge. I had my arm around my wife's waist; her hand was tucked somewhere inside my coat. The sign outside the café was lit with the warm red-and-white colors of the brand of beer they had on tap. "We're too early," I said to my wife. "I mean, if we go now, we'll be right on time."

"My wife." I should stop calling her that. Her name is Claire. Her parents named her Marie Claire, but in time Claire didn't feel like sharing her name with a magazine. Sometimes I call her Marie, just to tease her. But I rarely refer to her as "my wife" — on official occasions sometimes, or in sentences like "My wife can't come to the phone right now," or "My wife is very sure she asked for a room with a sea view."

On evenings like this, Claire and I make

the most of the moments when it's still just the two of us. Then it's as though everything is still up for grabs, as though the dinner date were only a misunderstanding, as though it's just the two of us out on the town. If I had to give a definition of happiness, it would be this: happiness needs nothing but itself; it doesn't have to be validated. "Happy families are all alike; every unhappy family is unhappy in its own way" is the opening sentence of Tolstoy's *Anna Karenina*. All I could hope to add to that is that unhappy families — and within those families, in particular the unhappy husband and wife — can never get by on their own. The more validators, the merrier. Unhappiness loves company. Unhappiness can't stand silence — especially not the uneasy silence that settles in when it is all alone.

So when the bartender at the café put our beers down in front of us, Claire and I smiled at each other in the knowledge that we would soon be spending an entire evening in the company of the Lohmans — in the knowledge that this was the finest moment of that evening, that from here on it would all be downhill.

I didn't feel like going to the restaurant. I never do. A fixed appointment for the immediate future is the gates of hell; the actual evening is hell itself. It starts in front of the mirror in the morning: what you're going to wear, and whether or not you're going to shave. At times like these, after all, everything is a statement, a pair of torn and stained jeans as much as a neatly ironed shirt. If you don't scrape off the day's stubble, you were too lazy to shave; two days' beard immediately makes them wonder whether this is some new look; three days or more is just a step from total dissolution. "Are you feeling all right? You're not sick, are you?" No matter what you do, you're not free. You shave, but you're not free. Shaving is a statement as well. Apparently you found this evening significant enough to go to the trouble of shaving, you see the others thinking — in fact, shaving already puts you behind 1–0.

And then I always have Claire to remind me that this isn't an evening like every other. Claire is smarter than I am. I'm not saying that out of some half-baked feminist sentiment or in order to endear women to me. You'll never hear me claim that "women in general" are smarter than men. Or more sensitive, more intuitive, that they are more "in touch with life" or any of the other horseshit that, when all is said and done, so-called sensitive men try to peddle more often than women themselves.

Claire just happens to be smarter than I am; I can honestly say that it took me a while to admit that. During our first years together, I thought she was intelligent, I guess, but intelligent in the usual sense: precisely as intelligent, in fact, as you might expect my wife to be. After all, would I settle for a stupid woman for any longer than a month? In any case, Claire was intelligent enough for me to stay with her even after the first month. And now, almost twenty years later, that hasn't changed.

So Claire is smarter than I am, but on evenings like this, she still asks my opinion about what she should wear, which earrings, whether to wear her hair up or leave it down. For women, earrings are sort of what shaving is for men: the bigger the earrings, the more significant, the more festive, the evening. Claire has earrings for every occasion. Some people might say it's not smart to be so insecure about what you wear. But that's not how I see it. The stupid woman is the one who thinks she doesn't need any help. What does a man know about things like that? the stupid woman thinks, and proceeds to make the wrong choice.

I've sometimes tried to imagine Babette asking Serge whether she's wearing the right

15

dress. Whether her hair isn't too long. What Serge thinks of these shoes. The heels aren't too flat, are they? Or maybe too high?

But whenever I do I realize there's something wrong with the picture, something that seems unimaginable: "No, it's fine, it's absolutely fine," I hear Serge say. But he's not really paying attention. It doesn't actually interest him, and besides, even if his wife were to wear the wrong dress, all the men would still turn their heads as she walked by. Everything looks good on her. So what's she moaning about?

This wasn't a hip café; the fashionable types didn't come here — it wasn't cool, Michel would say. Ordinary people were by far in the majority. Not the particularly young or the particularly old — in fact, a little bit of everything all thrown together, but above all ordinary. The way a café should be.

It was crowded. We stood close together, beside the door to the men's room. Claire was holding her beer in one hand; with the fingers of the other she was gently squeezing my wrist.

"I don't know," she said, "but I've had the impression recently that Michel is acting strange. Well, not really strange, but different. Distant. Haven't you noticed?"

"Oh yeah?" I said. "I guess it's possible."

I had to be careful not to look at Claire — we know each other too well for that — my eyes would give me away. Instead, I behaved as though I were looking around the café, as though I were deeply interested in the spectacle of ordinary people involved in lively conversation. I was relieved that I'd stuck to my guns, that we wouldn't be meeting the Lohmans until we reached the restaurant; in my mind's eye I could see Serge coming through the swinging doors, his grin encouraging the regulars above all to go on with what they were doing and pay no attention to him.

"He hasn't said anything to you?" Claire asked. "I mean, you two talk about other things. Do you think it might have something to do with a girl? Something he'd find it easier to tell you about?"

Just then the door to the men's room opened and we had to step to one side, pressed even closer together. I felt Claire's beer glass clink against mine.

"Do you think it has something to do with girls?" she asked again.

If only that were true, I couldn't help thinking. Something to do with girls . . . wouldn't that be wonderful, wonderfully normal, the normal adolescent mess. "Can

Chantal/Merel/Rose spend the night?" "Do her parents know? If Chantal's/Merel's/Rose's parents think it's okay, it's okay with us. As long as you remember . . . as long as you're careful when you . . . ah, you know what I mean . . . I don't have to tell you about that anymore. Right? Michel?"

Girls came to our house often enough, each one prettier than the next. They sat on the couch or at the kitchen table and greeted me politely when I came home. "Hello, Mr. Lohman." "You don't have to call me Mr. Lohman. Just call me Paul." And so they would call me "Paul" a few times, but a couple of days later it would be back to "Mr. Lohman" again.

Sometimes I would get one of them on the phone, and while I asked if I could take a message for Michel, I would shut my eyes and try to connect the girl's voice at the other end of the line (they rarely mentioned their names, just plunged right in: "Is Michel there?") with a face. "No, that's okay, Mr. Lohman. It's just that his cell phone is switched off, so I thought I'd try this number."

A couple of times, when I came in unannounced, I'd had the impression that I'd caught them at something, Michel and Chantal/Merel/Rose: that they were watching *The Fabulous Life* on MTV less innocently than they wanted me to think — that they'd been fiddling with each other, that they'd rushed to straighten their clothes and hair when they heard me coming. Something about the flush on Michel's cheeks — something heated, I told myself.

To be honest, though, I had no idea. Maybe nothing was going on at all, maybe all those pretty girls just saw my son as a good friend: a nice, rather handsome boy, someone they could show up with at a party — a boy they could trust, precisely because he wasn't the kind who wanted to fiddle with them right away.

"No, I don't think it's got anything to do with a girl," I said, looking Claire straight in the eye now. That's the oppressive thing about happiness, the way everything is out on the table like an open book: if I avoided looking at her any longer, she'd know for sure that something was going on — with girls, or worse.

"I think it's more like something with school," I said. "He's just done those exams; I think he's tired. I think he underestimated it a little, how tough his sophomore year would be."

Did that sound believable? And above all: did I look believable when I said it? Claire's gaze shifted quickly back and forth between my right and my left eye; then she raised her hand to my shirt collar, as though there were something out of place there that could be dealt with now, so I wouldn't look like an idiot when we got to the restaurant.

She smiled and placed the flat of her hand against my chest; I could feel two fingertips against my skin, right where the top button of my shirt was unbuttoned.

"Maybe that's it," she said. "I just think we both have to be careful that at a certain point he doesn't stop talking to us about things. That we'd get used to that, I mean."

"No, of course. But at his age, he kind of has a right to his own secrets. We shouldn't try to find out everything about him — then maybe he'd clam up altogether."

I looked Claire in the eye. My wife, I thought at that moment. Why shouldn't I call her my wife? My wife. I put my arm around her and pulled her close. Even if only for the duration of this evening. My wife and I, I said to myself. My wife and I would like to see the wine list.

"What are you laughing about?" Claire said. My wife said. I looked at our beer glasses. Mine was empty; hers was still three-quarters full. As usual. My wife didn't drink as fast as I did, which was another reason why I loved her, this evening perhaps more than other evenings.

"Nothing," I said. "I was thinking . . . I was thinking about us."

It happened quickly: one moment I was looking at Claire, looking at my wife, probably with a loving gaze, or at least with a twinkle, and the next moment I felt a damp film slide down over my eyes.

Under no circumstances was she to notice anything strange about me, so I buried my face in her hair. I tightened my grip around her waist and sniffed: shampoo. Shampoo and something else, something warm — the smell of happiness, I thought.

What would this evening have been like if, no more than an hour ago, I had simply waited downstairs until it was time to go, rather than climb the stairs to Michel's room?

What would the rest of our lives have been like?

Would the smell of happiness I inhaled from my wife's hair still have smelled only like happiness, and not, as it did now, like some distant memory — like the smell of something you could lose just like that?

21

3

"Michel?"

I was standing in the doorway to his room. He wasn't there. But let's not beat around the bush: I knew he wasn't there. He was in the garden, fixing the back tire of his bike.

I acted as though I hadn't noticed that; I pretended I thought he was in his room.

"Michel?" I knocked on the door, which was half-open. Claire was rummaging through the closets in our room; we would have to leave for the restaurant in less than an hour. She was still hesitating between the black skirt with black boots or the black pants with the DKNY sneakers. "Which earrings?" she would ask me later. "These, or these?" The little ones looked best on her, I would reply, with either the skirt or the pants.

Then I was in Michel's room. I saw right away what I was looking for.

I want to stress the fact that I had never

done anything like that before. Never. When Michel was chatting with his friends on the computer, I always stood beside him in such a way, with my back half-turned toward the desk, that I couldn't see the screen. I wanted him to be able to tell from my posture that I wasn't spying or trying to peek over his shoulder at what he'd typed on the screen. Sometimes his cell phone made a noise like panpipes, to announce a text message. He had a tendency to leave his cell phone lying around — I won't deny that I was tempted to look at it sometimes, especially when he had gone out. Who's texting him? What did he/she write? One time I had even stood there with Michel's cell phone in my hand, knowing that he wouldn't be coming back from the gym for another hour, that he had simply forgotten it. That was his old phone, a Sony Ericsson without the slide: the display showed **1 new message,** beneath an envelope icon. "I don't know what got into me; before I knew it, I had your cell phone in my hand and I was reading your message." Maybe no one would ever find out, but then again maybe they would. He wouldn't say anything, but he would suspect me or his mother nonetheless — a fissure that with the passing of time would expand into a substantial chasm. Our life as a happy

23

family would never be the same.

It was only a few steps to his desk in front of the window. If I leaned forward, I would be able to see him in the garden, on the flagstone terrace in front of the kitchen door, where he was fixing his inner tube — and if Michel looked up, he would see his father standing at the window of his room.

I picked up his cell phone, a brand-new black Samsung, and slid it open. I didn't know his pin code; if the phone was locked I wouldn't be able to do a thing, but the screen lit up almost right away with a fuzzy photo of the Nike swoosh, probably on one of his own clothes: his shoes, or the black knit cap he always wore, even at summertime temperatures and indoors, pulled down just above his eyes.

I scrolled down through the menu, which was roughly the same as the one on my own phone, a Samsung too, but six months old and therefore already hopelessly obsolete. I clicked on My Files and then on Videos. Sooner than expected, I found what I was looking for.

I looked and felt my head gradually grow cold. It was the sort of coldness you feel when you take too big a bite from an ice-cream cone or sip too greedily from an ice-cold drink.

The kind of coldness that hurt — from the inside out.

I looked again, and then I kept looking: there was more, I saw, but how much more was hard to say.

"Dad?"

Michel's voice came from downstairs, but then I heard him coming up the stairs. I snapped shut the slide on the phone and put it back on his desk.

"Dad?"

It was too late to hurry into our bedroom, to take a shirt or jacket out of the closet and pose with it in front of the mirror; my only option was to come out of Michel's own room as casually and believably as possible — as though I'd been looking for something.

As though I'd been looking for him.

"Dad." He had stopped at the top of the stairs and was looking past me, into his room. Then he looked at me. He was wearing his Nike cap; his black iPod nano dangled from a cord at his chest, and a set of headphones was slung around his neck. You had to give him credit — fashion and status didn't interest him. After only a few weeks, he had replaced the white earbuds with a standard set of headphones, because the sound was better.

Happy families are all alike: that popped into my mind for the first time that evening.

"I was looking for . . ." I began. "I was wondering where you were."

Michel had almost died at birth. Even these days I often thought back on that blue, crumpled little body lying in the incubator just after the caesarean. That he was here was nothing less than a gift — that was happiness too.

"I was patching my tire," he said. "That's what I wanted to ask you. Do you know if we've got valves somewhere?"

"Valves," I repeated. I'm not the kind of person who ever fixes a flat tire, who would even consider it. But my son — in the face of all evidence — still believed in a different version of his father, a version who knew where the valves were.

"What were you doing up here?" he asked suddenly. "You said you were looking for me. Why were you looking for me?"

I looked at him; I looked into the clear eyes beneath the black cap, the honest eyes that, I'd always told myself, formed a not-insignificant part of our happiness.

"Oh, nothing," I said. "I was just looking for you."

4

Of course they weren't there yet.

Without revealing too much about the location, I can say that the restaurant was hidden from the street by a row of trees. We were half an hour late already, and as we crossed the gravel path to the entrance, lit on both sides by electric torches, my wife and I discussed the possibility that for once, just this once, it might be we and not the Lohmans who arrived last.

"Want to bet?" I said.

"Why should I?" Claire said. "I'm telling you: they're not there."

A girl in a black T-shirt and a black floor-length pinafore took our coats. Another girl, in the same black outfit, was flipping through the reservations book lying open on a lectern.

She was only pretending not to recognize the name Lohman, I saw, and pretending badly at that.

"Lohman, was it?" She raised an eyebrow and made no effort to hide her disappointment at the fact that it wasn't Serge Lohman standing there in real life, but two people whose faces meant nothing to her.

I could have helped out by saying that Serge Lohman was on his way, but I didn't.

The lectern-with-book was lit from above by a thin, copper-colored reading lamp: Art Deco, or some other style that happened to be just in or just out of fashion at the moment. The girl's hair, black as the T-shirt and pinafore, was tightly tied up at the back in a wispy ponytail, as though it too had been designed to fit in with the restaurant's house style. The girl who had taken our coats wore her hair in the same tight ponytail. Perhaps it had something to do with regulations, I thought to myself — hygiene regulations, like surgical masks in an operating room: after all, this restaurant prided itself on serving "all-organic" products — the meat came from actual animals, but only animals that had led "a good life."

Across the top of the tight black hairdos, I glanced at the dining room — or at least at the first two or three visible tables. To the left of the entrance was the "open kitchen." Something was being flambéed at that very moment, from the looks of it, accompanied

28

by the obligatory clouds of blue smoke and dancing flames.

I didn't feel like doing this at all, I realized. Again, my aversion to the evening that lay ahead had become almost physical — a slight feeling of nausea, clammy hands, and the start of a headache somewhere behind my left eye — not quite enough, though, for me to actually become unwell or fall unconscious right there on the spot.

How would the black-pinafore girls react to a guest who collapsed before even getting past the lectern, I wondered. Would they try to haul me out of the way, drag me into the cloakroom — in any case somewhere where the other guests couldn't see me? They would probably prop me up on a stool behind the coatracks. Politely but firmly, they would ask whether they could call me a taxi. Off! Off with this man! — how wonderful it would be to let Serge stew, what a relief to be able to put a whole new twist on this evening.

I thought about what that would mean. We could go back to the café and order a plate of regular-person food. The daily special was ribs with fries, I'd seen on the blackboard above the bar — "Spareribs with fries €11.50" — probably less than a tenth of what we'd have to cough up here, each.

Another alternative would be to head straight for home, with at the very most a little detour past the video shop for a DVD, which we could then watch on the TV in the bedroom, lying on our roomy double bed: a glass of wine, some crackers, a few types of cheese to go with (one more little detour past the night shop), and a perfect evening would be complete.

I would be entirely self-effacing, I promised myself: I would let Claire choose the film, even though that meant it was bound to be some costume drama. *Pride & Prejudice, A Room with a View,* or something *Murder on the Orient Express*-ish. Yes, that was a possibility, I thought. I could pass out and we could go home. But instead I said: "Serge Lohman, the table close to the garden."

The girl raised her eyes from the page.

"But you're not Mr. Lohman," she said.

I cursed it all, right there: the restaurant, the girls in their black pinafores, this evening that was ruined even before it began — but most of all I cursed Serge, for this dinner he'd been so keen to arrange, a dinner for which he couldn't summon up the common courtesy to arrive on time. The way he never arrived on time anywhere; people in union halls across the country had to wait for him to show up too. The oh-so-busy Serge Loh-man was probably just running late — the meeting in the last union hall had run over, and now he was caught in traffic some-where. He didn't drive himself — no; driv-ing would be a waste of time for someone of Serge's status. He had a chauffeur to do that for him, so he could spend his precious time judiciously, reading important docu-ments.

"Oh, yes I am," I said. "Lohman is the name."

I kept my eyes fixed on the girl, who actu-ally blinked this time, and opened my mouth for the next sentence. The moment had come to cinch the victory, but it was a victory that smacked of defeat.

"I'm his brother," I said.

5

"The aperitif of the house, which we'd like to offer you today, is pink champagne."

The floor manager — or maître d', or supervisor, the host, the headwaiter, or whatever you call someone like that in restaurants like this — wasn't wearing a black pinafore. He had a three-piece suit on. The suit was pale green with blue pinstripes, and sticking out of the breast pocket was a blue hankie. What they call a pocket square.

His voice was subdued — almost too subdued to be heard above the hubbub in the dining room; there was something weird about the acoustics in this place, we'd noticed that as soon as we sat down at our table. (On the garden side! How did I guess!) If you didn't speak up, your words drifted away, up to the glass ceiling, which was also much higher than normal for a restaurant. Ridiculously high, you might say if you didn't know that the height of the ceiling had everything to do with the building's former use: a dairy, I thought I'd read somewhere, or a sewage disposal plant.

The floor manager stuck out his little finger and pointed at something on our table. At the tealight, I thought at first — instead of a candle or two, all the tables here had a tealight — but, no, the little finger was pointing out the plate of olives he had apparently just put there. In any case, I didn't remember it having been there before, not when he'd pulled back our chairs. When had he put the olives on the table? I was struck by a brief but intense wave of panic. This was happening to me more often lately: suddenly, pieces of the puzzle were gone — bites out of time, empty moments during which my thoughts must have been elsewhere.

"These are Greek olives from the Peloponnese, lightly doused in first-pressing, extra-virgin olive oil from Sardinia, and polished off with rosemary from . . ."

The floor manager leaned over our table slightly as he spoke, but we could still barely hear him: in fact, the last part of the sentence became completely lost, leaving us in the dark as to the origin of the rosemary.

Normally I don't give a damn about that kind of information — as far as I cared, the rosemary could have come from the Ruhr or the Ardennes, but it seemed like far too much fuss over one little plate of olives, and I had no intention of letting him off the hook that easily.

And then that pinky. Why would anyone point with their pinky? Was that supposed to be chic? Did it go with the suit with blue pinstripes, like the light-blue hankie? Or did he simply have something to hide? His other fingers, after all, were hidden the whole time. He kept them folded against the palm of his hand, out of sight — perhaps they were covered with flaky eczema or symptoms of some untreatable disease.

"Polished off?" I said.

"Yes, polished off with rosemary. Polished off means that they —"

"I know what it means," I said cuttingly — and perhaps a bit too loudly as well. A man and woman at the next table stopped talking for a moment and looked over at us: a man with a beard that was much too big, covering his face almost entirely, and a woman a little too young for him, in her late twenties, I figured; his second wife, I thought, or maybe some piece of fluff he was trying to impress by taking her to a restaurant like this. "Polished off," I repeated a little more quietly. "I know that doesn't mean that someone 'polished off' the olives. As in 'getting rid of them' or 'blowing them away.' "

From the corner of my eye I saw that Claire had turned her head and was gazing out the window. Things were not off to a good start: the evening was already ruined; there was no need for me to ruin it any further, especially not for my wife.

But then the manager did something I hadn't expected: I had more or less counted on seeing his mouth fall open, his lower lip start to tremble, and perhaps even the start of a blush, after which he would stammer some vague apology — something he'd been taught to rattle off, a protocol for dealing with rude and difficult guests — but instead he burst out laughing. What's more, it was a real laugh, not a fake or polite laugh.

"I'm sorry," he said, raising his hand to his mouth; the fingers were still curled up as they'd been when he pointed at the olives a minute ago; only the pinky was sticking out. "I never thought about it like that."

6

"What's with the suit?" I asked Claire after we had both said that we'd like the aperitif of the house and the floor manager had walked away from our table.

Claire raised her hand and brushed my cheek. "Sweetheart . . ."

"No, listen, it's weird. He's wearing it for a reason, right? You're not going to tell me that it's not on purpose?"

My wife gave me a lovely smile, the smile she always bestowed on me when she thought I was getting worked up about nothing — a smile that so much as said that she found all the fuss entertaining at best, but that I mustn't think for one second that she was going to take it seriously.

"And then the tealight," I said. "Why not a teddy bear? Or a silent vigil?"

Claire took a Peloponnesian olive from the plate and put it in her mouth. "Mmm," she said. "Lovely. Too bad, though — you really can taste that the rosemary has had too little sunlight."

Now it was my turn to smile; the rosemary, the manager had told us finally, was "homegrown," from a glassed-in herbarium behind the restaurant. "Did you notice how he points with his pinky all the time?" I said, opening the menu.

What I was in fact planning to do was look at the prices of the entrées: the prices in restaurants like this always fascinate me. Let me make it clear right away that I'm not stingy by nature; that has nothing to do with it. I'm also not going to claim that money is no object, but I'm light-years removed from people who say it's a "waste of money" to eat in a restaurant while "at home you can make things that are so much nicer." No, people like that don't understand anything, not about food and not about restaurants.

My fascination isn't that kind of fascination; it has to do with what, for the sake of convenience, I'd call the yawning chasm between the dish itself and the price you have to pay for it: as though the two variables — money on one side, food on the other — have nothing to do with each other, as though they inhabit two separate worlds and have no business being side by side on the same menu.

That was what I was planning to do: I was going to read the names of the dishes, and then the prices that were printed next to them, but my eye was caught by something on the left-hand page.

I looked, looked again, then peered around the restaurant to see if I could spot the manager's suit.

"What is it?" Claire asked.

"Did you see what it says here?"

My wife looked at me questioningly.

"It says: 'Aperitif of the house, ten euros.' "

"Oh?"

"But that's insane, isn't it?" I said. "The man said: 'We'd like to offer you the aperitif of the house,' right? 'The aperitif of the house is pink champagne.' So what are you supposed to think? You think they're offering you the pink champagne, or am I nuts? If they offer you something, you get it, right? 'Can we offer you the this-or-that of the house?' Then it shouldn't cost ten euros — it should be free!"

"No, wait a minute, not always. If the menu says 'Steak *à la maison*' — 'Steak of the house,' in other words — all it means is that it was prepared according to the recipe of the house. No, that's not a good example

38

. . . 'House wine' . . . 'Wine of the house' —
that doesn't mean you get the wine for free,
does it?"

"All right, okay, that's obvious. But this is
different. I hadn't even looked at a menu
yet. Someone in a three-piece suit pulls back
your chair for you, puts down a lousy little
plate of olives, and then says something
about offering you the aperitif of the house.
That's at least a little confusing, isn't it?
Then it sounds as though you're getting it,
not that you have to pay ten euros for it,
right? Ten euros! Ten! Look at it this way:
would we have ordered a little glass of bland
pink champagne if we'd known that it cost
ten euros?"

"No."

"That's what I'm saying. They trick you
into it with that horseshit about the 'aperitif
of the house.' "

"You're right."

I looked at my wife, but she looked back
earnestly. "No, I'm not pulling your leg,"
she said. "You're right. It really is different
from steak *à la maison* or a house wine. It is
weird. It's almost like they do it on purpose,
to see if you'll fall for it."

"It is, isn't it?"

In the distance I saw the three-piece suit
flash by, into the open kitchen; I raised my

hand and waved, but the only one who noticed was one of the black-pinafore girls. She hurried over to our table.

"Listen here," I said, and as I held up the menu for the girl to see, I glanced over at Claire — for support, for affection, perhaps only for an understanding look, a look that said you couldn't mess with the two of us, not when it came to so-called aperitifs of the house — but Claire's eyes were fixed on something a long way behind me: at the entrance to the restaurant.

"Here they come," she said.

7

Usually, Claire always sits facing the wall, but tonight we'd done it the other way around. "No, no, now it's your turn for a change," I said when the manager pulled back our chairs and she moved automatically toward the seat that looked out only on the garden.

Usually, I'm the one who sits with my back to the garden (or the wall, or the open kitchen), for the simple reason that I want to be able to see everything. Claire lets me have my way. She knows I don't like staring at walls or gardens, that I'd rather look at the people. "Come, now," she said as the floor manager stood waiting politely, his hands on the back of the chair, the chair with a restaurant view that he had pulled back for my wife, as a matter of principle, "this is where *you* want to sit, isn't it?"

It's not that Claire goes out of her way to appease me. It's just something she has

41

inside her, a sort of inner calm or depth that makes her content with blank walls and open kitchens. Or, like here: with a few patches of grass between gravel paths, with a rectangular pond and a few low hedges outside a window that stretches from the glass ceiling all the way to the floor. There must have been trees out there too, some-where, but the combination of falling dark-ness and reflecting glass made it impossible to tell.

That's all she seems to need: that, and a view of my face.

"Not tonight," I said. Tonight all I want to see is you, that's what I was planning to add, but I couldn't bring myself to say that out loud with the manager standing there in his pinstripes.

That evening all I wanted was to cling to my wife's familiar face, but there was another, not unimportant reason for me to sit facing the garden; it meant I could allow my brother's entrance to go unseen: the bustle at the door, the predictable groveling of the manager and the pinafore girls, the other guests' reactions — but when the mo-ment finally came, I turned in my chair and looked anyway.

Everyone, of course, had noticed the Loh-mans' arrival. There was even what you might describe as a stifled tumult around the lectern: no fewer than three girls in black pinafores were fussing over Serge and Babette. The manager was hovering around the lectern too — and there was someone else there as well, a little man with bristly gray hair, dressed not in black from head to toe, but simply in jeans and a white turtleneck. The restaurant owner, I suspected.

Yes, it had to be the owner, for now he stepped forward to extend a personal welcome to Serge and Babette. "They know me there," Serge had told me a few days ago. He knew the man in the white turtleneck, a man who didn't emerge from the open kitchen to shake hands with just anyone.

The guests, however, pretended not to notice; in a restaurant where you had to pay ten euros for the aperitif of the house, the rules of etiquette probably didn't allow for an open display of recognition. They all seemed to lean a few fractions of an inch closer to their plates, all apparently doing their best at the same time to forge ahead with their conversations, to avoid falling silent, because the volume of the general hubbub increased audibly as well.

And while the manager (the white turtleneck had disappeared back into the kitchen) was escorting Serge and Babette past the tables, no more than a barely perceptible ripple ran across the restaurant: a breeze falling across the still-smooth surface of a pond, a breath of wind through a field of grain, no more than that.

Serge smiled broadly and rubbed his hands together, while Babette remained a few steps behind. Judging by the little steps she took, her heels were probably too high for her to keep up with him.

"Claire!" He spread his arms, my wife was already out of her chair, and they were pecking each other three times on the cheek. There was nothing I could do but stand up: remaining seated would require too many explanations.

"Babette . . . ," I said, taking my brother's wife by the elbow. In fact, I had counted on her turning her cheek toward me for the obligatory three kisses and then kissing the air beside my own cheek, but instead I felt the soft pressure of her mouth, first on my one cheek, then the other; the third and final time she pressed her lips, no, not exactly to my mouth, but right beside it. Dangerously close to my mouth, one might say. We looked at each other; she was wearing glasses, as usual, but they looked different from the ones she'd been wearing last

44

time. I, at least, couldn't remember her glasses having such dark lenses.

Babette, as I mentioned earlier, is one of those women who look good in anything, including glasses. Yet there was something else, something different about her this time, like a room where someone has thrown out all the flowers while you were gone: a change in the interior you don't even notice at first, not until you see the stems sticking out of the garbage.

To call my brother's wife a "presence" would be putting it mildly. There were men, I knew, who felt intimidated or even threatened by her figure. She wasn't fat. No, fatness or thinness had very little to do with it — the proportions of her body were in perfect harmony. Everything about her, though, was big and broad: her hands, her feet, her head — too big and too broad, those men thought, and they went on to make insinuations about the size and breadth of other parts of her body, as if somehow to reduce the threat to human proportions.

In high school I'd had a friend who was six feet six inches tall. I remember how tiring it could be always to be standing next to someone who towered head and shoulders above you, as though you were literally standing in his shadow, and as though that shadow kept you from getting enough sunlight. Less sunlight than I deserved, I thought at times. Of course, there was the usual stiff neck from looking up all the time, but that was the least of it. In the summer we would go on vacation together. My high school buddy was not fat either, only tall, but still I experienced every movement of his arms and legs and the feet that stuck out of the sleeping bag and pressed against the inside of the canvas as a struggle for more space — a struggle for which I felt in part responsible and that physically drained me. Sometimes, in the morning, his feet would be sticking out of the entrance to the tent, and that made me feel guilty: guilty about the fact that tents weren't larger, so that people like him could fit in them completely.

When Babette is around, I always do my best to make myself bigger, taller than I really am. I stretch, so she can look me straight in the eye: as equals.

"You're looking good," said Babette, giving my arms a little squeeze. With most people, especially women, a compliment on your appearance means nothing at all, but with Babette it did — I'd found that out in the course of the years. When someone she liked looked bad, she said that too.

"You're looking good" could therefore mean that I did indeed look good, but it could also be an indirect request that I say something about her own appearance — in any event, to pay more attention to it than usual.

I took another look at her eyes, behind those lenses that reflected almost the entire restaurant: the diners, the white tablecloths, the teapot warmers . . . yes, dozens of teapot warmers were glittering in those lenses that, I saw now, were really only dark at the top. Below that they were only slightly tinted, so I could see Babette's eyes clearly.

They were red around the edges, and bigger than normal: unmistakable signs of a recent crying jag. Not a crying jag that had happened a few hours ago — no, crying that had happened just now, in the car, on the way to the restaurant.

Maybe she'd stopped in the parking lot and tried to cover up the worst of it, but it hadn't really worked. The dark lenses might have fooled the staff in the black pinafores, the floor manager in his three-piece suit, and the smart owner in the white turtleneck, but they didn't fool me.

And, at the same moment, I knew for certain that Babette wasn't trying to fool me at all. She had come closer to me than usual — she had almost kissed me on the lips. I'd had no choice but to look into her damp eyes and draw my own conclusions.

Now she blinked and shrugged, body language that could only mean "I'm sorry."

Before I could say anything, though, Serge forged ahead, almost pushing his wife aside as he seized my hand and shook it forcefully. He never used to have such a powerful handshake, but in the last few years he had realized that "the people of this country" had to be met with a firm grip — that they would never vote for a fishy handshake.

"Paul," he said.

He was still smiling, but there was no feeling behind it. Keep on smiling, you could see him thinking. The smile came from the same carload as the handshake. Together, in seven months' time, they were going to lead him to electoral victory. Even if this head were to be pelted with rotten eggs, the smile had to remain intact. Even behind the remains of a cream pie pressed into his face by an angry activist, the smile could never, ever fade from the voters' view.

"Hi, Serge," I said. "How're you doing?"

Meanwhile, behind my brother's back, Claire was seeing to Babette. They kissed — that is to say, my wife kissed her sister-in-law's cheeks — and hugged, then looked into each other's eyes.

Did Claire see what I had seen? Did she see the same red-rimmed despair behind the tinted lenses? But just then Babette laughed elatedly, and I missed seeing how she kissed the air beside Claire's cheeks.

We sat down, Serge diagonally across from me, beside my wife, while Babette — with the manager's assistance — sank into the chair beside me. One of the black-pinafore girls saw to Serge, who stood with one hand in his pocket for a moment, looking around the restaurant, before settling himself down.

"The aperitif of the house today is pink champagne," the manager said.

I took a deep breath, too deep, apparently, because the look my wife gave me was trying to tell me something. She rarely rolled her eyes or cleared her throat apropos of nothing, and she never, ever kicked me under the table to warn me that I was about to make a fool of myself or had already done so.

No, it was a very subtle something in her eyes, a shift invisible to the uninitiated, something between mockery and sudden earnest.

"Don't," the look said.

"Mmm, champagne," Babette said.

49

"Okay, sounds good," Serge said.

"Wait a minute," I said.

APPETIZER

8

"The crayfish are dressed in a vinaigrette of tarragon and baby green onions," said the manager: he was at Serge's plate now, pointing with his pinky. "And these are chanterelles from the Vosges." The pinky vaulted over the crayfish to point out two brown toadstools, cut lengthwise; the "chanterelles" looked as though they had been uprooted only a few minutes ago: what was sticking to the bottom, I figured, could only be dirt.

It was a well-groomed hand, as I'd established while the manager was uncorking the bottle of Chablis Serge had ordered. Despite my earlier suspicions, there was nothing for him to hide: neat cuticles without hangnails, the nail itself trimmed short, no rings — it looked freshly washed, no signs of anything chronic. For the hand of a stranger, though, I felt like it was coming too close to our food — it hovered less than an inch above the crayfish; the pinky itself came even closer, almost brushing the chanterelles.

I wasn't sure I would be able to sit still when that hand, with its pinky, was floating over my own plate, but for the sake of a pleasant evening I knew it would be better to restrain myself.

Yes, that's exactly what I would do, I decided: I would restrain myself. I would keep hold of myself, the way you hold your breath underwater, and I would act as though there were nothing strange at all about the hand of a perfect stranger waving over the food on my plate.

To be honest, though, there was something that was starting to get on my nerves, and that was how long everything took. Even while opening the bottle of Chablis, the manager mucked around. First as he installed the cooler — one of those buckets with two handles that you hook over the edge of the table, like a child's seat. Then, while presenting the bottle, the label — to Serge of course. Serge had asked our permission to choose the wine — at least he'd been civil enough to do that — but all this I-know-everything-about-wine business irritated the hell out of me.

I can't remember exactly when he first presented himself as a connoisseur; in my memory it seems to have happened quite suddenly. From one day to the next he became the one who picked up the wine list and mumbled something about the "earthy aftertaste" of Portuguese wines from the Alentejo: it had been a sort of coup, really, for from that day on, the wine list automatically ended up in Serge's hands.

After presenting the label and receiving my brother's nod of approval, the manager began uncorking the bottle. Operating a corkscrew, it became clear right away, was not his strong suit. He tried to disguise that a bit by shrugging and laughing at his own clumsiness, the whole time with a puzzled air that said this was certainly the first time anything like this had happened to him, but it was precisely that air that gave him away.

"Well, it doesn't seem to want to cooperate," he said as the top of the cork broke off and the wreckage came out with the corkscrew.

The manager was now faced with a dilemma. Should he try to ease the other half of the cork out of the bottle, here at the table, under our watchful eyes? Or would it be wiser to take the bottle back to the open kitchen for some expert help?

The simplest solution, unfortunately, was unthinkable: to push the stubborn half of the cork down into the bottle with the handle of a fork or spoon. You might find little crumbs of cork in your glass afterwards, but so what? Who cares? How much did this Chablis cost? Fifty-eight euros? The price meant nothing anyway. Or at most it meant that you had an excellent chance of coming across exactly the same wine on the supermarket shelf tomorrow, for €7.95 or less.

"Excuse me," the manager said. "I'm going to fetch another bottle for you." And before we could say a word, he went striding off past the other tables.

"Ah, well," I said. "I suppose it's like a hospital. You're better off praying that one of the nurses will take your blood, and not the specialist himself."

Claire laughed out loud. And Babette laughed too. "Oh, I felt so bad for him," she said.

Serge, though, sat there brooding. The look on his face was almost sorrowful, as though something had been taken away from him: his little toy, his self-important blather about wines and vintages and earthy grapes. Indirectly, the manager's bumbling reflected on him. He, Serge Lohman, had picked the Chablis with the rotten cork. He had been looking forward to an orderly

56

process: the reading of the label, the approving nod, the thimbleful that the manager would pour into his glass. That last bit, above all. That was, by now, one thing I couldn't stand to watch anymore, couldn't bear to hear: the sniffling, the gargling, the smacking of the lips, the wine that my brother would roll across his tongue, all the way to his gullet, and then back again. I always had to look the other way.

"Let's hope the other bottles don't have the same problem," he said. "That would be a pity: it really *is* an excellent Chablis."

He was clearly in a bad way. He was the one who had picked out this restaurant. They *knew* him here — the man in the white turtleneck knew him and had come out of the open kitchen specially to shake his hand. I wondered what would have happened if *I* had picked the restaurant, a different restaurant, one he'd never been to before, and the manager or a waiter had failed to uncork the wine at one go: you could bet your life on it that he would have smiled pityingly, then shaken his head. Oh, yes, I knew my brother well enough by now. He would have given me a look with a message only I could read — that *Paul,* he always takes us to the weirdest places . . .

You have big politicos who like to work in

the kitchen, who collect old comic books or have a wooden boat they've fixed up all by themselves. The hobby they choose usually clashes entirely with the face that goes with it, going completely against the grain of what everyone has made of them till then. The worst stick-in-the-mud, someone with all the charisma of a sheet of cardboard, suddenly turns out to cook splendid French meals at home in his free time; the next weekend supplement of the national newspaper features him in full color on the cover, his knitted oven mitts holding up a casserole filled with Provençal meatloaf. The most striking thing about the stick-in-the-mud, besides his apron with a reproduction of a Toulouse-Lautrec poster, is his completely implausible smile, meant to convey the joy of cooking to his constituency. Not so much a smile, really, as a fearful baring of the teeth, the sort of smile you wear when you've just been rear-ended and have lived to tell the tale, and which above all communicates relief at the simple fact that the Provençal meatloaf had not burned to a crisp in the oven.

What exactly had Serge been thinking when he chose wine as his particular hobby? I'd have to ask him sometime. Maybe this evening. I made a mental note; this wasn't the right moment, but the night was young.

When we were still living at home, all he ever drank was cola, huge amounts of it; he had no problem knocking back an entire king-size bottle at dinnertime. Then he would produce these gigantic belches, for which he was sometimes sent to his room, belches that lasted ten seconds or longer — like subterranean thunder rolling up and exploding from somewhere deep down in his stomach — and for which he enjoyed a certain schoolyard fame: among the boys, that is, for he knew even then that girls were only repulsed by burps and farts.

The next step had been the conversion of what was formerly a messy walk-in closet into a wine cellar. He bought racks to stack the bottles in, to let the wine age, as he put it. When guests came to dinner, he began to deliver lectures about the wine being served. Babette viewed it all with a kind of bemusement; perhaps she was the first to see through him, the first not to completely believe in him and his hobby. I remember calling to talk to Serge one afternoon and getting Babette on the line. Serge wasn't there. "He's tasting wine in the Loire Valley," she said. There was something in her voice, something about the way she said "tasting wine" and "Loire Valley" — the tone a woman uses when she says her husband is working late, even though she's known for a year that he's having an affair with his secretary.

Claire, as I noted earlier, is smarter than I am. But she doesn't blame me for not being her equal. What I mean to say is that she never looks down her nose at me; she doesn't sigh deeply or roll her eyes when I don't get something right away. Obviously I have no way of knowing how she talks about me when I'm not around, but I'm very sure, I have absolute faith in the fact, that Claire would never adopt the tone I detected in Babette's voice when she said: "He's tasting wine in the Loire Valley."

Babette, in other words, is also much smarter than Serge. That's not saying a hell of a lot, I might add — but I won't: some things speak for themselves. All I want to talk about here are the things I heard and saw during our little get-together at the restaurant.

9

"The lamb's-neck sweetbread has been marinated in Sardinian olive oil and is served with arugula," said the manager, who had by now arrived at Claire's plate and was pointing with his pinky at two minuscule pieces of meat. "The sun-dried tomatoes come from Bulgaria."

The first thing that struck you about Claire's plate was its vast emptiness. Of course, I'm well aware that, in the better restaurants, quality takes precedence over quantity, but you have voids and then you have voids. The void here, that part of the plate on which no food at all was present, had clearly been raised to a matter of principle.

It was as though the empty plate was challenging you to say something about it, to go to the open kitchen and demand an explanation. "You wouldn't even dare!" the plate said, and laughed in your face.

I tried to recall the price: the cheapest appetizer was nineteen euros; the entrées varied from twenty-eight to forty-seven. And then there were three set menus of forty-seven, fifty-eight, and seventy-nine euros each.

"This is warm goat's cheese with pine nuts and walnut shavings." The hand with the pinky was above my own plate now. I fought back the urge to say "I know, because that's what I ordered," and concentrated on the pinky.

This was the closest he had come to me this evening, even when pouring the wine. The manager had finally opted for the easiest solution and come back from the open kitchen with a new bottle, the cork already sticking halfway out of the neck.

After the wine cellar and the trip to the Loire Valley, there had been the six-week wine course. Not in France, but in a classroom at a night school. Serge had hung the diploma in the hallway, somewhere no one could possibly miss it. A bottle with the cork sticking out of it could contain something very different from what was on the label — that must have been dealt with during one of his very first lessons in that classroom. It could have been messed with: a malicious person could have diluted the wine with tap water, or dribbled saliva down the neck.

But after the aperitif of the house and the broken cork, Serge Lohman apparently was not in the mood for any more mucking about. Without looking at the manager, he had wiped his lips with his napkin and mumbled that the wine was "excellent."

At that moment I glanced over at Babette. Her eyes behind the tinted lenses were fixed on her husband: it was almost impossible to tell, but I would almost have sworn that she had raised an eyebrow when he passed his judgment on the pre-uncorked wine. In the car, on the way to the restaurant, he had made her cry, but by now her eyes were looking much less swollen. I hoped she would say something, something to get back at him: she was entirely capable of that; Babette could be very sarcastic when she put her mind to it. "He's tasting wine in the Loire Valley" had been one of the mildest expressions of that.

In my mind, I egged her on. Every unhappy family is unhappy in its own way. When it came right down to it, that might be the best thing — a huge, knock-down, drag-out fight between Serge and Babette before we moved on to the main course. I would speak soothing words, pretend not to take sides, but she would know that she could count on me.

To my regret, though, Babette said nothing at all. You could almost see the way she gulped back her undoubtedly murderous comment about the cork. But still, something had now taken place that kept alive my hopes of an explosion later in the evening. It's like a pistol in a stage play: when someone waves a pistol during the first act, you can bet your bottom dollar that someone will be shot with it before the curtain falls. That's the law of drama. The law that says no pistol must appear if no one's going to fire it.

"This is lamb's lettuce," the manager said; I looked at the pinky, which was no more than a centimeter away from the three or four curly little green leaves and the melted chunk of goat's cheese, and then at the entire hand, which was so close that I would only have had to lean forward a little to kiss it.

Why had I ordered this appetizer, when I don't even like goat's cheese? To say nothing of lamb's lettuce. This time the stingy portions worked in my favor. My plate too was mostly empty, although not as empty as Claire's. I could have devoured the three leaves in a single bite — or simply left them lying on the plate, which amounted to pretty much the same thing.

Whenever I see lamb's lettuce, I'm reminded of the little cage with the hamster or guinea pig that stood on the windowsill of our classroom in elementary school. It was there because it was good for us to learn about animals — to learn to take care of animals, I suppose. Whether the little leaves we pushed through the bars of the cage each morning were lamb's lettuce, I can't remember, but they looked a lot like it. The hamster or guinea pig nibbled at the leaves and then spent the rest of the day sitting in one corner of its cage. One morning it was dead, just like the little turtle, the two white mice, and the stick insects that had preceded it. What we were supposed to learn from this high mortality rate was never dealt with in the class.

The reason why I now had a plate of warm goat's cheese with lamb's lettuce in front of me was simpler than it seemed. I had been the last to order. We hadn't really talked beforehand about what we were going to have — or maybe we had, and I'd missed it. Whatever the case, I had settled on the *vitello tonnato,* but Babette, to my horror, ordered exactly the same thing.

No problem: at that point, I could always switch to my second choice — the oysters.

But the next-to-last person to order, right after Claire, was Serge. And when Serge ordered the oysters, I was stuck. I had no desire to order the same appetizer as someone else, but to have the same appetizer as my brother was out of the question. Theoretically speaking, I could have switched back to the *vitello tonnato,* but that was purely theoretical. It didn't feel right: not only would it look as though I wasn't original enough to choose an appetizer of my own, but it might, in Serge's eyes, raise the suspicion that I was trying to close ranks with his wife. Which was true, of course, but I couldn't be so obvious.

I had already closed the menu and laid it beside my plate. Now I opened it again. Reading like lightning, I skimmed down through the list of appetizers; I adopted a thoughtful expression, as though I was only looking for the dish I'd already chosen in order to point it out on the menu, but by then, of course, it was much too late.

"And for you, sir?" the manager asked.

"The melted goat's cheese with lamb's lettuce," I said.

It came out a little too readily, a little too sure-of-myself to sound credible. Serge and Babette didn't notice a thing, but across the table I saw the look of bewilderment on

66

Claire's face.

Would she try to protect me from myself? Would she say "But you don't like goat's cheese"? I wasn't sure; at that moment too many pairs of eyes were on me for me to shake my head at her, but I wasn't taking any chances.

"I hear the goat cheese is from an urban farm," I said. "From goats that live out in the open."

At last, after he had granted thorough attention to Babette's *vitello tonnato* — the *vitello tonnato* that, in the best of all worlds, could have been my *vitello tonnato* — the manager left and we were able to resume our conversation. *Resume* was not exactly the right word, though; as it turned out, none of us had the slightest idea what we'd been talking about before the appetizers arrived. That was one of the disadvantages of these so-called top restaurants: all the interruptions, like the exaggeratedly detailed review of every pine nut on your plate, the endless uncorking of wine bottles, and the unsolicited topping up of glasses made you lose track.

As far as that continual topping-up goes, let me say this: I have traveled a bit, I have been to restaurants in many countries, but nowhere — and when I say nowhere, I literally mean nowhere — do they top up your wine without your asking for it. They would consider that rude. Only in Holland do they come up to your table all the time; not only do they top up your glass, but they also cast a wistful eye at the bottle when it seems to be getting empty. "Isn't it about time to order another one?" is what those looks are meant to say. I know someone, an old friend, who spent a few years working in Dutch "top restaurants." Their tactic, he told me once, is to actually force as much wine as possible down your throat, wine they sell for seven times what the importer charges for it, and that's why they always wait so long between bringing the appetizer and taking orders for the entrée: people will order more wine out of pure boredom, just to kill time — that's the way they figure it. The appetizer usually arrives quite quickly, my friend said, because if the appetizer takes too long, people start complaining. They start to doubt their choice of restaurant, but after a while, when they've had too much drink between appetizer and entrée, they lose track of time. He knew of cases where the entrées had been ready for a long time but remained on the plates in the kitchen because the people at the table in question weren't complaining. Only when

68

there was a lull in the conversation and the customers began to look around impatiently were the plates shoved into the microwave.

What had we been talking about before the appetizers came? Not that it really mattered, it couldn't have been anything important, but that was what made it so irritating. I could remember what we'd said after all the fuss with the cork and the placing of our orders, but I had no idea what had been going on right before our plates arrived.

Babette had joined a new gym — we'd talked about that a bit: about losing weight, the importance of remaining active, and which sport was best for which person. Claire was thinking about joining a health club, and Serge had said he couldn't stand the obtrusive music at most places like that. That's why he had taken up running, he said, where you could be out on your own in the fresh air, and he acted as though he had come up with the idea all by himself. He conveniently forgot that I had started running years ago, and how he had never missed an opportunity to make snide comments about his "little brother out trotting around."

Yes, that's what we had talked about at first, for rather too long for my taste, but an innocent subject to be sure, a fairly typical prelude to a standard restaurant evening. But for the rest of the evening? Not if my life depended on it. I looked at Serge, at my wife, and then at Babette. At that moment, Babette jabbed her fork into her *vitello tonnato,* cut off a slice, and raised it to her mouth.

"But now I've completely forgotten," she said, the fork poised in the air. "Did you say you two have already seen the new Woody Allen, or not?"

10

When the conversation turns too quickly to films, I see it as a sign of weakness. I mean: films are more something for the end of the evening, when you really don't have much else to talk about. I don't know why, but when people start talking about films, I always get a sinking feeling in the pit of my stomach, like when you wake up in the morning and find that it's already getting dark outside.

The worst are those people who describe entire films. They get right into it — they have no qualms about taking up fifteen minutes of your time: fifteen minutes per film, that is. They don't really care whether you haven't yet seen the film in question or whether you saw it a long time ago. Such considerations don't bother them — they're already right in the middle of the opening scene. To be polite, you feign interest at first, but soon you bid farewell to courtesy:

You yawn openly, stare at the ceiling, and squirm around in your chair. You do everything in your power to make the narrator shut up, but nothing helps. They're too far gone to notice the signals. Above all, they're addicted to themselves and their own crap about films.

I believe it was my brother who started in about the new Woody Allen. "A masterpiece," he said, without asking whether we — that is, Claire and I — might have seen it already. Babette nodded emphatically at this — they had seen it together last weekend; they were in agreement about something for a change. "A masterpiece," she said. "Really, you two have to go."

To which Claire said that we had already been. "Two months ago," I added, which in fact was unnecessary — it was just something I felt like saying. It wasn't aimed at Babette, but at my brother. I wanted to let him know that he was running pretty far behind with his masterpieces.

At that moment, a bevy of girls in black pinafores arrived with our appetizers, followed by the manager and his pinky, and we lost track of where we were — until Babette picked up the thread again with her question about whether or not we had already seen it, the new Woody Allen.

"I thought it was a great film," Claire said as she dipped a sun-dried tomato in the olive oil on her plate and raised it to her lips. "Even Paul liked it. Didn't you, Paul?"

Claire does that all the time: draws me into things in a way that I can't back out. Now, the others already knew that I had liked it, and "even Paul" meant something along the lines of "even Paul, who usually doesn't like any film, especially something by Woody Allen."

Serge looked at me, a morsel of appetizer still in his mouth. He was chewing on it, but that didn't stop him from addressing himself to me. "A masterpiece, right? No, really, fantastic." He went on chewing and then gulped. "And that Scarlett Johansson, I wouldn't kick her out of bed for eating crackers. Good Lord, what a beauty!"

Hearing your older brother refer to a film you yourself think is pretty good as a "masterpiece" is kind of like having to wear that brother's old clothes: the hand-me-downs that have become too small for him, but which in your eyes are above all *old*. My options were limited: admitting that Woody Allen's film was a masterpiece would be like wriggling into those old clothes, and was therefore out of the question. There was no superlative for "masterpiece" — the most

73

I could do was try to prove that Serge hadn't understood the film, that he considered it a masterpiece for all the wrong reasons, but that would involve a lot of effort. It would be laying it on rather thick for Claire, and probably for Babette as well.

In fact, there was only one option left, and that was to run Woody Allen's film into the ground. It wouldn't be too hard — there were enough weaknesses I could point out, weaknesses that don't really matter when you like a film but that you can make use of in an emergency in order to dislike the same film. Claire would raise her eyebrows at first, then hopefully realize what I was doing: that my betrayal of our shared appreciation for the film was in the service of the struggle against spineless, show-offy crap about films in general.

I reached for my glass of Chablis, intending first to take a thoughtful sip before carrying out this latter strategy, when suddenly I saw another way out. What was it my idiot brother had said, anyway? About Scarlett Johansson? "Kick her out of bed for eating crackers . . . a beauty" — I didn't know what Babette thought of that kind of crass macho talk, but Claire always got up on her hind legs when men started in about "sweet asses" and "nice tits." I'd been looking at my brother when he said that about the crackers and had missed her reaction, but that wasn't really even necessary.

Sometimes, recently, I have had the impression that he's starting to lose touch with reality, that he seriously thinks the Scarlett Johanssons of this world would like nothing more than to eat crackers in his bed. I suspected him of viewing women in more or less the same way that he viewed food, his daily hot meal in particular. That was how he used to be, and to be honest, it's never really changed. "I need to eat something," Serge says when he's hungry. He'll say that when you're out hiking somewhere in a national park, far from civilization, or driving down the highway, between two exits. "Sure," I say then, "but right now we don't have anything to eat." "But I'm hungry right now," Serge will say. "I need to eat now."

There was something pitiful about it, this dumb resolve that would make him forget everything else — his surroundings, the people he was with — and focus on only one objective: sating his own hunger. At moments like this he reminded me of an animal that encounters an obstacle in its path: a bird that doesn't understand that the glass in the windowpane is made of solid matter and flies into it again and again.

And when we would finally find a place to eat, it was never a pretty sight. He would eat the way one fills the tank with gas: he would devour his cheese sandwich with white bread or his almond cake quickly and efficiently, to make sure the fuel reached his stomach as soon as possible; without fuel there was no way you could go on. The real fine dining came much later, like his knowledge of wine; at a certain point he decided it was necessary, but the speed and efficiency remained: even these days, he was always the first to empty his plate.

I would have paid a fortune to see and hear just once how things went in the bedroom between him and Babette. On the other hand, there is a part of me that would actually resist that with every fiber of my being, that would pay an equally great fortune never to have to find out.

"I need to fuck." And then Babette saying she has a headache, that she's having her period, or that this evening she doesn't even want to think about it, about his body, his arms and legs, his head, his smell. "But I need to fuck right now." I bet my brother fucks the way he eats, that he stuffs himself into a woman in the same way he stuffs a beef croquette into his mouth — and that his hunger is then stilled.

"So you were mostly sitting there looking at Scarlett Johansson's tits," I say, much more crudely than I'd planned. "Or do you mean something else when you say 'a masterpiece'?"

A miraculous kind of silence fell then, the kind you only hear in restaurants: a sudden, raised awareness of the presence of others, the buzzing and the click of cutlery on plates at thirty other tables, the one or two becalmed seconds when background noises become foreground noises.

The first thing to break the silence was Babette's laughter; I glanced up at my wife, who was staring at me in dismay, and then back at Serge; he was trying to laugh too, but his heart wasn't in it — what's more, he still had food in his mouth.

"Come, come, Paul, not so holier-than-thou!" he said. "She just happens to be a babe — a man has eyes in his head, doesn't he?"

"A babe." Claire wouldn't like that one either — I knew that. She would always say "a good-looking man," never "tasty," let alone "nice ass." "All that fashionable talk about 'nice asses' — it's too contrived for me when women start talking like that," she'd said once. "It's like when women suddenly start smoking pipes or spitting on the ground."

With every fiber of his being, Serge had remained a yokel, a boorish lout: the same boorish lout who used to get sent from the table for farting.

"I also think Scarlett Johansson is a very attractive woman," I said. "But it sounded sort of like you thought that was the most significant thing about the film. Do correct me if I'm wrong."

"Well, things go completely wrong with that, what's his name, that Englishman, the tennis teacher, because he can't get her off his mind. He even has to shoot her just to get what he wants."

"Hey!" Babette said. "Don't say that — that ruins it if you haven't seen it yet!" Another brief silence descended, during which Babette looked from Claire to me. "Oh shit, I think I must have been asleep . . . you two *did* see it already!"

11

We all laughed, all four of us, a moment of release. But too much release was not good — one had to remain on one's toes. The simple truth was that Serge Lohman had a nice ass himself. You heard women say it often enough. He was all too aware that they found him attractive, and there was nothing wrong with that. He was photogenic; he possessed a certain — again, loutish — attractiveness. A bit too in your face and a bit too much rough timber, if you asked me, but of course there are women who prefer plain furnishings: tables or chairs made from "authentic materials" — scrap wood from old stall doors in northern Spain or Piedmont.

Serge's girlfriends had usually given up on him after a few months. There was a boring, matter-of-fact side to that attractiveness — they soon tired of his "pretty face." Babette was the only one who had stuck it out with him, about eighteen years now, which in itself was something of a miracle. They had been squabbling for eighteen years, and it was pretty clear that they didn't really suit each other at all, but you often see that — couples for whom constant friction is the real engine of their marriage, every fight the foreplay to the moment when they can make up in bed.

But sometimes I couldn't help but think that it was all much simpler than that, that Babette had merely signed up for something, for a life at the side of a successful politician, and that it would have been a waste of all the time she'd invested to stop now — the way you don't put aside a bad book when you're halfway through it. You finish it reluctantly — that's the way she'd stayed with Serge. Perhaps the ending would make up for some of it.

They had two children of their own: Rick, who was Michel's age, and Valerie, a slightly autistic thirteen-year-old with an almost translucent, mermaid-like beauty. And then there was Beau, exact age unknown, but probably somewhere between fourteen and seventeen. Beau came from Burkina Faso and had ended up with Serge and Babette via a "development project": one of those where you support schoolchildren in the

Third World by buying them books and other necessities and then "adopt" them — at a distance to start with, by means of letters and photographs and postcards, but later in real life as well. The chosen child then lives with the Dutch foster family for a while, and if that goes well, he is allowed to stay. A sort of rent-to-own agreement, in other words. Or like a cat you bring home from the animal shelter; if the cat scratches the sofa to bits or pisses all over the house, you take it back.

I remember a few of the photographs and postcards Beau had sent from faraway Burkina Faso. In the photo that stayed with me longest, you saw him standing in front of a red-brick building with a corrugated iron roof, a pitch-black boy in a striped pajama top that reached to just below his knees, like a nightgown, his bare feet in rubber sandals.

"Merci beaucoup mes parents pour notre école!" was written beneath it in a graceful schoolboy hand.

"Isn't he darling?" Babette had said when she showed it to us. They had traveled to Burkina Faso and lost their hearts, as Serge and Babette themselves put it.

A second trip followed, forms were filled in, and a few weeks later Beau landed at

Schiphol Airport. "Do you two know what you're getting into?" Claire had asked them once, back in the days when the whole adoption was still at the postcard stage. They had reacted indignantly. They were helping someone, weren't they? A child who would never have the opportunities in his own country that he would in Holland? Yes, they knew very well what they were getting into. There were already far too many people in the world who thought only about themselves.

You couldn't accuse them of outright egotism. Rick was three at the time, and Valerie was only a few months old. They weren't like most adoptive parents, who couldn't have children of their own. In completely selfless fashion they were taking a third child into their home — not their own flesh and blood, but a needy child who was being offered a new life in Holland.

So then what was it? What, indeed, *were* they getting into?

Serge and Babette made it clear to us that this question was not to be posed, so we didn't pose the other questions either. Did Beau still have parents of his own? Or was he an orphan? I have to say that Babette was more fanatical about the adoption than Serge was. It was her "project" from the start, something she planned to carry out successfully no matter what the cost. She did everything she could to give her adopted child just as much love as her own children.

In the end, the word *adoption* itself became taboo. "Beau is our son, that's all," she said. "There is no difference." At such moments, Serge would nod in agreement. "We love him just as much as we do Rick and Valerie," he said.

There's a possibility, of course, that he knew even then — I wouldn't want to pass judgment or accuse him of having acted with forethought — but later on it worked to his advantage, that black child from Burkina Faso whom he loved as one of his own. It was a different sort of thing from his knowledge of wine, but it had the same effect. It gave him a face: Serge Lohman, the politician with the adopted African son.

He began to pose more frequently for family photographs. It looked good, Serge and Babette on the couch with the three children at their feet. Beau Lohman became living proof that there was one politician who didn't act purely out of self-interest — that he, at least at one point in his life, had not acted out of self-interest. His other two children, after all, had been conceived in standard fashion, so it hadn't been an act of desperation, this adoption of a child from Burkina Faso. That was the message: on other issues as well, perhaps, Serge Lohman would not act purely out of self-interest.

A waitress topped up Serge's glass, then mine; Babette's and Claire's were still half full. The waitress was a pretty girl, as golden-blonde as Scarlett Johansson. It took her a long time, filling the glasses. It was clear that she was fairly new at it and probably hadn't been working here long. First she took the bottle from the cooler and dried it completely with the white napkin draped over the bottle neck and the edge of the bucket. The pouring itself didn't go too smoothly, either: she stood beside Serge's chair at such an angle that she accidentally elbowed Claire in the head.

"Oh, I'm so sorry," she said, and blushed deeply. Of course Claire said right away that it was no problem, but the girl was now so flustered that she filled Serge's glass all the way to the brim. No problem there either — except for a wine connoisseur.

"Hey, hey, hey," my brother said. "Are you trying to get me drunk or something?" He slid his chair back a couple of feet, as though the girl hadn't filled his glass too full but had actually spilled half the bottle over his pants. Now she blushed even more deeply. She blinked her eyes, and for a moment I thought she was going to burst into tears. Like the other girls in black pinafores, she had her hair tied up tightly in a regulation ponytail, but its golden-blondeness made it look less severe than the others'.

She had a sweet face. I couldn't help myself; I thought about the moment when she would pull the elastic band from her ponytail and shake her hair loose, later tonight when her day at the restaurant was over — her terrible day, as she would tell a girlfriend (or maybe a boyfriend): "You know what happened to me today? So stupid, just like me! You know how I hate all that stiff etiquette stuff with the wine bottles? Well, tonight I completely lost it. That wouldn't even be so bad, but you know who was at the table?" The girlfriend or boyfriend would look at the golden-blonde hair hanging loose and say: "No, tell me. Who was at the table?" For maximum effect, the girl would pause for a moment. "Serge Lohman!" "Who?" "Serge Lohman! That cabinet minister! Or maybe he's not a real minister, but you know who I mean — he was on the news yesterday — the one who's going to win the election. It was so dumb . . . there was a woman at the table too, and I smacked her in the head with my

85

elbow." "Oh, him . . . Jesus! And what happened then?" "Well, nothing. He was really nice, but I could have curled up and died!"

Really nice . . . Yes, Serge had been really nice, after he'd slid his chair back a couple of feet and then raised his head and seen the girl for the first time. In a hundredth of a second, too fast to be seen by the naked eye, I saw his expression change — from feigned dismay and annoyance at the unskilled handling of his Chablis to totally empathetic friendliness. How he melted, in short — the resemblance to the only recently discussed Scarlett Johansson could not have escaped even him. He saw a "sweet thing," a blushing and stammering sweet thing who was completely at his mercy. He gave her his most charming smile. "But that's okay," he said, lifting his glass and causing a substantial slug of white wine to land on his half-empty plate of oysters. "I should be able to finish it anyway."

"I'm so sorry, sir," the girl said again.

"Nothing to worry about. How old are you? Are you old enough to vote?"

At first I thought my ears were playing tricks on me. Was I actually hearing this? But just at that point my brother turned his head in my direction and gave me a big, fat wink.

"I'm nineteen, sir."

"Okay, tell you what. If you vote for the right party when the elections come up, we'll do our best to overlook your wine-pouring abilities."

The girl blushed again, the skin on her face turned an even darker red than before — and, for the second time within a couple of minutes, I thought she was going to burst into tears. I looked over at Babette, but there was nothing to suggest that she disapproved of her husband's behavior. In fact, she seemed rather amused by it — the nationally famous politician Serge Lohman, leader of the largest opposition party, a shoo-in for prime minister, openly flirting with nineteen-year-old waitresses and making them blush. Maybe this was cute; maybe this only confirmed his irresistible charm; or maybe she, Babette, just happened to like being married to a man like my brother. In the car on the way here, or in the parking lot, he had made her cry. But what did that amount to, anyway? Was she suddenly going to leave him in the lurch, now, after eighteen years? Six or seven months before the elections?

I tried to reestablish eye contact with Claire, but she seemed engrossed by Serge's brimming wineglass and the waitress's stammering. She ran her hand over the back of her head, over the place where the girl's elbow had hit her — who knows, maybe harder than it had appeared — then asked: "Are you two going to France again this summer? Or don't you have any plans yet?"

12

Every year, Serge and Babette went to their house in the Dordogne with the children. They belonged to that class of Dutch people who think everything French is "great": from croissants to French bread with Camembert, from French cars (they themselves drove one of the top-end Peugeots) to French chansons and French films. At the same time, they failed to see that the local French population of the Dordogne fairly retched at the sight of Dutch people. Anti-Dutch slogans had been scrawled on the walls of many *résidences secondaires,* but according to my brother, this was the work of "a tiny minority" — after all, wasn't everyone nice to you when you went to a shop or a restaurant?

"Uh . . . that depends," Serge said. "It's still a bit up in the air."

We had visited them there for the first time a year ago, the three of us, on our way to Spain — the first time and the last, as Claire put it after we resumed our trip three days later. My brother and his wife had insisted so often that we drop by that it had become almost embarrassing to put it off any longer.

The house was in a lovely location, on a hill, tucked away amid the trees. Glinting in the distance through the branches, in the valley below, you could see a bend in the Dordogne River. It was muggy the whole time we were there, not a breath of wind. Huge beetles and blowflies, of a size never seen in the Netherlands, buzzed loudly amid the leaves, or flew against the windows with smacks so hard they made the glass rattle in its sashes.

We were introduced to the "mason" who had built the open kitchen for them, to the "Madame" who ran the bakery, and to the owner of a "completely ordinary little restaurant" along a tributary of the Dordogne, "where all the locals go." Serge introduced me to everyone as *"mon petit frère."* He seemed at ease among the French, each and every one of them just regular people, after all. Regular people were his specialty in Holland, so why not here as well?

What barely seemed to register with him

90

was that those regular people were earning large sums of money off him, off the Dutchman with his summer home and his money, and it was in part for that reason that they continued to exercise a modicum of courtesy. "So kind," Serge said. "So normal. Where would you find that in Holland these days?" He failed to notice, or maybe he just shut his eyes to it, how the "mason" hocked a green tendril of chewing tobacco onto their tiled patio after mentioning the price of a shipment of authentic rural roofing tiles for the lean-to above their outdoor kitchen. How the "Madame" at the bakery actually wanted to go on serving her customers but stood waiting while Serge introduced his *petit frère,* and how those same customers exchanged knowing nods and winks — nods and winks that spoke volumes concerning the despicable boorishness of these Dutch people. How the jovial owner of the little restaurant squatted beside our table and said in a conspiratorial tone that he had, that very day, received a bag of escargots from a local farmer who normally kept them for himself. This time he had been able to buy some, though, and the owner wanted to offer them exclusively to Serge and his "lovely family" at a "special price" — the taste was something we would encounter nowhere else. Meanwhile, Serge overlooked the fact that the French customers were all handed the carte du jour, an inexpensive three-course menu at less than half the price of a single helping of snails. And concerning the wine tasting in that little restaurant, I prefer to say nothing at all.

We stayed for three days. During those three days we also visited a château, where we had to stand in line in front of a house with hundreds of other foreigners, mostly Dutch, before being guided through twelve swelteringly hot rooms with old poster beds and tub chairs. The rest of the time we spent largely in the airless garden. Claire tried to do some reading. It was too hot for me to even open a book — the white of the pages hurt your eyes — but it was difficult to do nothing at all. Serge was always busy with something; there were things around the house he did himself, things for which he did not have a local craftsman at his beck and call. "The people here start to respect you when you work on your own house," he said. "You notice that after a while." And so he pushed his wheelbarrow forty times up and back between the outdoor kitchen and the provincial highway, where the rural roofing tiles had been dropped. It never occurred to him for a moment that his do-ityourselfing might be cheating the local mason out of a considerable chunk of his paid working hours.

He sawed his own wood for the fireplace as well. Sometimes it looked almost like a publicity shot for his election campaign: Serge Lohman, the people's candidate, with a wheelbarrow, a saw, and burly blocks of wood — a regular man like any other, the only difference being that few regular men could afford a summer home in the Dordogne. Perhaps that was the real reason why he never allowed a camera crew onto his "property," as he referred to it. "This is my place," he himself said. "My place, for me and my family. It's no one else's business."

When he wasn't lugging roofing tiles or sawing wood, he was out picking blackberries or blueberries. Blackberries and blueberries from which Babette then made jam. With her hair up in a kerchief, she spent days ladling out hot, sickly-sweet substances into hundreds of canning jars. Claire had no choice but to ask if she needed help, just as I felt obliged to help Serge with his roofing tiles. "Can I give you a hand?" I asked after the seventh barrowful went by. "Well, now that you mention it" was his reply.

"When can we leave?" Claire asked me that night in bed, when we were finally alone and could cuddle up close. Not too close, though — it was too hot for that. The berries had turned her fingers blue; a darker version of the blue was in her hair and streaked across her cheeks.

"Tomorrow," I said. "Oh, no, I mean the day after tomorrow."

On our last night, Serge and Babette invited friends and acquaintances over for dinner in the garden. They were Dutch friends and acquaintances, all of them, and they all had summer homes close by. "Nothing special," Serge said. "Just a little group of friends. Nice people, all of them, really."

Seventeen Dutch people, not counting the three of us, stood around the garden that evening with plates and glasses. There was an aging actress ("with no work and no husband," Claire filled me in the next morning) and a skinny choreographer who drank only Vittel water from half-liter bottles he had brought himself, and a pair of married homosexual writers who spent the whole evening carping at each other.

On the table, Babette had laid out a buffet of salads, French cheeses, cured meats, and bread. Meanwhile, Serge turned his attention to the barbecue; he was wearing a red-and-white-check apron and grilling hamburgers and shish kebabs with bell peppers and onions. "The secret of a good barbecue is to build a good fire," he'd told me a few hours before the dinner with the little circle of friends. "The rest is a piece of cake." My job was to collect dry twigs. Serge was drinking more than usual — a wicker bottle of wine stood beside him in the grass next to the barbecue. Maybe he was more nervous about how the evening would go than he was letting on. "In Holland, they're all sitting down to potatoes and gravy right now," he said. "Can you imagine it? This is the life, man!" He waved his fork at the trees and bushes that kept the garden hidden from prying eyes.

All the Dutch people I spoke to that evening told more or less the same story, often in the very same words. They didn't envy their countrymen, who were forced, by financial considerations or other obligations, to stay behind in Holland. "Around here, we're as happy as God in France," said a woman, who told me she had worked for years in the "diet industry." I thought she was joking, until I realized that she had uttered the phrase entirely in earnest, as though she had come up with it herself.

I looked around at the other figures cradling their wine-glasses in the golden-yellow glow from the braziers and torches positioned strategically around the garden, and in my mind I heard the voice of the old actor who figured in that TV commercial ten — or was it twenty? — years ago: "Yes, that's right, you too can be happy as God in France. With a good glass of cognac and real French cheese . . ."

The mere thought brought with it a whiff of Boursin, as though someone had spread a slice of toast with that filthiest of all fake French cheeses and shoved it under my nose. It was the combination of the lighting and the odor of Boursin that kept me from seeing my brother and sister-in-law's garden party as anything but an old, outdated TV commercial from twenty years ago or longer. As imitation cheese that had nothing whatsoever to do with French cheese, just like here, in the heart of the Dordogne, where everyone was only playing at being in France, while the French themselves were most conspicuous by their absence.

Whenever I mentioned the anti-Dutch graffiti, they all shrugged it off. "Juvenile delinquents!" was the verdict of the unemployed actress, while a copywriter who had sold his ad agency "lock, stock, and barrel" in order to settle in the Dordogne assured me that the slogans were mostly aimed at Dutch campers, who brought all their groceries from Holland in their trailers and didn't spend a cent in the local shops.

"We're not like that," he said. "We eat in their restaurants, have a Pernod in their cafés, and read their newspapers. Without people like Serge, and a lot of others, there would be plenty of masons and plumbers around here without work."

"And let's not forget the local winemakers!" said Serge, raising his glass. "Cheers!"

Back in the shadows, in the darkest part of the garden beside the hedge, the skinny choreographer was making out with the younger member of the writer couple. I saw a hand slip inside a shirt and looked the other way.

But what if the slogan-scrawlers didn't stop at mere slogans? I asked myself. It probably wouldn't take much to scare off this band of cowards. The Dutch had a tendency to shit in their pants at the mere threat of real violence. You could start off by throwing rocks through windows, and if that didn't work, you could burn down a couple of *résidences secondaires.* Not too many, because the real objective was to let those houses pass back into the hands of people who had first claim on them: the young French newlyweds who for years now had been forced by skyrocketing property

97

prices to live with their parents. The Dutch had ruined the housing market for the local people; astronomical sums were being paid even for ruins. With the help of relatively inexpensive French masons, the ruin was then rebuilt, only to remain uninhabited for most of the year. When you looked at it that way, in a clear, cold light, it was a miracle that there had been so few real incidents, that the native population had been content merely to scrawl a little graffiti.

I let my gaze travel over the lawn. Someone had put on a CD by Édith Piaf. Babette, who had chosen a wide, translucent black dress for the party, was executing a few unsteady, tipsy dance steps to the tune of *"Non, je ne regrette rien. . . ."* If broken windows and arson didn't do it, you could always take things up a notch, I thought to myself. You could lure one of these Dutch pussies away from his home under the pretense that you knew where there was another, even cheaper winemaker, then pound him to a pulp in some cornfield. Not just slap him up against the side of the head — no, sterner stuff, baseball bats and flails.

Or if you saw one out walking on his own, at a bend in the road, coming back from the supermarket with a shopping bag full of baguettes and red wine, you could let your car make a little skid. Almost by accident. "He was suddenly right there, right in front of my bumper," you could say later — or you could say nothing at all. You could leave the Dutchman lying on the edge of the road like roadkill, and when you got home, you could wash any telltale traces off the bumper and fender. All was fair, as long as the message got across: You people don't belong here! Fuck off back to where you came from! Go home and play at being in France in your own country, with your baguettes and red wine, but not here, not where we come from!

"Paul . . . ! Paul . . . !" From the middle of the lawn, with her flapping gown dangerously close to the flame of one of the braziers, Babette was holding out her arms to me. "Milord" was booming from the loudspeakers. Dancing. To be dancing on the grass with my brother's wife. Happy as God in France. I looked around and saw Claire standing at the table with the cheeses — and at that same moment, she saw me.

She was talking to the unemployed actress and threw me a desperate glance. At parties back in Holland, that meant "Can't we go home, please?" But we couldn't go home. We were doomed to press on to the bitter end. Tomorrow. Tomorrow we would be allowed to go away. "Help!" was all Claire's look was saying now.

I gestured to my sister-in-law — a gesture that said something like "I can't right now," but that later I would be sure to come and dance with her across the lawn — and walked toward the table with the cheeses. *"Allez riez, Milord! Chantez, Milord!"* Edith Piaf sang. There were, of course, stubborn characters among all those hundreds of Dutch people with summer homes in the Dordogne, I thought to myself. Characters who closed their eyes to the truth, who simply wouldn't admit the fact that they were unwanted foreigners around here. Who, despite all evidence to the contrary, kept insisting that it was all the work of a "tiny minority," the smashed windows and the acts of arson and the battered and run-over countrymen. Perhaps those last bull-heads would have to be freed from their illusions with a little more force.

I thought about *Straw Dogs* and *Deliverance,* films that come to mind whenever I am out in the sticks, but never more than here, in the Dordogne, on the hilltop where my brother and his wife had created what they called their "little French paradise." In *Straw Dogs,* the local population — after limiting themselves at first to a little badgering — take horrible revenge on the newcomers who think they've bought a cute little house in the English countryside. In *Deliverance,* it's the American hillbillies who rudely interrupt a group of city slickers on a canoeing trip. Rape and murder feature prominently in both films.

The actress looked me over from head to toe before speaking. "Your wife tells me you will be leaving us tomorrow." Her voice had something artificially sweet to it, like the substance in Diet Coke, or the filling they use in diabetic chocolates, which say on the package that they won't make you fat. I looked at Claire, who rolled her eyes slightly, up at the star-studded sky. "And that you're going to Spain, of all places."

I thought about one of my favorite scenes from *Straw Dogs.* What would this artificial voice sound like if its owner were to be dragged into a barn by a pair of drunken French bricklayers? So drunk they could no longer tell the difference between a woman and the ruins of a cottage with only the walls still standing. Would she still be shooting her mouth off when the bricklayers set about rectifying her foundation? Would the voice come loose of its own accord once it was being peeled off, layer by layer?

At that very moment, a commotion arose

at the edge of the garden, not the darkened edge with bushes where the choreographer had been groping the younger of the two writers, but closer to the house, along the pathway leading to the paved road.

It was a group of about five men. Frenchmen, I saw right away, although I'd be hard pressed to say why — their clothes probably, which had something rural about them without being as emphatically sloppy and disheveled as these Dutch people playing at being in France. One of the men had a shotgun slung over his shoulder.

Perhaps the children really had said something. Maybe they actually had asked permission to leave the party and go "into the village," as our Michel continued to insist the following day. On the other hand, I hadn't really noticed that they had been gone for the last few hours. Serge's daughter, Valerie, had been in the kitchen for most of the evening, watching TV; at a certain point, she had come out and said goodnight to all of us, and given her uncle Paul two pecks on the cheek.

Now Michel was standing between two Frenchmen, his head bowed. His black hair, which he had let grow to shoulder length that summer, hung lankly along his face. One of the two men was holding him by the upper arm. Serge's son, Rick, was being held too, albeit a bit more loosely. One of the Frenchmen had his hand resting lightly on his shoulder, as though he no longer posed a threat.

It was, in fact, Beau — Serge's adopted son from Burkina Faso who had arrived here among the Dutch people in the Dordogne by way of the relief project for his corrugated-iron school building and his new parents, with a layover in Holland — who had to be held tight. He was kicking and flailing. Two other Frenchmen had twisted his arms up behind his back and finally got him onto the ground, face down in the grass of my brother's garden.

"Messieurs . . . ! Messieurs!" I heard Serge call out as he hurried with giant steps toward the group. But he had already knocked back quite a bit of the local red and was clearly having a hard time walking straight at all. *"Messieurs! Qu'est-ce qu'il se passe?"*

13

I went to the men's room, but when I came back, the main course still hadn't arrived. A new bottle of wine, however, was already on the table.

The furnishings of the men's room had been thought about a bit too much — one could even wonder whether terms like "men's room" or "toilet" quite fit the bill. Water was gurgling everywhere, not only along the stainless-steel peeing wall, but also down the full-length mirrors in their granite frames. You could say — rightly — that they were all consistent parts of a whole: consistent with the waitresses' tight ponytails, their black pinafores, the Art Deco lamp on the lectern, the organic meat, and the manager's pinstripe suit — the only problem being that it was never exactly clear what that whole might boil down to. It was sort of like certain designer glasses, glasses that add nothing to the personality of the person wearing them. On the contrary, they draw attention first and foremost to themselves: I am a pair of glasses, and don't you ever forget it!

It wasn't that I'd really needed to go to the toilet. I just had to get away for a moment, away from our table and all the gabbing about movies and holiday destinations. But when I took up position at the stainless-steel urinal, purely for form's sake, and opened my fly, the gurgling water and the tinkling of piano music in the background suddenly made me have to go really badly.

It was at that moment that I heard the door open and a new visitor enter the men's room. Now, I'm not one of those men who suddenly can't pee anymore when someone else is in the room, but it does take longer: it takes longer, above all, for me to get going. I cursed myself for having gone to the urinal and not into a stall.

The new visitor cleared his throat a couple of times; he was also humming something that sounded vaguely familiar, a melody I recognized only a second later as "Killing Me Softly."

"Killing Me Softly with His Song" . . . by . . . goddamn it, what was that woman's name again? Roberta Flack! Bingo! I prayed to God that the man would go find a toilet of his own, but from the corner of my eye I saw him step up to the peeing wall just a few feet away from me. He made the usual motions, and after only a few seconds I heard the sound of a steady, powerful jet of urine clattering against the water streaming down the wall.

It was the sort of jet that seems particularly pleased with itself, that wants nothing more than to demonstrate its own boundless good health and that probably, once, back in primary school, belonged to the little boy who could pee farther than anyone else, all the way across the ditch.

I looked up and saw that the owner of the jet was the man with the beard, the man with the beard who had been sitting with his objectionably young girlfriend at the table next to ours. Just then, the man looked over too. We both nodded vaguely, as is customary when two men stand three feet apart to take a piss. From within the beard, the man's mouth twisted into a grin. A triumphant grin, I couldn't help thinking, the typical grin of a man with a powerful jet, a grin that was amused by men who had more trouble peeing than he did.

After all, wasn't a powerful jet also a sign of manliness? Didn't it, perhaps, give its owner right of primacy when it came to the available women? And, conversely, wasn't a cowardly dribble an indication that there were probably other things that didn't flow right down there? Indeed, that the survival of the species would be endangered were women to shrug indifferently at such dribbling and no longer let themselves be drawn to the healthy sound of a powerful jet?

There were no partitions between us — all I would have had to do was lower my eyes to catch sight of the dick that went along with the bearded man. Judging from the clatter, it had to be a big dick, I thought to myself, a big cock of the shameless variety, with thick blue veins right below the surface of darkish-gray skin that was ruddily healthy yet still rather rough: the sort of dick that might tempt a man to spend his holidays at a nudist camp, or in any event to purchase the smallest model *slip de bain,* of the flimsiest material possible.

The reason why I had excused myself and gone to the men's room was because it was all becoming too much for me. By way of holiday destinations and the Dordogne, we had ended up at racism. My wife had supported me in my position that muffling away racism and pretending it wasn't there only made the problem worse. Out of the blue, and without even looking at me, she came to my aid. "I think that what Paul means is . . ." That was how she started: by putting into words what she thought I was trying to say. Coming from anyone but Claire, it could have sounded denigrating, or patronizing or condescending, as though I were unable to express my own opinions in words another person could understand. But coming from Claire, "I think that what Paul means is . . ." meant nothing more and nothing less than that the others were too slow on the uptake, too thick to grasp a point that her husband was holding up before their eyes in an extremely clear and obvious fashion — and that she was starting to lose patience.

After that, we went back to films for a little bit. Claire said that *Guess Who's Coming to Dinner?* was "the most racist movie ever." Everyone knows the story, set in the late 1960s. The daughter of a wealthy white couple (played by Spencer Tracy and Katharine Hepburn) brings her new fiancé home to meet her parents. To their great dismay, the fiancé (played by Sidney Poitier) turns out to be black. During dinner, the truth gradually becomes clear: the black man is a good black man, an intelligent black man in a nice suit, a university professor. In intellectual terms, he is far superior to the white parents of his fiancée, who are mediocre, upper-middle-class types chock-full of prejudices concerning Negroes.

"And that's precisely where the racist hook comes in, in those prejudices," Claire had said. "The black people the parents know about, from TV and the neighborhoods where they're afraid to go, are poor and lazy and violent criminals. But their future son-in-law, fortunately, is a well-adapted Negro who has put on the white man's neat three-piece suit. In order to look as much like the white man as he can."

Serge looked at my wife with the look of an interested listener, but his body language betrayed the fact that he found it hard to listen to any woman he couldn't immediately place in simple categories like "tits," "nice ass," or "wouldn't kick her out of bed for eating crackers."

"It wasn't until much later that the first unadapted blacks appeared in movies," Claire said. "Blacks who wore baseball caps and drove flashy cars: violent blacks from the worst neighborhoods. But at least they were themselves. They were no longer some watered-down version of a white man."

At that point, my brother coughed and cleared his throat. He sat up straight, then leaned over the table — as though he were searching for the microphone. That's exactly what it looked like, I thought to myself. In all his movements he was suddenly the national politician again, the shoo-in to be our country's next leader, and he was about to put in her place a woman in the audience in some provincial union hall.

"And what's so bad about adapted black people, Claire?" he said. "I mean, to hear you tell it, you'd rather have them remain themselves, even if that means they go on killing each other in their ghettos over a few grams of crack. With no prospect of improvement."

I looked at my wife. In my thoughts I egged her on, to deliver my brother the coup de grâce. He had set it up, and she could knock it in, as they say. It was just too ghastly, the way he tried to inject his own party platform into a normal discussion about people and the differences between them. *Improvement* . . . a word, nothing more: crap dished up for the constituency.

"I'm not talking about improvement, Serge," Claire said. "I'm talking about the way we — Dutch people, white people, Europeans — look at other cultures. The things we're afraid of. If a group of dark-skinned men was coming toward you down the sidewalk, wouldn't you feel a stronger urge to cross the street if they were wearing baseball caps, rather than neat clothing? Like yours and mine? Or like diplomats? Or office clerks?"

"I never cross the street. I believe we should approach everyone as equals. You mentioned the things we're afraid of. I agree with you about that. If we would just stop being afraid, then we could go on to cultivate more understanding for each other."

"Serge, I'm not some debating partner you need to wow with hollow terms like *improvement* and *understanding.* I'm your sister-in-law, your brother's wife. It's just the four of us here now. As friends. As family."

"What it's about is the right to be a prick," I said.

A brief silence fell, the proverbial silence in which you could hear a pin drop, had that not been ruled out already by the noise of the busy restaurant. It would be going too far to claim that all heads turned in my direction, the way you read sometimes. But attention was being paid. Babette giggled. "Paul . . . !" she said.

"No, but I was suddenly reminded of a TV program that was on years ago," I said. "I can't remember the name of it anymore." I remembered very well but had no desire to mention the name of the program — that would only be a distraction. The name of the program might prompt my brother to make some sarcastic comment, to try to take the edge off my real message before I even had a chance to deliver it. "I didn't know you watched things like that" . . . that kind of comment. "It was about homos. They interviewed an older lady who lived downstairs from two homosexual men, two young men who lived together and took care of her cats sometimes. 'Such sweet boys!' the lady said. What she really meant to say was that even though her two neighbors were homosexual, the way they took care of her cats when she was gone showed that they were still people like you and me. That lady sat there beaming smugly, because now everyone could see how tolerant she was. Her upstairs neighbors were sweet boys, even if they did do dirty things to each other. Objectionable things, actually, unhealthy and unnatural. Perversions, in other words, that were nonetheless mitigated by the boys' selfless care for her cats."

I paused for a moment. Babette smiled. Serge had raised his eyebrows a couple of times. And Claire, my wife, looked amused — the look she gave me when she knew where things were going from here.

112

"In order to understand what this lady was saying about her upstairs neighbors," I went on, because no one else was saying anything, "you have to turn the situation around. If the two sweet homosexuals hadn't fed the cats at all but instead had pelted them with stones or tossed poisoned pork chops down to them from their balcony, then they would have been just plain dirty faggots. I think that's what Claire meant about *Guess Who's Coming to Dinner?* That the friendly Sidney Poitier was a sweet boy too. That the person who made that movie was absolutely no better than the lady in that program. In fact, Sidney Poitier was supposed to serve as a role model. An example for all those other nasty Negroes, the uppity Negroes. The dangerous Negroes, the muggers and the rapists and the crack dealers. When you people put on a good-looking suit like Sidney's and start behaving like the perfect son-in-law, we white folks will be your friends."

14

The man with the beard was drying his hands. I pulled up my zipper, as a sign that I was finished peeing, even though it had produced no sound, and made straight for the exit. My hand was already on the stainless-steel door handle when I heard the man with the beard say: "Isn't it difficult for that friend of yours sometimes, going to a restaurant when he has such a familiar face?"

I stopped. Without letting go of the handle, I turned and looked at him. The man with the beard was still drying his hands with a clump of paper towels. Within the abundant growth of his beard, his mouth had once again twisted itself into a grin — but not a triumphant grin this time, more like a cowardly baring of the teeth. I have no bad intentions, the grin was saying.

"He's not my friend," I said.

The grin vanished. The hands stopped

their drying as well. "Oh, excuse me," he said. "I just saw you sitting there. We, my daughter and I, we figured: just keep acting normal, let's not gawk at him."

I said nothing. The revelation about the daughter had done me more good than I cared to admit. The beard, despite his unabashed jet, had not succeeded in hooking a woman thirty years his junior. He tossed the wet clump of paper into a stainless-steel trash bin; it was one of those bins with a spring-loaded lid, which made it hard for him to get it all in in one shot.

"I was wondering," he said. "I was wondering whether perhaps it was possible . . . My daughter and I, we both feel that our country is in need of a change. She's studying political science. I was wondering whether maybe she could have her picture taken with Mr. Lohman, later on?"

He had pulled a flat, shiny camera from the pocket of his jacket. "It would only take a second," he said. "I realize that it's a private dinner for you and everything, and I don't want to bother him. My daughter . . . my daughter would never forgive me if she knew I'd even dared to ask this. She was the one who said it wasn't right to stare at a famous politician in a restaurant. That you should leave him alone during his few private moments. And that you absolutely shouldn't try to have your picture taken with him. But on the other hand, I know how wonderful it would be for her. To have her picture taken with Serge Lohman, I mean."

I looked at him. I wondered what it would be like to have a father whose face you couldn't see. Whether a day would finally come when, as the daughter of a father like that, you simply lost patience — or whether you got used to it, like bad wallpaper.

"No problem at all," I said. "Mr. Lohman is always pleased to come in contact with his supporters. We're in the middle of an important discussion right now, but just keep your eye on me. When I give you the sign, that will be the right moment for a photo."

15

The first thing I noticed when I came back from the men's room was the silence at our table: the kind of tense silence that tells you right away that you've missed something important.

I had come back into the dining room along with the beard. He was in front of me, so I only noticed the silence once I was already close to our table.

Or no, there was something else that I noticed first: my wife's hand, reaching out diagonally across the tablecloth, holding Babette's. My brother was staring at his empty plate.

And it was only after I settled down in my chair that I realized Babette was crying. A soundless weeping, a barely perceptible shaking of the shoulders, a tremble in her arm — the arm attached to the hand that Claire was holding.

I sought and made eye contact with my

wife. Claire raised her eyebrows and tossed a meaningful glance in the direction of my brother. At that same moment, Serge raised his head, looked at me sheepishly, and shrugged. "Well, Paul, you're in luck," he said. "Maybe you should have stayed in the bathroom a little longer."

Babette yanked her hand away from Claire's, seized her napkin from her lap, and tossed it on her plate.

"You are such an unbelievable shithead!" she said to Serge, sliding back her chair. The next moment, she was walking past the other tables, heading for the toilets — or the exit, I thought. But it didn't seem likely that she would leave us. Her body language, the subdued pace at which she moved past the tables, told me she was hoping one of us would come after her.

And indeed, my brother began getting up from his chair. Claire laid a hand on his forearm. "Let me go to her for a moment, Serge," she said, and stood up. She too hurried off past the other tables. By now Babette had disappeared from view, so I couldn't tell whether she had gone for the toilets or a breath of fresh air.

My brother and I looked at each other. He made an attempt at a feeble smile, but it didn't really work. "It's . . . ," he began.

"She has . . ." He looked around, then brought his head closer to mine. "This isn't what you think," he said then, so quietly that I could barely understand him.

There was something about his head. About his face. It was still the same head (and the same face), but it was like it was suspended in air, with no clear link to a body, without even a coherent thought. He reminded me of a cartoon character who has just had a chair kicked out from under him. The cartoon character remains hanging in space for a moment before he realizes that the chair is no longer there.

If he wore this face while passing out flyers on the street, I thought, flyers calling upon ordinary, everyday people to be sure to vote for him in the coming elections, no one would give him a second look. The face made you think of a brand-new car, fresh from the showroom, that rounds the first corner, swipes a lamppost, and gets a big scratch down its side. No one would want a car like that.

Serge got up and moved to the chair across from me. The chair was Claire's. It belonged to my wife. Without a doubt, he could now feel her body heat, left behind on the seat, right through the cloth of his trousers. The thought of it made me furious.

"Okay, that makes it easier for us to talk," he said.

I didn't say a thing. I won't deny that this was how I liked to see my brother: floundering. I wasn't about to throw him a life buoy.

"She's been having a hard time lately with . . . well, you know . . . I've always hated that word," he said. "The menopause. It sounds like something that would never happen to our wives."

He paused. The pause was probably meant for me to say something about Claire. About Claire and the menopause. "Our wives," that's what he'd said. But it was none of his business. Whatever was wrong or right with Claire, that was private.

"It's the hormones," he went on. "First the room's too warm and all the windows have to be opened. The next moment she's suddenly all weepy." He turned his head, his still visibly shaken head, toward the restrooms, the door, and then back to me. "Maybe it's good for her to talk about it with another woman. You know what I mean, girl talk. At moments like this, I can't do anything right anyway."

He grinned. I didn't grin back. He raised his arms from the tabletop and flapped his wrists. Then he leaned his elbows on the table and pressed his fingertips together. He looked over his shoulder again.

"There's something else we should really talk about, though, Paul," he said.

I felt something cold and hard inside me — something cold and hard that had been there all evening — grow a little colder and harder.

"We need to talk about our children," said Serge Lohman.

I nodded. I looked across the aisle and nodded again. The man with the beard had already looked our way a few times. For clarity's sake, I nodded a third time. The man with the beard nodded back.

I saw him put down his knife and fork, lean over to his daughter and whisper something to her. The daughter grabbed her handbag and began rummaging through it. Meanwhile, her father pulled the camera out of his coat pocket and rose from his chair.

Main Course

16

"Grapes," said the manager.

His pinky was hovering less than a quarter of an inch over a minuscule bunch of fruitlets that I thought at first were berries — white currants or something. I didn't know anything about berries really, except that most types were inedible to humans.

The "grapes" were lying beside a deep-purple piece of lettuce, a full two inches of empty plate away from the actual main course — "filet of guinea fowl wrapped in paper-thin sliced German bacon." Serge's plate featured the tiny cluster and the shred of lettuce too, but my brother had ordered the tournedos. There's not a whole lot you can say about a tournedos except that it's a piece of meat, but because something had to be said, the manager provided a brief account of where the tournedos came from. Of the "organic farm" where the animals "lived in freedom," until they were butchered.

I could see Serge's impatience. He was hungry in the way only Serge can be hungry. I recognized the symptoms: the tip of his tongue sweeping across his upper lip like the tongue of a ravenous dog in a cartoon, the rubbing together of the hands that an outsider could take for delighted anticipation, but which was absolutely anything but. My brother was not delighting in anticipation. There was a tournedos on his plate, and that tournedos had to be wolfed down as quickly as possible. He needed to eat — now!

The only reason I had asked the manager about the grapes was to torment my brother.

Babette and Claire weren't back yet, but what did he care? "They'll be here any minute now," he'd said when no less than four girls in black pinafores had showed up with our main courses, trailing the manager in their wake. The manager asked whether we would like them to wait with this course until our wives had returned, but Serge quashed that immediately. "Please, just put it down," he said. His tongue was already moving across his upper lip, and the hand rubbing was beyond his control.

The manager's little finger pointed first to my guinea-hen filet rolled in German bacon, and then at the side dishes: a little heap of "lasagna slices with eggplant and ricotta," held together with a toothpick, that reminded me of a miniature club sandwich, and an ear of corn impaled at both ends on a spring. The spring was probably meant to enable you to pick up the corn without getting your fingers greasy, but it had, above all, something laughable about it — or no, not laughable, more like something intended to be funny, an ironic nod from the chef, something like that. The spring was chrome plated and stuck out about an inch from either end of the corncob, which glistened with butter. I'm not particularly fond of corn that way. Gnawing at an ear of corn I've always found disgusting — you get too little to eat, and too much remains stuck between your teeth, while the butter goes dripping down your chin. Besides, I've never been able to shake the idea that corncobs, first and foremost, are pig feed.

After the manager had described the organic conditions on the farm, the farm where Serge's tournedos had been cut from a cow, and promised that he would come back in a bit to elucidate the contents of our wives' plates, I pointed to the little bunch of berries. "Are those by any chance white currants?" I asked.

Serge had already plunged his fork into the tournedos. He was poised to cut off a piece; his right hand holding the steak knife was hovering over his plate. The manager had already turned to walk away, but now he turned back. As his pinky approached the bunch of grapelets, I looked at Serge's face.

That face radiated impatience, that above all. Impatience and irritation at this new delay. He'd had no qualms about starting in on his little filet of beef in the absence of Babette and Claire, but he couldn't stand the idea of sinking his teeth into it with a stranger hanging around.

"What was all that about berries?" he asked after the manager had finally walked away and we were alone at last. "Since when are you interested in berries?"

He cut off a large chunk of his tournedos and stuck it in his mouth. The chewing took ten seconds, at the very most. After swallowing, he stared into space for a few moments; it looked as though he were waiting for the meat to hit his stomach. Then he applied his knife and fork to the plate again.

I got up.

"What is it now?" Serge asked.

"I'm going to see what's taking them so long," I said.

17

I tried the ladies' room first. Carefully, so I wouldn't startle anyone, I pushed the door open a crack.

"Claire . . . ?"

Except for the absence of a peeing wall, the room was identical to the men's. Stainless steel, granite, and piano music. The only difference was the vase of white daffodils positioned between the two sinks. I thought about the owner of the restaurant, about his white turtleneck.

"Babette?" Calling my sister-in-law's name was only a formality, an excuse for being in the doorway of the ladies' toilet at all, should anyone actually be in one of the stalls, which didn't seem to be the case.

I walked to the front door, past the cloakroom and the girls at the lectern. It was pleasantly warm outside. A full moon hung between the treetops, and it smelled of herbs, a smell I couldn't quite place but that seemed almost Mediterranean. A little farther along, at the edge of the park, I saw the lights of cars, and a passing tram. And farther still, through the bushes, the lighted windows of the bar where, at this very moment, the regular people were settling down to their spareribs.

I walked down the gravel pathway with its electric torches and turned left along a path that cut around the restaurant. To my right was the footbridge across a ditch, which led to the street with its traffic and the bar serving spareribs; to my left was a rectangular pool. Farther back, where the pool dissolved into darkness, I saw something that I took at first to be a wall, but which on closer inspection turned out to be a head-high hedge.

Turning left again, I walked along the edge of the pool; the light from the restaurant was reflected in the dark water; from here you could see the diners at their tables. I went on a bit, then stopped.

There was no more than thirty feet between us, but I could see my brother sitting at our table and he couldn't see me. As we had waited for the main dish, I had looked outside any number of times but with the falling of darkness had been able to see less and less. From where I sat, however, I was able to see almost the entire restaurant reflected in the glass. Serge would have to press his face up against the window, and then perhaps he would see me standing here, but even then it wasn't certain he would see anything more than a dark form across the pool.

I looked around. As far as I could tell in the dark, the park was deserted. Not a sign of Claire and Babette. My brother had put down his knife and fork and was wiping his mouth with a napkin. From here I couldn't see his plate, but I would have bet there was nothing left on it: the eating had been done, the feeling of hunger was a thing of the past. Serge raised his glass to his lips and drank. Just at that moment, the man with the beard and his daughter stood up from their table. On their way to the door, they paused beside Serge's table. I saw the man with the beard raise his hand; the daughter smiled at him, and Serge raised his glass by way of greeting.

Undoubtedly, they had wanted to thank him again for the "meet and greet." Serge had indeed been the very picture of courtesy. He had passed seamlessly and in an instant from his role as diner in need of privacy to that of nationally known face — a nationally known face that had always remained itself, a regular person, a person like you and me, someone you could come up and talk to anytime and anywhere, because he never placed himself on a pedestal.

I suppose I was the only one who noticed the wrinkle of irritation on his brow when the man with the beard had come over to him the first time. "Please do excuse me, but your . . . your . . . this gentleman assured me that it would be no problem if we . . ." The wrinkle was there for no more than a second. After that, we were shown the Serge Lohman anyone could feel good about voting for, the prime-ministerial candidate who felt at ease among the common people.

"Of course! Of course!" he'd cried jovially when the beard showed him the camera and pointed to his daughter. "And what's your name?" Serge had asked the girl. She wasn't a particularly pretty girl, not the kind who produced that naughty glint in my brother's eye: not a girl for whom he would try to show off, as he had earlier with the clumsy waitress, the Scarlett Johansson look-alike. She did have a nice face, though — an intelligent face, I corrected myself — too intelligent in fact to want to have her picture taken with my brother. "Naomi," she replied.

"Come sit next to me, Naomi," Serge said, and when the girl had settled down in the empty chair he put his arm around her shoulders. The beard took a few steps back. "And now one for the scrapbook," he said after the camera had flashed once, and he took another one.

The photo moment had caused a certain amount of commotion. The people at the tables next to ours had, it's true, acted as though there had been no photo moment, but it was just as with Serge's entrance earlier that evening. Even when you act like nothing is happening, something happens — I don't know how to put it any more clearly. It's like walking right past an accident because you don't like the sight of blood. Or, no, let's scale it down a bit: like an animal that's been hit and is lying dead at the side of the road. You see it, you saw the dead animal from a ways back already, but you don't look at it anymore. You don't feel like seeing the blood and guts spilling out. And so you look at something somewhere else — at the sky, for example, or a flowering bush in the field farther along, at anything except the side of the road.

Serge had been awfully jovial, putting his arm around her shoulders like that: he had pulled the girl over a little closer and then leaned his head to one side, leaned his head so far that their heads almost touched. The result was probably a wonderful photo — the beard's daughter probably couldn't have asked for a better photo — but I had the distinct impression that Serge wouldn't have been so jovial if it had been Scarlett Johansson (or a Scarlett Johansson look-alike) beside him, instead of that girl.

"We'd like to thank you very much," the man with the beard had said. "We won't bother you anymore. You're here in a private capacity."

The girl — Naomi — hadn't spoken a word; she pushed her chair back and went to stand beside her father.

But they still didn't go away.

"Does this happen often?" the beard asked, leaning over a little so that his head was just over our table. He was also speaking more quietly, more confidentially. "That people just come up to you and ask to have their picture taken with you?"

My brother stared at him; the wrinkle between his eyebrows was back. What more did they want from him? the wrinkle said. The beard and his daughter had had their jovial moment — now they should just fuck off.

For once, I couldn't blame him. I had seen it happen before, the way people hung around Serge Lohman too long. They couldn't take leave of him; they wanted the moment to last longer. Yes, they almost always wanted a little bit more. A photograph or an autograph wasn't enough. They wanted something exclusive, an exclusive treatment. A distinction had to be made between them and all those others who came up and asked for a photo or an autograph. They were looking for a story. A story they could tell everyone the next day: You know who I met last night? Yeah, that's the one. So nice, so normal. We thought that after the picture was taken, he would want to be left alone. But he didn't, not at all! He invited us to sit down at his table and insisted we have a drink with him. I don't think everyone with a famous face would do that. But he did. And it was late by the time we left.

Serge looked at the man with the beard. The wrinkle between his eyebrows had become more pronounced, but an outsider might have mistaken it for the frown of someone whose eyes were pained by looking into the light. He slid his knife across the tablecloth, away from his plate, then back again. I knew the dilemma he was

135

struggling with. I had been there more often, more often than I liked: my brother wanted to be left alone. He had shown the sunniest side of his character. He had let the father immortalize him with his arm around the daughter's shoulder. He was normal, he was human: anyone who voted for Serge Lohman was voting for a normal and human prime minister.

But now, now that the beard just kept standing there, waiting for even more free chitchat with which he could show off in front of his colleagues on Monday morning, Serge had to control himself. One cutting or even mildly sarcastic comment could ruin everything, and the entire charm offensive would have been pointless. On Monday, the beard would tell his colleagues what an arrogant shit Serge Lohman had turned out to be, a man who put on airs. After all, the beard and his daughter hadn't been bothering him; all they did was ask for a picture and then left him to his little private dinner party. Among those colleagues there would be two or three who wouldn't vote for Serge Lohman after hearing that. In fact, it was quite possible that those two or three colleagues would pass along the story about the arrogant, unapproachable party leader — the so-called

136

snowball effect. As with all slander, the story would take on increasingly grotesque form every time it was told. The highly reliable gossip would spread like wildfire, telling how Serge Lohman had treated someone with contempt, an ordinary father and his daughter who had asked politely to have their picture taken with him. In a later version, the candidate for prime minister would have thrown the two out of the restaurant on their ears.

Even though he had only himself to blame for this, at that moment I felt sorry for my brother. I had always sympathized with the movie stars and rock idols who went after the paparazzi lying in wait for them outside the club and broke their cameras. Had Serge decided to take a swing and smack the beard right in the face, wherever that might be hidden behind those despicably laughable or laughably despicable leprechaun bristles, he could have counted on me one hundred percent. I would have twisted the beard's arms behind his back, I thought to myself, so that Serge could concentrate on smashing his face. He would, after all, have to throw a little more weight into the punches in order to damage anything behind all that hair.

Without exaggerating, you could say that

Serge was of two minds when it came to public attention. At those moments and on those occasions when he is the public's sweetheart, during his speeches in provincial union halls, when he answers questions from an audience of the "rank and file," or in front of the TV cameras or radio microphones, when he stands in a street market in a windbreaker handing out campaign flyers and talking to regular people, or when he stands at the lectern and lets the applause roll over him — no, what am I saying: the continuous standing ovation that lasted for minutes at the last party congress (flowers were thrown onto the podium, spontaneously, it was said, but in fact carefully stage-directed by his campaign manager), at moments like that, he shines. It's not just a matter of beaming with pride, or self-importance, or because politicians who want to get ahead simply have to beam, because otherwise the campaign might end tomorrow. No, he really shines: he radiates something.

Every time I've seen it, it has surprised me. It is surprising and amazing to behold how my brother — the oaf, the lumpen boor who "has to eat now" and scarfs down his tournedos joylessly in three bites, the easily bored dullard whose eyes start to wander at every subject that doesn't have to do with *him* — how this brother of mine on a podium and in the spotlights and on TV literally begins to shine — how, in other words, he becomes a politician with charisma.

"It's his magic," said the hostess of a young people's program, in an interview with a women's magazine. "When you get close to him, something happens." I happened to see that particular episode of the young people's program, and it was clear what Serge did. First of all, he never stops smiling. He's taught himself to do that — his eyes don't smile along, which is how you can tell it's not for real. But still: he smiles, and people like that. For the rest, throughout most of the interview, he stood with his hands in his pockets, not bored or blasé, but casual, as though he were standing in a schoolyard (a schoolyard was not far off the mark, actually, because the interview was done in some noisy and poorly lit youth club, after a speech there). He was too old to pass for a schoolboy, but he was the nicest teacher of them all: the teacher you could confide in, who sometimes says "shit" or "cool"; the teacher without a tie who, during the field trip to Paris, gets a little tipsy at the hotel bar along with everyone else. Occasionally, Serge took a hand out of his pocket to illustrate with a gesture some point from the party program, and then it was as though he was going to run that hand through the hostess's hair, or say that her hair was nice.

But in private, that all changes. Like everyone with a famous face, he also has the look: whenever he goes into someplace in a private capacity, he never looks straight at anyone. His eyes dart around without fixing on any living person — he looks at ceilings, at the lamps hanging from those ceilings, at tables, at chairs, at the framed prints on the wall. What he would really like to do is to look at nothing at all. And the whole time, he grins; it's the grin of someone who knows that everyone is looking at him — or purposely not looking at him, which boils down to the same thing. Sometimes it's hard for him to keep those two things — the public property and the private circumstances — separate. Then you see him thinking that maybe it's not such a bad idea to profit a little from the public interest during his private moments — like tonight, in the restaurant.

He looked at the man with the beard and then at me. The wrinkle was gone. He winked, and the next moment he reached into his coat pocket and pulled out his cell phone.

"Excuse me, would you?" he said, taking a look at the display. "I'm afraid I have to take this." He smiled apologetically at the beard, pressed a key, and raised the phone to his ear.

There had been no sound, no old-fashioned ringing, no special ringtone with a little tune — but it was possible. There was plenty of background noise that could have prevented the beard and Naomi and me from hearing anything — or who knows, maybe he had the phone set to vibrate.

Who could say? Certainly not the beard. For him, the moment had arrived to slink away empty-handed. Of course, he might have had his doubts about the phone call — he had every reason to think he was being flimflammed — but experience showed that people didn't do that. It ruined their story: they'd had their picture taken with the future prime minister of the Netherlands; they had talked to him a little, but he was a busy man too.

"Oh," Serge said into the phone. "Where?" He was no longer looking at the beard and his daughter, he was looking outside; as far as he was concerned, they had already left. It was, I must admit, a great bit of acting.

"I'm having dinner at the moment," he said, and looked at his watch; he mentioned the name of the restaurant. "No, I won't be able to do that before midnight," he said.

I felt it was my duty to look at the man with the beard. I was the receptionist who shows the patient to the door, because the doctor himself has to deal with the next patient. I gestured, not an apologetic gesture, but one that more or less said that he and his daughter could now withdraw without suffering any loss of face.

"These are the times when you ask yourself what you do it for," my brother sighed when we were alone again and he had put away his cell phone. "Jesus Christ, those are the worst! The ones who just won't go away. If the girl had at least been a little bit pretty . . ." He winked. "Oh, I'm sorry, Paul, I forgot. You like them like that, the wallflowers."

He grinned at his own little joke, and I grinned along with him, looking toward the door to see if Claire and Babette were on their way back. But then, before I expected it, Serge grew serious again. He put his elbows on the table and formed a little bridge with his fingertips. "So what were we talking about?" he said.

And then they came with the main course.

18

And then? Then I was standing outside, looking from a distance at my brother, who was sitting at our table all alone. I was sorely tempted to spend the rest of the evening out here — or at least not go back inside.

I heard an electronic beep that I couldn't place at first, followed by other beeps that together seemed to form a melody; what it resembled most was the ringtone coming from a cell phone, but not my own.

Still, undeniably, it was coming from the pocket of my own blazer — the right pocket. I'm left-handed; I always put my cell in my left-hand pocket. I slid my hand — my right hand — into the pocket and felt, in addition to the familiar key ring and something hard that I knew to be an open pack of Stimorol, an object that could only be a phone.

Before I had time to even pull it out, I realized what was going on. How Michel's phone had ended up in my pocket was something I couldn't reconstruct immediately, but I still found myself faced with the simple fact that someone was calling Michel. On his cell phone. Now that it was no longer muffled by the fabric of my blazer, the ringtone was awfully loud, so loud I was afraid people might hear it all over the park.

"Fuck," I said.

The best thing, of course, would be to let the phone go on ringing until it switched to voice mail. On the other hand, I wanted it to stop making that noise right away.

On the other hand, I was curious about who was calling.

I looked at the display to see whether I might recognize a name, but reading proved unnecessary. The display lit up in the dark, and even though the features were a bit blurry, I had no trouble recognizing my own wife's face.

Claire, for some reason, was calling her son, and there was only one way to find out what that reason was.

"Claire?" I said after sliding the phone open.

There was no sound. "Claire?" I said again. I looked around a few times; it wasn't hard to imagine that my wife would suddenly pop out from behind a tree — surprise, it was all a joke, even if it was a joke I didn't quite get at the moment.

"Dad?"

"Michel! Where are you?"

"At home. I was . . . I couldn't . . . But where are you?"

"At the restaurant. We told you. But how —" But how did I get your cell phone, I wanted to say, but suddenly that didn't seem like a good question to ask.

"But what are you doing with my cell?" my son asked then; he didn't sound upset, more surprised, like me.

His room, earlier that evening, his phone on the table . . . What were you doing up here? You said you were looking for me. Why were you looking for me? Did I have his phone in my hand at that moment? Or had I already put it back on the table? I was just looking for you. Could I really have . . . ? But then I would have had to have my blazer on already. I never wear blazers around the house. I tried to think why I would have gone upstairs wearing my blazer, to my son's room. "I have no idea," I said meanwhile, sounding as casual as I could. "I'm just as surprised as you are. I mean, they sort of look alike, our cell phones, but I can hardly imagine that I —"

"I couldn't find it anywhere," Michel butted in. "So I called my own number to

145

see if I could hear it ring somewhere."

His mother's picture on the screen. He had called from home — the screen on his phone showed a picture of his mother when anyone called him from our land line. Not a picture of his father, it flashed through my mind. Or of the two of us. At the same moment, I realized how ridiculous that would be, a picture of his parents on the couch in the living room, smiling with their arms around each other: a happy marriage. Daddy and Mommy are calling. Daddy and Mommy want to talk to me. Daddy and Mommy love me more than anyone else in the world.

"I'm sorry, guy. I guess I was stupid enough to put your cell phone in my pocket. Your father must have had a senior moment." Home was Mama. Home was Claire. I didn't feel left out, I noted; somehow it was actually a comfort. "We won't be home late. You'll have it back in a couple of hours."

"Where are you guys? Oh yeah, you went to dinner. You said that already. Isn't that the restaurant in that park, across from . . ." Michel mentioned the name of the regular-people café. "That's not very far."

"Don't bother. You'll have it back before you know it. An hour or so, max." Did I still sound lighthearted? Cheerful? Or could you tell from my voice that I didn't really want him to come to the restaurant and pick up his phone?

"I can't wait that long. I've got . . . I need some numbers. I have to call someone." Did I actually hear him hesitate there, or was it just that the connection was lost for a moment?

"I'll look for you if you want. If you tell me which number you need . . ."

No, that was completely the wrong tone. I had no desire to be that kind of easygoing, fun-to-be-around dad: a father who's allowed to poke around in his son's cell phone because father and son, after all, "have nothing to hide from each other." I was already so grateful that Michel still called me "Dad" and not "Paul." There was something about that first-name-basis business that had always appalled me: children of seven who called their father "George" or their mother "Wilma." It was freeness and easiness of the wrong sort, and at the end of the day it always backfired on the all-too-free-and-easy parents. It was only a small step from "George" and "Wilma" to "But I said I wanted peanut butter, didn't I, George?" After which the sandwich with chocolate sprinkles is sent back to the kitchen and disappears into the garbage.

I've seen them often enough in my own surroundings, parents who laugh rather sheepishly when their children speak to them in that tone of voice. "Oh, you know, these days they hit adolescence a lot earlier" is how they try to smooth it over, but they are too shortsighted, or simply too cowardly, to realize that they have called this reign of terror down upon themselves. In their heart of hearts, of course, what they hope is that their children will go on liking them for longer as George and Wilma than they would as Dad and Mom.

A father who looked at the contents of his fifteen-year-old son's cell phone was getting too close. He could see right away how many girls were in the contacts, or which raunchy photos had been downloaded as screen wallpaper. No, my son and I did have things to hide: We respected each other's privacy. We knocked on the door of the other's room when it was closed. And we did not, for example, walk in and out of the bathroom naked without towels around our waists simply because there was nothing to hide, as was common in George-and-Wilma families — no, not that, not that at all!

But I had already snooped around in Michel's cell phone. I had seen things that weren't meant for me. From Michel's point of view, it was mortally dangerous for me to hold onto his phone any longer than was absolutely necessary.

"No, that's okay, Dad. I'm coming right now to get it."

"Michel?" I said, but he had already hung up. "Fuck!" I shouted for the second time that evening, and at that moment I saw Claire and Babette emerging from behind the tall hedge. My wife had her arm around her sister-in-law's shoulder.

It took only a few blinks of an eye: during those blinks, I thought about stepping back and making myself fade into the shrubbery. But then I remembered why I had gone into the garden in the first place: to find Claire and Babette. It could have been worse. Claire could have seen me using Michel's cell phone. She could have wondered who I was calling, here, outside the restaurant — in secret!

"Claire!" I waved. Then I walked toward them.

Babette was still holding a hankie to her nose, but there were no more tears to be seen. "Paul . . . ," my wife said.

She looked straight at me as she spoke my name. First she rolled her eyes, then breathed an imaginary sigh. I knew what that meant, because I had seen her do it before — the time, for example, when her mother tried to take an overdose of sleeping pills at the rest home.

It's a lot worse than I thought, the eyes and the sigh said.

Now Babette looked at me as well. She took the hankie away from her face. "Oh, Paul," she said. "Dear, sweet, Paul . . ."

"The . . . the main course has arrived," I said.

19

There was no one in the men's room.

I tried all three cubicles: they were unoccupied.

You two go ahead, I'd said to Claire and Babette when we reached the entrance. Go ahead and start — I'll be there in a minute.

I went into the cubicle farthest from the door and locked it behind me. For appearances' sake, I pulled my trousers down around my ankles and sat: my underpants I kept on.

I took Michel's cell phone out of my pocket and slid it open.

On the display I saw something I hadn't seen before — at least, something I hadn't noticed out in the garden.

At the bottom of the screen, a little white box had appeared:

2 missed calls
Faso

Faso? Who the hell was Faso?

It sounded like a made-up name, a name that couldn't really belong to anyone . . .

And suddenly I knew. Of course! Faso! Faso was the nickname Rick and Michel had given their adopted half brother and half cousin. Beau. Because of the country where he was born. And because of his first name: Beau.

Beau Faso. B. Faso from Burkina Faso.

They had started it a couple of years back — at least that was the first time I'd heard them use the nickname, at Claire's birthday party. "You want some, Faso?" I heard Michel say as he held up to Beau a red plastic bowl of popcorn.

And Serge, who was standing close by, heard it too. "Please," he said. "Cut that out. His name is Beau."

Beau himself seemed to be the last person to be bothered by his nickname. "It's okay, really, Dad," he said to my brother.

"No, it's not okay," Serge said. "Your name is Beau. Faso! I don't know, I just think it's . . . I think it's not nice."

Serge had probably meant to say "I just think it's discrimination" but had bitten his tongue at the last moment.

"Everyone's got a nickname, Dad."

Everyone. That was what Beau wanted. He wanted to be like everyone.

After that I had rarely heard Michel and Rick use the nickname when other people were around. But apparently it had lived on: all the way to Michel's list of contacts.

What had Beau/Faso been calling Michel about?

I could listen to the voice mail, if he'd left a message, but then Michel would see right away that I'd been poking around in his phone. We were both on Vodafone, and I could have recited the voice mail lady's message in my sleep. "You have ONE new message" changed, after the first time it was listened to, into "You have ONE old message."

I pushed the Select button, clicked on through to File Manager, and then to Videos.

A drop-down menu appeared:

1. **Videos**
2. **Downloaded videos**
3. **Favorite videos**

Just as I had a few hours (an eternity) ago in Michel's room, I clicked on **3. Favorite videos.** Even more than an eternity, it had been a turning point — a turning point as in *before* the war or *after* the war.

The still of the most recent video was outlined in blue; this was the film clip I had already watched an eternity ago. I clicked back one video, pushed Options, then Play.

A station. The platform at a station, a subway station by the looks of it. Yes, an aboveground subway station out in one of the suburbs, judging from the high-rise apartments in the background. Maybe the southeast side of town, or else Slotervaart.

I might as well be frank. I recognized the subway station. I knew right away which subway station it was, and where, and along which line — only I'm not going to shout it from the rooftops. At this point, there's no one who would benefit from my mentioning the name of the station.

The camera panned down and began following the heels of a pair of white sneakers that were moving down the platform with a certain degree of haste. After a while, the camera swung up again and you saw a man, an older man, around sixty, I figured, although with people like him it's always hard to tell. It was clear in any case that this was *not* the owner of the white sneakers. When the camera moved in closer you could see his unshaven, rather spotty face. A panhandler, probably, a homeless person. Something like that.

I felt the same cold that I had felt earlier that evening in Michel's room, the cold that came from inside.

Beside the homeless person's head, Rick's face appeared. My brother's son grinned at the camera. "Take one," he said. "Action!"

Then, with no warning, he struck the man on the side of his head with the palm of his hand, on the ear. It was a real rabbit punch: The head lurched to the side. The man winced and raised his hands to cover his ears, as though to ward off the next blow.

"You're a piece of shit, motherfucker!" Rick screamed in English, with a hint of that giveaway accent, like a Dutch actor in a British or American movie.

The camera moved in even closer; the homeless man's unshaven face filled the little screen. He blinked his watery red eyes. His lips mumbled something incomprehensible.

"Say 'Jackass,' " said another voice off-camera, a voice I immediately recognized as my son's.

The homeless man's head disappeared,

and there was Rick again. My nephew looked into the camera and put on an intentionally stupid grin. "Don't try this at home," he said, and took another swing, or at least his arm made a punching movement. The actual blow landed off-camera.

"Say 'Jackass,' " said Michel's voice.

The homeless man's head appeared on-screen again. This time, judging from the camera angle — there were no longer apartment blocks in the background, only a stretch of gray concrete along the platform and rails behind — lying on the ground. His lips trembled. His eyes were closed.

"Jack . . . jack . . . ass," the man said.

There the frame froze. In the ensuing silence, I heard only the sound of water rushing down the peeing wall.

"We need to talk about our children," Serge had said — how long ago?

An hour? Two?

What I really felt like was staying here until tomorrow morning: until the cleaners found me.

I got up.

20

At the entrance to the dining room, I hesitated.

Michel could arrive any moment to pick up his cell phone. He hadn't yet, in any case, I saw as I took a few steps forward, then stopped; the only people at our table were Claire, Babette, and Serge.

I ducked behind a large potted palm. Peeking through the foliage, I didn't have the impression that they'd seen me.

By far the best thing, I reflected, would be to intercept Michel. Here in the entranceway, or at the cloakroom; even better, of course, would be outside in the garden. Yes, I needed to go to the garden; that way I could walk up and meet Michel partway, give him his cell phone there. Not hindered by the looks and possible questions from his mother, uncle, and aunt.

I turned and walked outside, past the girl at the lectern. I had no fixed plan. I would

157

have to say something to my son. But what? I decided to wait and see whether he would bring anything up himself — I would pay close attention to his eyes, I resolved, his honest eyes that had always been so bad at lying.

Following the path with the electric torches, I took the turn to the left, just as I had earlier in the evening. The most obvious thing would be for Michel to take the same route we had, across the footbridge opposite the regular-people's bar. There was another entrance to the park — in fact that was the main entrance — but then he would have to cycle a lot farther in the dark.

When I reached the bridge, I stopped and looked around. There was no one in sight. The light from the restaurant's torches was no more than a weak yellowish glow here, no brighter than a pair of candles.

The darkness had an advantage too. In the dark, when we couldn't see each other's eyes, Michel might be more willing to speak the truth.

And then what? What was I going to do with that "truth"? I rubbed my eyes. I needed to appear lucid, in any case, later. Cupping a hand in front of my mouth, I exhaled and smelled. Yes, my breath smelled of alcohol, of beer and wine. But until now,

I calculated, I had had a total of no more than five drinks. I'd resolved beforehand to remain in control; I didn't want to give Serge the chance to score off me this evening just because I was sloppy. I knew myself well enough. I knew that a dinner out had a certain limited curve of concentration, and that by the end of that curve I would no longer have the oomph to come back at him if he started in about our children again.

I looked at the other side of the bridge and the lights of the bar behind the bushes, on the far side of the street. A tram rode past the stop without slowing down. After that, it was silent again.

"Hurry up, now!" I said out loud.

And it was there and at that precise moment, as I heard the sound of my own voice — was jolted awake by the sound of my own voice, I should perhaps say — that I suddenly knew what I had to do.

I took Michel's cell phone out of my pocket and slid it open.

I pressed Show.

I read both text messages: the first one contained a phone number, and the comment that no message had been left; the second said that the same number had left **1 new message.**

159

I compared the times under the two texts. Between the first and the second there had been only two minutes. Both had arrived just a little more than fifteen minutes ago — while I was talking to my son on the phone, in this same park, just a little ways from here.

I pressed Options twice, then hit Delete.

Then I called the number on the voice mail.

When Michel got his phone back later, there would be no missed calls listed on the display, I reasoned, and therefore no reason for him to consult his voice mail — at least not for the time being.

"Yo!" I heard then, after the voice mail lady had announced that there was one new message (and two old ones). "Yo! You gonna call me back, or what?!"

Yo! About six months ago, Beau had started adopting the Afro-American look, with a New York Yankees cap and matching lingo. He had been taken from Africa and brought here, and until a short while ago he had always spoken proper, standard Dutch. Not the Dutch spoken by ordinary people, but the Dutch of the circles surrounding my brother and his wife. Supposedly quite neutral, but in fact with the accent recognizable among thousands as that of the elite —

160

the Dutch you hear on the tennis court and in the canteen at the hockey club.

There must have been a day when Beau had looked in the mirror and decided that Africa was synonymous with pitiful and needy. But despite his prim diction, he would never be a Dutchman either. So it was perfectly understandable for him to go looking for his identity elsewhere, on the far side of the Atlantic, in the black neighborhoods of New York and Los Angeles.

From the very beginning, though, there had been something about this act that annoyed me terribly. It was the same thing that had always annoyed me about my brother's adopted son — something about his aura of sainthood, if you could call it that, the shrewdness with which he exploited his differentness from his adoptive parents, his adoptive brother, his adoptive sister, and cousin.

As a little boy he had climbed onto "Mother's" lap much more often than Rick or Valerie did — usually in tears. Babette would caress his little black head and speak comforting words, but she was already looking around to find who to blame for Beau's sorrow.

The guilty party was usually not far away.

"What happened to Beau?" she would

demand accusingly of her biological son.

"Nothing, Mama," I heard Rick say once. "All I did was look at him."

"In fact," Claire had said when I aired my dislike of Beau, "you're a racist."

"No I'm not!" I said. "I would be a racist if I liked that little hypocrite simply for the color of his skin or where he comes from. Positive discrimination. I would only be a racist if our adopted nephew's hypocrisy made me draw conclusions about Africa in general, or Burkina Faso in particular."

"I was only kidding," said Claire.

A bicycle was coming across the bridge. A bicycle with a headlight. I could see the rider only in silhouette, but I could have picked my own boy out of a crowd of thousands, even in the dark. The way he sat hunched down over the handlebars like a racing cyclist, the supple nonchalance with which he let the bike sway left and right while the body itself barely moved: these were the ways and moves of . . . of a predator. The thought popped into my mind without my being able to stop it. "Of an athlete" was what I had meant to say — to think. A sportsman.

Michel played soccer and tennis, and six months ago he had joined a gym. He didn't smoke, was very moderate with alcohol, and he had on more than one occasion expressed his disdain for drugs, both soft and hard. "Those losers" was what he called the pot-heads in his class, and we, Claire and I, were all too pleased to hear it. Pleased to have a son who was not a delinquent, who rarely skipped school and always did his home-work. He was not an exceptionally good student. He never went out of his way to excel — in fact, he barely did more than the bare minimum — but on the other hand, there were never any complaints. His marks and exam scores were usually "average"; it was only for gym that he ever received an A+.

"Old message," the voice mail lady said.

I realized only then that I was still holding his cell phone to my ear. Michel was already halfway across the bridge. I turned my back to him and began walking toward the restau-rant; whatever happened, I had to break the connection as quickly as possible and stuff the phone back into my pocket.

"Tonight's okay," Rick's voice said. "We'll do it tonight. Call me. Ciao."

After that, the voice mail lady announced the time and date that the message had been left.

I heard Michel behind me, his bike tires crunching on the gravel.

"Old message," she said again.

Michel cycled past me. What did he see? A man rambling through the park all alone? Holding a cell phone to his ear? Or did he see his father? With or without the cell phone?

"Hi, love," I heard Claire's voice say now, at the same moment that my son went by. He cycled on to the lit gravel path and climbed off the bike. He looked around quickly, then walked his bike to the rack to the left of the entrance. "I'll be home in an hour. Your father and I are going to the restaurant at seven. I'll make sure we stay away till after midnight. So you two have to do it tonight. Your father doesn't know about any of this, and I want to keep it that way. Bye, love. See you in a bit. Big smooch."

Michel had locked his bike and was walking toward the door. The voice mail lady mentioned the date (today) and the time (two in the afternoon) that this last message had been left.

Your father doesn't know about any of this.

"Michel!" I shouted. I slid the cell phone into my pocket. He stopped and looked around. I waved.

And I want to keep it that way.

My son came toward me along the gravel. We met precisely at the top of the path. It was awfully well lit. But maybe I was going to need this much light, I thought.

"Hi," he said. He was wearing his black knit cap with the Nike logo. The headphones were slung around his neck, the cable running down the collar of his jacket — a green quilted Dolce & Gabbana jacket he had bought with his own clothes allowance only recently, after which there was no money left for socks and underpants.

"Hi, guy," I said. "I figured I'd walk up a bit and meet you."

My son looked at me. His honest eyes. Frank, that was how you would have to describe his gaze. Your father doesn't know about any of this.

"You were talking on the phone," he said.

I said nothing.

"Who were you talking to?"

He was trying to sound as casual as possible, but there was an urgent undertone to his voice. It was a tone I had never heard there before, and I could feel the hair standing up on the back of my neck.

"I was trying to call you," I said. "I was wondering what was taking you so long."

21

This is what happened. These are the facts.

One night, about two months ago, three boys were on their way home from a party. It was a party in the canteen of the high school two of the three boys attended. Those two were brothers. One of them was adopted.

The third boy went to a different school. He was their cousin.

Although the cousin never drank alcohol, that evening he had had a couple of beers. Just like the other two. Both cousins had danced with girls. Not their steady girl-friends, because they didn't have them at that point — all different girls. The adopted brother did have a steady girlfriend. He spent most of the evening kissing her in a darkened corner.

The girlfriend had not gone along when the three boys left. They all had to be home by one. The girl was waiting for her father to come and pick her up.

It was, in fact, already one thirty, but the boys knew that this fell within the limits their parents allowed. It had been agreed beforehand that the cousin would sleep over at the home of the two brothers — the cousin's parents were spending a few days in Paris.

They had decided to drink one last beer at a café on their way back. But because they didn't have enough money on them, they needed to stop first at a cash machine. A few streets farther down — they were now about halfway between the school and home — they found an ATM. It was one of those with an outer door made of safety glass; the machine itself was inside, in a cubicle.

One of the two brothers, the biological brother as it were, goes in to withdraw cash. The adopted brother and the cousin wait outside. But then the biological brother comes back outside almost immediately. So quick? the other two ask. No, man, the brother says, man, I flipped my shit. What is it? the others ask. Inside there, the brother says. There's someone lying there. Someone's lying there asleep, in a sleeping bag. Jesus, man, I almost stepped on his head.

As to what precisely happened after that, and above all as to who was the first to come up with the disastrous plan, accounts differ. All three of them agreed that it stank inside the ATM cubicle. A horrible stench: a mixture of barf and sweat, and something else that one of the three described as being like the smell of a rotting corpse.

That stench is significant. A person who stinks cannot count on much sympathy. A stench can be blinding. No matter how human those odors are, they can actually obscure the perception of the one who stinks as a real person of flesh and blood. That is no excuse for what happened, but it would also not be right simply to omit it.

Three boys are out to get some cash — not a lot, a few ten-euro notes for a final beer at the café. But there was no way they were going to hang around in that stench. You couldn't be around it for more than ten seconds without gagging — it was like a torn-open garbage bag was lying there.

But what is lying there is a person: a person who breathes, yes, who even snores and snorts in his sleep. Come on, we'll find another ATM, the adopted brother says. Forget it, say the other two. That's crazy, if you can't even get some cash because someone's lying in front of the machine, stinking and sleeping off his rotgut. Come on, the adopted brother says again, let's go.

But the other two think that's spineless. They're going to withdraw their money here. They're not going to go off and walk however many blocks to some other machine. Now the cousin goes inside. He starts yanking on the sleeping bag. Hey, hey, wake up! Get up!

I'm leaving, says the adopted brother. I'm not into this.

Don't be such a wimp, say the other two. We'll be done in a minute, and then we'll grab a beer. But the adopted brother says again that he's not into it, that he's tired anyway and doesn't feel like a beer anymore — and then he goes off on his bike.

The biological brother tries to stop him. Wait a minute, he shouts after him. But the adopted brother only waves back, then disappears around the corner. Let him go, the cousin says. He's a bore. He's squeaky clean. He's a boring asshole.

The two of them go back inside. The brother tugs at the sleeping bag. Hey, wake up! Oh, blecch . . . man, that stinks, he says. The cousin kicks the foot end of the sleeping bag. It's not really the smell of a corpse, more like garbage bags — that's right, garbage bags full of leftover food, gnawed-off chicken bones, moldy coffee filters. Wake up! A kind of stubbornness comes over both

169

of them now, the cousin and the brother. They're going to withdraw cash here, at this ATM, and nowhere else. Of course, they'd had a little to drink at the school party. And it is in fact that same stubbornness, the stubbornness of the tipsy driver who says he's perfectly capable of taking the wheel himself — and the stubbornness of the guest who hangs around too long at the end of your birthday party, who grabs one last beer ("one for the road"), then tells you the same story for the seventh time that evening.

You got to get up, mister — this is a cash machine. They remain polite: despite the stench, so horrific it brings tears to their eyes, they still call him mister. The stranger, the invisible man in the sleeping bag, is undoubtedly older than they are. A mister, in other words, probably a tramp, but still a mister.

Now, for the first time, sounds start to come from inside the sleeping bag. They are the kinds of sounds you'd pretty much expect in the circumstances: moaning, groaning, unintelligible mumbling. It is coming to life. It still sounds like a child who doesn't want to get up yet, who maybe doesn't really want to go to school today, but then the sounds are followed by movements: someone or something stretches and

170

seems about to poke a head or some other body part out of the sleeping bag.

They don't have a clear plan, the brother and the cousin. They realize, perhaps too late, that they really don't want to know precisely what's hidden away inside the sleeping bag. So far it has been only an obstacle, something that was in the way. It gave off a monstrous stench, it didn't belong there, it had to go away, but now they actually have to talk to that something (or someone) who's been woken up against its will, woken from its dreams. Who knows what the stinking homeless dream about — about a roof over their head, probably, a warm meal, a wife and children, a house with a driveway, a sweet dog wagging its tail and running toward them across a lawn complete with sprinkler.

Fuck off!

It's not the curse that shocks them so much at first, but the voice. It shatters certain expectations. You would expect to see something unshaven appear from the sleeping bag: sweaty hair glued to the skull, a mouth toothless but for a couple of black stumps. But this sounds almost like a woman . . .

But what if it *was* a . . . At that same moment, the sleeping bag starts moving even more: a hand, another hand, a whole arm, and then a head. You can't really tell right away, or yes you can, because of the hair with bald spots — black hair, gray here and there, with the scalp shining through. A man goes bald differently. The face itself is grimy, unshaven, or no — it has facial hair, but clearly not like a man's. Fuck off! Bastards! The voice is shrill. The woman flails around with one arm, the way you chase away flies. A woman. The brother and the cousin look at each other. It's time to knock off. Later, they will both recall that exact same moment. The discovery that it is a woman in the sleeping bag changes everything. Come on, let's go, the brother actually says. Goddamn it! the woman screams. Fuck off! Fuck off!

Shut your face! the cousin says. I said, Shut your face! He kicks the sleeping bag hard, but there isn't much space for kicking. He can barely keep his balance, and he slips. His foot shoots out too far. The tip of his shoe grazes the sleeping bag and hits the woman right under the nose. A hand with greasy, swollen fingers and black nails is raised to the nose. There is blood. Bastards! they hear. The voice is now so loud and shrill that it seems to fill everything. Murderers! Scumbags! The brother pulls the

172

cousin toward the door. Come on, let's get out of here. Then they are out the door and standing outside. Dirty, rotten bastards, they can still hear from the cash-machine cubicle, a bit quieter now, but probably still loud enough to be heard down at the corner. It's late, though. The street is deserted. There are only three or four windows still lit in the entire area.

I wasn't going to . . . , the cousin said. My foot slipped. Jesus Christ, what a filthy bitch! Sure, the brother says. Of course you didn't. Jesus, I wish she'd shut up! Noise is still coming from the cubicle, but the door has fallen shut now; it's already more muffled — a spluttering, a vague, injured spluttering.

Then suddenly they can't help laughing; they're able to remember precisely the way they looked at each other, their own indignant, flushed faces — that, and the muffled grumbling from behind the glass door, and how they had burst out laughing. In stitches. There's no stopping it. They have to lean against the wall to keep from falling down, and then they lean on each other. They throw their arms around each other's necks, their bodies shaking with laughter. Bunch of scumbags! The brother imitates the woman's shrill voice. Bastards! The cousin

173

squats down, then falls to the ground. Stop it please! Please! You're killing me!

Leaning against a tree are a few garbage bags, and a couple of other objects obviously put there for the morning trash collection: an office chair on casters, a cardboard box that once contained a wide-screen TV, a desk lamp, and a picture tube. They're still laughing as they pick up the office chair and carry it over to the cubicle. Dirty, rotten shit-whore! They throw the chair, in as far as it can go into the little cubicle, at the sleeping bag, which the woman has now crawled back into. The cousin holds the door open. The brother goes back for the desk lamp, and two full garbage bags. The woman pokes her head out of the sleeping bag again. Her hair really is stuck together in thick, greasy mats. She has a beard, or else it's just caked-on filth. She tries to push the office chair away with one hand but doesn't really succeed. Then the first garbage bag hits her full in the face: her head rocks back, strikes hard against the steel wastepaper container on the wall. Now the cousin throws the desk lamp. It's an old-fashioned kind with a round shade and a retractable arm. The metal shade hits the woman on the nose. It is perhaps strange that she has stopped screaming, that the brother and the cousin are no longer hearing her shrill voice. She is merely sitting there, nodding groggily, when the second garbage bag hits her in the face. Stupid whore, go pass out somewhere else, then! Get a job! That "Get a job!" cracks them up again. Get a job! the brother shouts. Get a job, job, job! The cousin is back outside again. He goes over to the tree where the garbage bags were. He pushes aside the wide-screen box and sees the gas can. It's one of those army gas cans, a green one like the kind you see on the backs of jeeps. The cousin picks up the gas can by the handle. Empty. What else would he have expected — who would put a full gas can out with the trash? No, no, what do you think we're gonna do? the brother cries when he sees the cousin coming with the gas can. Nothing, man — it's empty, right? The woman has come back to her senses a little. You delinquents, you should be ashamed of yourselves, she says in a voice that is suddenly and unexpectedly prim, a voice from the distant past, perhaps, before the free fall started. It stinks in here, the cousin says. We're going to smoke it out a little bit. He holds up the gas can. Cute, she says, but can I go back to sleep now? The blood under her nose has already dried up. The cousin throws the empty gas can — perhaps on purpose, who knows — beside her head, at a safe distance. It makes a lot of noise, it's true, but all things being equal, it's not as bad as the garbage bags and the desk lamp.

Later — a few weeks later — the footage on the weekly *Opsporing Verzocht,* a Dutch version of the *Most Wanted* series, clearly showed how both boys, after throwing the gas can, go back outside. They remain off-camera for a fairly long time. The images registered by the camera in the cash-machine cubicle never actually show the woman in the sleeping bag. The camera is pointed at the door, at the people who come in for money. You can see those who make a withdrawal, but it's a fixed camera. The rest of the cubicle is out of sight.

The evening Claire and I saw that footage for the first time, Michel was upstairs in his room. We were sitting next to each other on the couch in the living room, with the newspaper and a bottle of red wine left over from dinner. The story had been in all the papers. It was on the evening news a number of times, but it was the first time the footage itself was broadcast. The images were jerky, out of focus, immediately recognizable as from a security camera. Until then, the general reaction had been one of outrage.

176

What was the world coming to? A defense-less woman . . . young people . . . stiffer sentences — yes, even the appeal to restore the death penalty had raised its hoary head again.

That was all before that evening's broadcast. Until then, it had been little more than a news report, a shocking report, true enough, but still — like all news reports — one that was fated to wear thin. With the passing of time, the sharp edges would be dulled, until the story finally disappeared altogether, not important enough in any case to be stored in our collective memory.

But the security-camera footage changed all that. The boys — the offenders — were given a face, albeit a face that was hard to recognize because of the bad quality of the images and the fact that both wore knit caps pulled down over their eyebrows. What the viewers did recognize, however, was something else: they saw all too clearly that the boys were having a good time, that they almost creased up with laughter as they pelted their helpless — or at least invisible — victim, first with the office chair, then the garbage bags, the desk lamp, and finally the empty gas can. You saw — jerkily, in black and white — them high-five each other after throwing the garbage bags, how they screamed things, undoubtedly abuse, at the homeless woman off-camera, even though there was no sound.

Above all, you saw them laughing. That was the moment when the collective memory came into play. It was the key moment — the laughing boys demanded their place in that collective memory. In the top ten of the collective memory, they came in at number eight, probably right below the Vietnamese colonel summarily executing a Vietcong soldier with a bullet through the head, but perhaps even above the Chinese man with his carrier bags trying to stop the tanks at Tiananmen Square.

And there was something else that played a role. The two were wearing knit caps, but they were upper-middle-class boys. They were white. It wasn't easy to say how you could tell. It was hard to put your finger on it — something about their clothing, their movements. The boys down the street. Not the kind of trash who torch cars in order to start a race riot. Comfortably enough off, well-to-do parents. Boys like the ones we all know. Boys like our nephew. Like our son.

Looking back, I can recall the exact moment when I realized that this was not about boys like our nephew or our son, but about our son himself (and about our nephew). It was a cold and deathly quiet moment. Down to the very second, I could still point out the moment in the footage when I tore my eyes away from the TV and looked at Claire's face in profile. Because the investigation is still under way, I'm not going to talk here about what made me realize, with a shock of recognition, that I was sitting on the couch watching our own son pelt a homeless woman with office chairs and garbage bags. And laughing. I'm not going into it any further, because technically I can still deny everything. Do you recognize this boy as Michel Lohman? At this point in the proceedings, I can still shake my head. That's hard to say . . . the images are pretty unclear . . . I couldn't swear to it.

More images came afterwards, a compilation — the moments when little was happening had been edited out. You saw the two boys come back into the cubicle again and again and throw things.

The worst part came at the end, the key image as it were: the picture that caught the attention of half the world. First you saw the gas can being thrown — the empty gas can — and then, after they had gone outside again and come back, something else. On film, it was hard to see what it was: a lighter? a match? You saw a flash of light, a flash that overexposed everything at once, that blinded you for a few seconds. The screen turned white. When the picture came back, you could just see the boys beating a hasty retreat.

They didn't come back. The final images registered by the security camera didn't show much at all. No smoke or flames. The explosion of the gas can had not been followed by a fire. Yet it was precisely this seeing nothing that made the images so terrifying. Because the most important thing was happening off-camera, and you had to fill in the rest for yourself.

The homeless woman was dead. Died right then and there, most probably. At the moment the gas vapors from the gas can exploded in her face. Or at most a couple of minutes later. Perhaps she had tried to wriggle out of the sleeping bag — perhaps not. Off-camera.

I looked, as I said before, at Claire's face in profile. If she turned her head and looked at me, I would know. Then she would have seen the same thing I did.

Claire turned her head and looked at me.

I held my breath — or rather, I took a deep breath, so that I could be the first to say something. Something — I didn't know exactly which words I would use — that

180

would change our lives.

Claire held up the bottle of red wine: there was only a bit left in the bottom, just enough for half a glass.

"Do you want this?" she asked. "Or should I open another one?"

22

Michel put his hands in his coat pockets. It was hard to tell whether he had gone for my lie. When he turned his head to one side, his face was lit by the glow from the restaurant.

"Where's Mama?" he asked.

Mama. Claire. My wife. Mama had told her son that his father didn't know about any of this. And that she wanted to keep it that way.

Earlier in the evening, at the regular-people café, my wife had asked whether I too thought our son had been acting strangely of late. *Distant* — that was the word she'd used. The two of you talk about things Michel and I don't talk about, she had said. Could it have something to do with a girl?

Had Claire been feigning concern about Michel's behavior? Were her questions meant only to get me to reveal how much I knew: whether I had any idea at all what our son and nephew were up to in their spare time?

"Mama is inside," I said. "With . . ." I started to say "With Uncle Serge and Aunt Babette," but, in the light of recent events, that suddenly sounded so ridiculously childish. "Uncle" Serge and "Aunt" Babette were things of the past . . . the distant past, when we were still happy, it crossed my mind, and I had to bite my tongue. I had to be careful not to let my lip start trembling, or to let Michel see my wet eyes. "With Serge and Babette," I finished my sentence. "The main course just arrived."

Was I mistaken, or did I see Michel feeling around for something in his coat pocket? For his cell phone, perhaps? He didn't wear a watch — he used his phone to tell the time. I'll make sure we stay away till after midnight, Claire had assured him on his voice mail. So you two have to do it tonight. Did he, at this moment, after my announcement that the main course had just arrived, feel the need to check the time? The amount of time left until "after midnight," to do what they had to do?

When he asked about his mother, the tone that had frightened me only thirty seconds earlier vanished from Michel's voice.

183

Where's Mama? "Uncle" and "aunt" were childish, reminiscent of birthday parties and questions like "What do you want to be when you grow up?" But "Mama" was Mama. Mama would always remain Mama.

Without thinking about it any further, I decided that the moment had arrived. I pulled Michel's phone out of my pocket. He looked at my hand, then raised his eyes to meet mine.

"You looked," he said. His voice didn't sound threatening at all anymore, more like fatigued, resigned.

"Yeah," I said. I shrugged, the way you shrug over something that can't be changed anymore anyway. "Michel . . . ," I began.

"What did you look at?" He took his phone out of my hand, slid it open, then closed it again.

"Well . . . the ATM machine . . . and the vagrant at the subway station . . ." I grinned — a fairly stupid grin, I imagined, and completely out of place, but I had decided to do it that way, that this would be my approach: I would act the ignoramus, a rather naïve father who didn't think it was such a big deal that his son beat up vagrants and set fire to the homeless. Yes, naïveté was the right way to do it. It shouldn't be too hard for me to play the naïve father — after all,

184

that was what I was: naïve. "Jackass . . . ," I said, still with a grin.

"Does Mama know?" he asked.

I shook my head. "No," I said.

What *does* Mama know about was what I really wanted to ask, but it was still too soon for that. I thought back to the evening when the footage from that ATM cubicle had first been broadcast. Claire had asked whether I wanted the last of the wine or whether she should open a new bottle. Then she had gone — that's right — to the kitchen. Meanwhile, the female presenter of *Opsporing Verzocht* had made an urgent appeal to viewers to call the number at the bottom of the screen if they had any information that might lead to the arrest of the culprits. "You can, of course, also alert your local police," she said, turning her noble and offended expression on me. "What is the world coming to?" that expression said.

That evening, after Claire had crawled into bed with a book, I went upstairs to Michel's room. I saw a strip of light under his door. I remember standing there in the hallway for a full sixty seconds. I asked myself in all seriousness what would happen if I said nothing at all. If I just carried on with my life, like everyone else. I thought about happiness — about happy couples,

185

and about my son's eyes.

But then I thought about all those other people who had watched the program: students at Rick and Beau's high school who had been at that party on the same night — and who may have seen the same thing I had. I thought about the people here in the neighborhood, here on our street: neighbors and shopkeepers who had seen the somewhat reserved but always-friendly boy traipsing past with his sports bag, his quilted jacket, and his knit cap.

Last of all, I thought about my brother. He was no genius. In a certain sense you could even call him mentally deficient. If the opinion polls were right, after the upcoming elections he would be sworn in as our new prime minister. Had he been watching? And Babette? An outsider would never recognize our children from the security-camera footage, I told myself. But there is something about parents that makes them able to pick their children out of thousands: on a crowded beach, a playground, in fuzzy black-and-white footage . . .

"Michel! Are you still up?" I knocked on his door, and he opened it. "Jesus, Dad!" he said when he saw my face. "What is it?"

After that, it had all gone fairly quickly, at

least more quickly than I had expected. In fact, he seemed almost relieved that now there was someone else who knew too. "Jesus," he said a few times. "Jesus, man. This is really weird, you know, to be talking about this now, the two of us."

He made it sound as though that was all it was, weird: as though, for example, we had been discussing the most intimate details of how he had tried to pick up a girl at a school party. In a way, of course, he was right. I never had tried to bring up things like this before. But the weirdest thing of all was the reticence I noticed in myself from the very start. As though I were giving him the liberty not to tell everything to me, his father, should that prove too painful for him.

"We didn't know, right?" he said. "How were we supposed to know that there was still something in that gas can? It was empty. I swear it was empty."

Did it matter whether he and his cousin were actually ignorant of the fact that empty gas cans can explode too? Or whether they were only feigning ignorance of something that can be assumed to be common knowledge? Gasification, gasoline fumes. Never hold a match up to an empty tank. Why else weren't you allowed to use your cell phone at the pumps? Because of gas fumes and the danger of an explosion.

Right?

But I didn't say any of that. As I said before, I didn't try to refute the arguments with which Michel tried to prove his innocence. After all, how innocent was he, anyway? Are you innocent when you throw a desk lamp at someone's head, but guilty when you accidentally set that same person on fire?

"Does Mama know?" Yes, he had asked me that. Even back then.

I shook my head. And that's how we stood there for a while in his room, saying nothing, both of us with our hands in our pockets. I didn't press on. I didn't, for example, ask what had gotten into him. What he and his cousin had been thinking when they started pelting the homeless woman with objects.

Looking back on it, in fact, I know for certain that then and there, during those few minutes of silence, as we stood with our hands in our pockets, I had already made up my mind. I couldn't help thinking about the time Michel had kicked a ball through the window of a bike shop, when he was eight. Together we had gone to the owner to offer to pay for the damage. But the owner

188

wasn't satisfied with that. He had burst into a tirade about "the riffraff" who played soccer in front of his store, each and every day, and who kicked the ball against the window "on purpose." "Sooner or later, it was bound to break," he said. "You could count on that." "And that's exactly what those punks were hoping for," he added.

I had been holding Michel's hand as we listened to the owner of the bike shop. My eight-year-old son had looked down at the floor guiltily, and occasionally squeezed my fingers.

It was that combination, the combination of the bitter bike dealer who numbered Michel among the punks and my son who responded so guiltily to his tirade, that threw the switch inside my head.

"Why don't you just shut up?" I said.

The shop owner was standing behind his counter. He seemed at first to think he had misunderstood me. "What did you say?" he asked.

"You heard me loud and clear, asshole. I came here with my son to offer to pay for your shitty window, not to listen to your crap about kids playing soccer. What's the big deal, you fucking idiot? A ball through the window. That doesn't give you any right to call an eight-year-old boy a punk. I came

189

here to pay for the damage, but now you're not getting a cent. Go figure out for yourself where the money's coming from."

"Excuse me, my good man, but I'm not going to stand here and let myself be insulted," he said as he started to come around from behind the counter. "Those boys broke my window — I didn't do it myself."

Beside the counter was a bicycle pump, an old-fashioned upright model. The pump itself was bolted at the bottom to a wooden plank. I leaned down and picked it up.

"I'd stay where I am if I were you," I said calmly. "The only thing that's been damaged so far is a window."

There was something about my voice, I still remember, that made the bike dealer stop, then step back behind the counter. It had, indeed, sounded unnaturally calm. I was not on edge. The hand with which I gripped the pump was not shaking in the slightest. The bike dealer had called me a good man, and maybe I looked like one, but I was not a good man.

"Oh, hold on," he said. "We're not going to do anything crazy, are we?"

I felt Michel's hand around my fingers. He squeezed them again, harder than the first few times. I squeezed back.

"How much is the window?"

He blinked his eyes. "I've got insurance," he said. "It's just that —"

"That's not what I asked. I asked how much it cost."

"A hundred . . . a hundred and fifty guilders. Two hundred in total, with labor, etcetera."

In order to take the money out of my pocket, I had to let go of Michel's hand. I laid two one-hundred-guilder bills on the counter.

"This is it," I said. "This is what I came for. Not to listen to your sick bullshit about a couple of kids kicking a ball."

I let go of the pump as well now. I registered a sense of fatigue. And regret. It was the same fatigue and regret you feel when you miss a tennis ball. You were planning to smash it, but you swing hard and miss; the arm holding the racket meets no resistance and lashes wildly through the air.

I knew for sure, and in the depths of my being I still know, that I was sorry the bike dealer had backed off so quickly. I would have felt less tired had I been able to use the pump.

"So, we fixed that nicely, didn't we, buddy?" I said on the way home.

Michel took my hand again, but said nothing. When I looked down, I saw that there were tears in his eyes.

"What is it, fella?" I asked. I stopped and squatted down in front of him. He bit his lower lip, and then he really began to cry.

"Michel!" I said. "Michel, listen. There's no reason to be sad. That was a nasty man. I told him that. You didn't do anything wrong. All you did was kick a ball through a window. It was an accident. Accidents happen, but that's no reason for him to talk about you like that."

"Mama," he said now, between sobs. "Mama . . ."

I felt something inside my body stiffen, or perhaps what I felt was the way something nameless and indefinable unfolded: a folding trellis, tent poles, an umbrella — I was afraid I wouldn't be able to stand up straight again.

"Mama? Do you want to go to Mama?"

He nodded emphatically and wiped his teary cheeks with his fingers.

"Shall we hurry up and go to Mama, then?" I said. "Shall we tell Mama about everything? What the two of us did?"

"Yeah," he peeped.

When I stood up, I really did think that I heard something snap — in my spine, or maybe deeper than that. I took his hand,

and we set off. At the corner of our street, I looked down; his face was still red and wet with tears, but the crying had stopped.

"Did you see how scared that guy was?" I said. "We almost didn't have to do a thing. We wouldn't even have had to pay him for that window. But I don't think that would have been right. When you break something, even if it's an accident, you have to pay for the damage."

Michel said nothing until we arrived at the front door.

"Daddy?"

"Yeah?"

"Were you really going to hit that man? With the bicycle pump?"

I had already put the key in the lock, but now I squatted down in front of him again. "Listen," I said. "That man is not a good man. That man is just a piece of trash who hates kids who are playing. It doesn't matter whether I would have hit him over the head with that pump. Besides, if I had, he would only have had himself to blame. No, what matters is that he *thought* I was going to hit him, and that was enough."

Michel looked at me earnestly. I had chosen my words carefully, because I didn't want to make him cry again. But his eyes were already almost dry. He was listening carefully, and then he nodded slowly.

I put my arms around him and hugged him. "How about if we don't tell Mama about the bicycle pump?" I said. "Shall we keep that as our little secret?"

He nodded again.

Later that afternoon, he went into town with Claire to buy some clothes. At the table that evening, he was quieter and more serious than usual. I winked at him once, but he didn't wink back.

When his bedtime arrived, Claire had just sat down on the couch to watch a movie she really wanted to see. "Sit back and enjoy it. I'll take him up," I said.

And so we lay beside each other on his bed and chewed the fat a little: innocent chitchat, about soccer and a new computer game he was saving up for. I had resolved not to bring up the incident in the bike shop, not unless he started in about it himself.

I kissed him goodnight and was about to turn off the night-light when he leaned over and threw his arms around me. He squeezed hard — he had never put that much force behind a hug before. He pressed his head against my chest.

"Dad," he said. "Dear old dad."

23

"You know what the best thing would be?" I said that evening in his room, after he had told me the whole story and swore again that he and Rick had never been planning to set anyone on fire. "It was a joke," he'd said. "And it was . . ." He grimaced in disgust. "You should have smelled how that stank," he said.

I nodded. My mind was already made up. I did what I thought I had to do as a father: I put myself in my son's shoes. I put myself in Michel's position: how he had been on his way home from the school party, along with Rick and Beau. And how they had decided to withdraw some cash — and what they found in the ATM cubicle.

I put myself in his shoes. I formed an idea of how I myself would have reacted to the living creature in the sleeping bag, lying in my way there. To the stench. To the simple fact that someone, a person (I am purposely avoiding words here like *homeless person* or *vagrant*), how a person thinks that ATM cubicles are a place to sleep. A person who then reacts indignantly when two boys try to convince her otherwise. A person who becomes tetchy when disturbed in her sleep. A spoiled reaction, in other words, the kind of reaction you see more often from people who think they have a right to something.

Hadn't Michel told me that the woman had sounded prim? A prim accent, a good family, someone from the upper classes. Until now, little had been revealed about the homeless woman's background. Perhaps for good reason. Maybe this was the black sheep of a well-to-do family whose members were completely used to ordering around the people who worked for them.

And then there was something else. This was the Netherlands. This was not the Bronx. We were not in the slums of Johannesburg or Rio de Janeiro. In Holland, you had a social safety net. No one *had* to lie around and get in the way in an ATM cubicle.

"You know what the best thing would be?" I said. "To just forget it for the time being. As long as nothing happens, nothing is happening."

My son looked at me for a few seconds.

Maybe he felt he was too big to say "dear old Dad" anymore, but beside the fear in his eyes, I also saw thankfulness.

"You think maybe?" he said.

24

And now, in the restaurant garden, we were standing across from each other again, not speaking a word. Michel slid his cell phone open and closed a few times, then put it in his coat pocket.

"Michel," I began.

He didn't look at me. He had his head turned to the other side now, toward the darkened park. His face remained in darkness too. "I don't have time for this right now," he said. "I have to get going."

"Michel. Why didn't you tell me? About those videos? Or at least about that one video. Back then? Back when there was still time?"

He ran his fingers over his nose, scuffed his white tennis shoes in the gravel, and shrugged.

"Michel?"

He looked at the ground. "It doesn't make any difference," he said.

For one single moment, I thought about the father I could have been, perhaps the one I should have been, the father who would now say "It makes a big difference!" The time for sermonizing was past, though. That bridge had already been crossed: back then, on the night of the TV broadcast, in his room. Or maybe even before that.

A few days ago, not long after Serge had called me about the get-together at the restaurant, I had watched the episode of *Opsporing Verzocht* again on the Internet. It seemed like a good idea. It might make me better prepared for the dinner.

"We need to talk," Serge had said.

"About what?" I replied. Playing ignorant — that seemed the best thing to me.

At the other end of the line, my brother breathed a deep sigh.

"I think we're past the stage of my needing to tell you that," he said.

"Does Babette know?"

"Yes. That's why I want to talk about it with the four of us. It has to do with all of us. They're our children."

It struck me that he had not asked in turn whether Claire knew. Apparently he assumed she did — or else he didn't care. After that, he had named the restaurant, the restaurant where they knew him. The seven-month waiting list, he said, would pose no obstacle.

Did Claire know too? I thought now as I looked at my son walking toward his bike, getting ready to leave.

"Michel, wait a minute," I said. We need to talk, that other father would have said, the father I was not.

I had watched the footage again, with this evening in mind, the laughing boys who threw a desk lamp and garbage bags at the invisible homeless person. And finally the flash of exploding gas fumes, the boys running away, the telephone numbers you could call — or the local police you could also alert.

I watched it one more time, especially the last bit, with the gas can and the tossing of what I knew by then was a lighter. A Zippo, a lighter with a lid, the kind of lighter that only goes out when you click the lid shut. What were two boys, neither of whom smoked, doing with a lighter? There were questions I hadn't asked, purely because I didn't feel the need to know everything. From an urgent need not to know everything, you could also say — but this one I had. "To give people a light," Michel had replied without hesitation. "Girls," he added when I suppose I looked at him a bit blankly.

"Girls ask you for a light, for a joint or a Marlboro Light. You miss a chance when you don't have anything in your pocket."

As I said, I watched that last part twice. After the flash of light, the boys disappeared out the glass door. You saw the door shut; then the footage stopped.

The second time, though, I suddenly saw something I hadn't noticed before. I clicked the video back to the point where Michel and Rick ran out the door. From the moment the door fell shut, I put the player on slow, and then slower, frame by frame.

Do I have to go into detail about the physical symptoms that accompanied my discovery? I believe they should be obvious. The pounding heart, the dry lips and tongue, the icicle inside the head, at the back, its point jamming into the topmost vertebra, into the hollow space without bone or cartilage where the skull starts, at the moment when I froze the very last frame from the security camera.

There, at the bottom right: something white. Something white that no one would notice the first time they saw it, because everyone assumed they had already seen the worst of it. The lamp, the garbage bags, the gas can . . . the time had come to shake one's head and murmur words of disapproval: young people; the world; defense-less; murder; video clips; computer games; labor camps; stiffer sentences; the death penalty.

The image froze, and I stared at the white thing. Outside it was completely dark. In the glass door you could see a reflection of part of the inside of the ATM cubicle: the gray tile floor, the machine itself with its keyboard and screen, and the brand — the logo, I believe one should say — of the bank to which the ATM machine belonged.

In theory, the white thing could just have been a reflection, the reflection of fluorescent lighting off something inside the cubicle itself — off one of the objects with which the boys had pelted the homeless woman, for example.

But that, indeed, was entirely theoretical. The white thing was outside — the camera made it clear that it was outside, on the street. A random viewer would never have noticed, especially not on the broadcast of *Opsporing Verzocht.* You had to freeze the film, or view it frame by frame, as I had done, and even then . . .

Even then you had to know what you were seeing. That's what it boiled down to. I knew what I was seeing, because I had immediately recognized the white thing for what it was.

I clicked on Full Screen. The image was larger now, but also more blurry and formless. I couldn't help but think of *Blowup,* the Michelangelo Antonioni film in which a photographer, while enlarging a picture, sees a pistol lying under a bush: a murder weapon, as it turns out later. But here, on this computer, enlargement didn't help at all. I clicked on Minimize and picked up the magnifying glass that was lying on my desk.

With the magnifier, it was only a matter of adjusting the distance. As I moved it in and out in front of the screen, the image became sharper. Sharper and bigger.

Ever sharper and ever bigger. I saw confirmed what I had seen correctly the first time I looked: a tennis shoe. A white tennis shoe of the kind countless people wear; countless people like my son and my nephew.

That last thought made me pause for a moment, but no more than a tenth of a second: one tennis shoe could point to tens of thousands of tennis-shoe wearers, but conversely, tens of thousands of tennis shoes would be hard to trace back to one specific wearer.

No, that wasn't really what had made me

stop and think. It was about the signal being given, or better yet: the meaning of the white tennis shoe outside the glass door of the cubicle. Or even better yet: the meanings.

I took another close look — I zoomed in and out with the magnifying glass. Upon closer examination, you could see a slight shift in color above the tennis shoe; the blackness of the street outside was here just a tad less black. That was probably the leg, the trouser leg of the tennis-shoe wearer who was stepping into the frame.

They had come back. That was the first meaning. The second meaning was that the police, possibly in collaboration with the makers of *Opsporing Verzocht,* had decided not to include this final moment in the broadcast.

Anything was possible, of course. The tennis shoe might belong to someone other than Michel or Rick, a chance passerby who happened to arrive thirty seconds after the boys had left the cubicle. But that didn't seem very likely, not at that hour of the night, on that street, somewhere in an outlying neighborhood. Besides, that would make this passerby a witness who might have seen the boys. A material witness, someone the police would have wanted to summon via

204

the broadcast to report what he knew.

All in all, there was only one likely explanation for the white tennis shoe: the one explanation that I had hit upon immediately (all this — the zooming in on the tennis shoe with the magnifying glass and the drawing of the conclusion — had actually taken less than a couple of seconds). They had come back. Michel and Rick had come back to see with their own eyes what they had done.

This was all fairly disturbing, albeit no more than that. The truly frightening thing had to do with how this final footage had been cut from the broadcast of *Opsporing Verzocht.* I tried to figure out what reason they might have not to show the images. Perhaps there was something there that made Michel or Rick (or both) easier to recognize? But wouldn't that have been an additional reason to actually *show* the images?

And what if the footage was simply too unimportant, I thought for all of a hopeful three seconds. A trivial afterthought that wouldn't help the viewer at all? No, I realized right away. The fact that they had come back was too important to simply omit.

So there was something to be seen there,

something that might be kept from the viewer — something only the police and the culprits knew about.

You sometimes read about the police leaving certain facts out of the publicity surrounding an investigation — the precise nature of the murder weapon, or a sign that the murder had left beside, or on, his victim. To prevent mentally disturbed individuals from claiming a crime — or copying it.

For the first time in weeks, I wondered whether Michel and Rick themselves had actually seen the security-camera footage. I had told Michel about it on the evening of the broadcast. I told him they had been filmed by a security camera, but that they were almost unrecognizable. So for the time being, I'd added, there was nothing to worry about. During the days that followed, we hadn't touched on the subject of the security camera either. I was acting on the basis that it was better not to come back to any of it, not to rake up our secret.

I was hoping, in fact, that it would blow over, that with the passing of time, the interest would fade, that people would be occupied by other, newer news, and that the exploding gas can would be erased from their collective memory. A war needed to break out somewhere; a terrorist attack

206

might be even better — plenty of fatalities, lots of civilian casualties over whom people could shake their heads in dismay. Ambulances driving up and away, the twisted steel of train or subway cars, a ten-story building with the facade blown out — that was the only way the homeless woman in the ATM cubicle could vanish into the background, become an occurrence, a minor incident amid greater incidents.

That was what I had hoped for during those first few weeks. The news would become old news, perhaps not within a month, but definitely within six months — in any case, after a year. By that time, the police, too, would be occupied with other, more urgent matters. Fewer and fewer detectives would be assigned to the case, as they referred to it, and I was under no illusions about that lone, dogged detective who sinks his teeth into an unsolved crime and doesn't let go for years: such detectives exist only in TV series.

After those six months, after that year, we would be able to go on living as a happy family. A scar would remain somewhere, true enough, but a scar does not have to get in the way of happiness. In the meantime, I would act as normally as possible. Do normal things. Go out to dinner occasionally, to the movies, take Michel to a soccer match. At the table, during our evening meals, I kept a close eye on my wife. I was searching for tiny changes in her behavior, anything that might show that she, in turn, suspected a connection between the images from the security camera and our own happy family.

"What is it?" she asked on one of those evenings. Apparently I had taken the keeping a close eye a bit too literally. "What are you looking at?"

"Nothing," I said. "Was I looking at something?"

Claire couldn't help but laugh; she laid her hand on mine and squeezed my fingers gently.

At such moments, I meticulously avoided looking at my son. I didn't want any knowing glances. I wasn't going to wink at him or show in any other way that we were still sharing a secret. I wanted everything to be normal. A shared secret would have excluded Claire — his mother, my wife — and that would create a greater threat to our happy family than the entire incident in the ATM cubicle.

Without knowing glances — without winks — there was in fact no secret — that was my reasoning. It might be hard for us to put the events in the cubicle out of our minds, but in the course of time, they would start to exist outside us — just as they did for other people. But what we did have to forget was the secret. And the best thing was to start forgetting as soon as possible.

25

That was the plan. That had been the plan before I reran the broadcast of *Opsporing Verzocht* and saw the white tennis shoe.

The next step I took simply on a hunch. Perhaps there was more footage to be found, I thought to myself. Or rather: perhaps the missing footage, accidentally or not, had ended up on another site.

I clicked onto YouTube. The chances were slim, but it was worth a try. In Search, I typed the name of the bank to which the ATM machine belonged, and after that the words "homeless" and "death."

No fewer than thirty-four hits appeared. I scrolled down past the little screens. On all of them, the opening frame was more or less the same: the heads and knit caps of two laughing boys. Only the accompanying titles and the brief descriptions of the clip itself were any different. "Dutch Boys Bank Murder" was one of the most straightforward. "Don't Try This at Home — Fire Bomb Kills Homeless Woman" was another. Each and every one of the clips was extremely popular — the counter showed that most of them had been viewed thousands of times.

I clicked on one at random and watched again — albeit in a choppier, edited version — the throwing of the desk lamp, the garbage bags, and the gas can. I looked at a couple more. In one montage titled "Hottest New Tourist Attraction: Set Your Money on Fire!" someone had added canned laughter to the images. Each time a new object was thrown at the homeless woman, a wave of laughter followed. The laughter reached a hysterical climax when the lighter was thrown, and ended with thundering applause.

Most of the videos did not include the shot of the white tennis shoe. They stopped right after the flash of light and the boys running away.

Looking back, I don't know exactly why I clicked on the next video too. It didn't look any different from the other thirty-three. The opening shot was roughly the same: two laughing boys in knit caps, although here they were already picking up the office chair.

211

Perhaps it was the title, "Men in Black III." Not a jokey title for starters, not like most of the others. But it was also the first and, as I found out consequently, the only title that did not refer to the events shown but indirectly to the culprits themselves.

"Men in Black III" began with the throwing of the office chair; then came the garbage bags, the lamp, and the gas can. But there was an essential difference. Whenever both or either of the two boys came into reasonably sharp focus, the film slowed down. And every time that happened, you heard ominous music, more a sort of zooming tone, a deep, gurgling noise that is associated primarily with submarine and shipwreck disaster movies. As a result, all attention was focused on Michel and Rick, and less on the throwing of the things they had found beside the tree.

Who are these boys? the slow-motion images, in combination with the doomsday music, seemed to ask. What it is they're doing — we know that by now. But who are they?

The zinger came all the way at the end. After the flash and the slamming door, the screen went black. I was getting ready to click to the next video, but the time line at the bottom of the screen showed that "Men in Black III" lasted a total of 2 minutes and 58 seconds, and that we were now only at 2 minutes and 38.

As I said, I had almost clicked away. I wasn't expecting anything more than for the screen to remain black for another 20 seconds. The music had swelled again. The only thing left would probably be credits, I figured — nothing more than that.

How would this evening, our dinner at the restaurant, have proceeded, had I indeed quit right then and there?

In ignorance, that was the answer. At least, in relative ignorance. I could have lived on for a few more days, or maybe a few weeks or months, in my dreams about happy families. I would only have needed to hold my own family up for comparison with my brother's for the space of one evening. I could have seen how Babette tried to cover up her tears behind her tinted glasses and how joylessly my brother wolfed down his meat in a couple of bites. Then I would have walked home with my wife. I would have placed my arm around her waist and, without looking at each other, we would both have known that happy families really were all alike.

The screen shifted from black to gray. You saw the door of the ATM cubicle again, but this time from the outside. The quality of the images was a lot worse, like the resolution of the camera on a cell phone, I realized right away.

The white tennis shoe.

They had come back.

They had come back to record what they had done.

"Holy shit!" said a voice off-camera. (Rick)

"Aw, yuck!" said a second voice. (Michel)

The camera was now pointed at the foot end of the sleeping bag. The cubicle was filled with a bluish haze. Excruciatingly slowly, the camera panned up along the sleeping bag.

"Let's go." (Rick)

"At least it doesn't smell as gross here anymore." (Michel)

"Michel . . . come on . . ."

"Come on, yourself. Go and stand beside it. You have to say 'Jackass.' At least, then, we've got that."

"I'm goin' . . ."

"No, asshole! You're staying!"

At the top of the sleeping bag, the camera stopped. The image froze there, then faded to black. In red letters, the following text appeared on-screen:

MEN IN BLACK III

The Sequel

COMING SOON

I waited a few days. Michel went out often. He always took his cell phone with him; the chance presented itself only today — only this evening, right before we were to leave for the restaurant. While he was fixing his tire in the garden, I went to his room.

I had actually assumed he would have deleted it. I was hoping, praying, that he had deleted it. Somehow I also hoped that, having seen the images on YouTube, I had now seen everything — that they had stopped there.

But that wasn't the case.

It was only a few hours ago that I saw the rest.

26

"Michel," I said to my son, who had already turned to leave, who had said that it didn't make any difference, "Michel, you have to delete those films. You should have done it a long time ago, but now it's really important."

He stopped. Again he scraped his white Nikes through the gravel.

"Aw, Dad," he began. It seemed as though he was going to say something, but he only shook his head.

In both videos, I had seen and heard how he pushed his cousin around, and sometimes even snarled at him. That was precisely what Serge had always insinuated, and would doubtless repeat tonight: that Michel was a bad influence on Rick. I had always denied that. I had always thought it an easy way for my brother to duck his own responsibility for his son's actions.

But since a few hours ago — in fact since

much longer ago than that, of course — I had known it was true. Michel was the leader of the two: Michel called the shots. Rick was the subservient goon. And, deep in my heart, that division of roles pleased me. Better that than the other way around, I thought. Michel had never been pestered at school. Even then, he'd gathered around him a whole crew of submissive friends who wanted nothing more than to be around my son. I knew from experience how parents could suffer when their children were bullied. I had never suffered.

"You know what would be even better?" I said. "For you to throw away that whole cell phone. Somewhere where they'll never find it again." I looked around. "Here, for example." I pointed at the little bridge over which he had just come cycling up. "In the water. If you want, we'll go buy a new one on Monday. How long have you had this one, anyway? We'll just say it got ripped off. We'll renew the subscription, and on Monday you'll have the newest Samsung, or a Nokia, whatever you want . . ."

I held out my hand, palm up.

"Do you want me to do it for you?" I asked.

He looked at me. I saw the eyes I had been seeing all my life, but also something I would rather not have seen: he looked at me in a way that said I was getting worked up about nothing, that I was just a fussy, worried father, a worried father who wants to know what time his son will be coming home from a party.

"Michel, this isn't about a party or something," I said, faster and louder than I'd meant to. "This is about your future —" Another one of those abstract terms: the future. I was sorry right away that I had said it. "Why the hell did you two put that footage on the Internet?" Don't swear, I admonished myself. When you start swearing, you sound like those second-rate movie hams you hate so much. But I was almost screaming now. Anyone at the door of the restaurant, anyone close to the lectern or the cloakroom could have heard it. "Was that cool too? Or tough? Didn't that make any difference either? 'Men in Black III'! For God's sake, what were you two thinking?"

He had put his hands in the pockets of his jacket and bowed his head, so that I could just barely see his eyes beneath the edge of the black knit cap.

"That wasn't us," he said.

The door of the restaurant swung open. There was laughter, and a group of people came outside. Two men and a woman. The men wore tailored suits and had their hands in their pockets. The woman was wearing a silvery, almost backless dress and carried a matching shoulder bag.

"Did you really say that?" the woman asked, taking a couple of unsteady steps in her high heels, which were silver as well. "To Ernst?"

One of the men pulled a set of car keys from his pocket and tossed them in the air. "Why not?" he said. He had to stretch his arm out to catch the keys again. "You must be crazy!" the woman shrilled. Their shoes squeaked on the gravel as they passed. "Which of us is still in any state to drive?" said the other man, and all three of them burst out laughing.

"Okay, wait a minute," I said after the threesome had reached the end of the gravel path and turned left toward the footbridge. "The two of you set a homeless person on fire and then you film it. On your cell phone. Just like with that alcoholic at the subway station." I noticed that the man who had been smacked around on the platform had now become an alcoholic. In my words. Perhaps an alcoholic really did deserve to be smacked around more than someone who drinks two or three glasses a day. "And then suddenly it's right there on the Internet, because that's what you guys want, isn't it? For as many people as possible to see it?" Had they put the alcoholic on YouTube as well? it occurred to me then. "Is that alcoholic on there too?" I asked right away, for good measure.

Michel breathed a sigh. "Dad! You're not listening!"

"I am listening. I listen too much. I . . ." Again the door of the restaurant opened. A man in a suit came out and looked around, took a few steps to one side so that he was beside the entrance but out of the light, and lit a cigarette. "Goddamn it," I said.

Michel turned around and walked to his bike.

"Michel, where are you going? I'm not finished yet."

But he kept on walking. He pulled a key out of his pocket and stuck it in the lock, which sprang open with a bang. I looked quickly at the man smoking beside the entrance. "Michel," I said, quietly but urgently, "you can't just walk away from this. What are we going to do about it? Are there more of those films I haven't seen? Will I have to see them later on, on You-Tube, first? Or are you going to tell me now whether —"

"Dad!" Michel spun around and grabbed

my forearm. He yanked it hard and said: "Now just shut up!"

Stunned, I looked into my son's eyes. His honest eyes in which — there was no use denying it — I now saw only hatred. I caught myself glancing to one side as well, at the smoking man.

I grinned at my son. I couldn't see it myself, but it must have been a stupid grin. "Okay, I'll shut up," I said.

Michel let go of my arm; he bit his lower lip and shook his head. "Christ! When are you going to start acting normal?"

I felt a cold stabbing in my chest. Any other father would now have said something like "Who's acting normal here? Huh? Who? Who's acting normal?" But I wasn't a father like all other fathers. I knew what my son was getting at. I wished that I could put my arms around him and press him against me. But he would probably push me away in disgust. I knew for certain that a physical rejection like that would be too much, that I would burst into tears right there and wouldn't be able to stop.

"Oh, buddy," I said.

I needed to stay calm, I told myself. I had to listen. I remembered now that Michel had said I wasn't listening. "Okay, I'm all ears," I said.

He shook his head again. Then he pulled his bike resolutely from the rack.

"Wait a minute!" I said. I kept hold of myself. I even stepped to one side, as though I didn't want to get in his way. But before I knew it, I had my hand on his forearm.

Michel looked at the hand as though some strange insect had landed on his arm. Then he looked at me.

At that point we were very close to something, I realized. Something that couldn't be undone later on. I took my hand off his arm.

"Michel, there's something else," I said.

"Dad, please."

"Someone called you."

He stared at me. It wouldn't have surprised me much to have felt his fist in my face a moment later: his knuckles hard against my upper lip, or higher, against my nose. Blood would flow, but it would make a number of things clearer. More out in the open.

But nothing happened. "When?" he asked quietly.

"Michel, I hope you'll forgive me, I shouldn't have, but . . . it was because of those films, I wanted to . . . I was trying to . . ."

"When?" My son took his foot off the pedal and planted both feet firmly on the gravel.

"A little while ago. It was a message. I listened to the message."

"Who was it from?"

"From B — from Faso." I shrugged. I grinned. "That's what you guys call him, right? Faso?"

I saw it plainly. There could be no mistake about it: my son's expression hardened. There wasn't enough light here, but I could have sworn that his face also turned a few shades paler.

"What did he want?" He sounded calm. Or no, not calm. He was trying to sound casual, bored almost, as though the fact that his adopted cousin had called him tonight was of no significance.

But he had given himself away. The significance lay in something very different: in the fact that his father had been listening to his messages. That wasn't normal. Any other father would have thought twice before doing that. In fact, that's what I had done. I had thought twice. Michel should have been enraged. He should have screamed, "What gives you the right to listen to my voice mail!" That would have been normal.

"Nothing," I said. "He asked you to call

back." In that fake, chummy tone of his, I almost added.

"Okay," Michel said. He nodded slightly. "Okay," he said again.

Suddenly, I remembered something. Just a bit ago, when he had called his own phone and gotten me on the line, he had said he was looking for a number. That he was coming to get his cell phone because he needed a number. I thought I knew now which number that was. But I didn't ask him. Because there was something else I remembered too.

"You said I wasn't listening," I said. "But I did listen. When we were talking about the two of you putting that video up on You-Tube."

"Yeah."

"You said that wasn't you."

"That's right."

"So who was it? Who put it there?"

Sometimes you answer a question by asking it out loud.

I looked at my son. And he looked back.

"Faso?" I said.

"Yeah," he said.

27

In the silence that fell then, the only sounds were those from the park and the street across the water: the brief flap of birds' wings in the branches, a car accelerating, a church bell striking once — a silence during which my son and I looked at each other.

I couldn't be absolutely certain, but I thought I saw a moistness in Michel's eyes. His look, in any case, left no room for misinterpretation. You finally get it? that look said.

During the same silence, a cell phone began ringing, in my left pocket. Ringing and buzzing. My hearing seemed to be getting worse lately, so I had chosen "Old Phone" as my ringtone, an old-fashioned ringing that reminded you of a classic, black Bakelite telephone, and that I could hear no matter what.

I pulled the phone out of my pocket,

intending to dismiss the call, until I saw the name on my screen: Claire.

"Hello?"

I gestured to Michel not to go, but he had already crossed his arms and leaned them on the handlebars. Suddenly he seemed in less of a hurry to get away.

"Where are you?" my wife asked. Her voice was quiet, but insistent. The restaurant noises in the background almost drowned it out. "What's taking you so long?"

"I'm outside."

"What are you doing out there? We've almost finished the main course. I thought you were going to come back right away."

"I'm out here with Michel."

I had actually meant to say "with our son," but I didn't.

We were silent for a moment.

"I'm coming," Claire said.

"No, wait! He's got to . . . Michel was just getting ready to go . . ."

But the connection had already been broken.

Your father doesn't know about any of this, and I want to keep it that way. I thought about my wife, who would be coming out the door of the restaurant any moment, and about the way I would look at her then. Or rather: whether I would be able to look at her in the same way I had a couple of hours ago, in the bar for regular people, when she'd asked if I also thought Michel had been acting strange lately.

I was wondering, in other words, whether we were still a happy family.

My next thought was about the video of the homeless woman who had been set on fire. And then, most of all, about how it got onto YouTube.

"Is Mama coming?" Michel asked.

"Yeah." Maybe I was imagining things, but I thought I heard relief in his voice when he asked whether "Mama" was coming. As though he'd been standing here with his father long enough. His father who couldn't do anything for him anyway. Is Mama coming? Mama's coming. I had to be quick. I had to look out for him, in the only department in which I could still look out for him.

"Michel," I said, laying my hand on his forearm again. "What does Beau . . . Faso . . . how did Faso find out about that video? He had already gone home, right? I mean . . ."

Michel glanced at the entrance, as though hoping that his mother was already coming out to save him from this painful tête-à-tête with his father. I looked over at the door too. Something had changed, but I didn't know right away what it was. The smoking man, I realized the next instant. The smoking man was gone.

"Just did," Michel said. Just did. The same two words he used to say when he had lost his coat, or left his book bag somewhere on a playground and we asked him how he could have done that. Just did . . . Just forgot. Just left it lying there. "I e-mailed those videos to Rick. And then Faso saw them too. He pulled them off of Rick's computer. He put some of it on YouTube, and now he says he's going to put the rest on there too if we don't pay him."

There were any number of questions I could have asked then: for a full second I asked myself which one other fathers would have asked.

"How much?" I asked.

"Three thousand."

I looked at him.

"He wants to buy a scooter," he said.

28

"Mama."

Michel threw his arms around Claire's neck and buried his face in her hair. "Mama," he said again.

Mama had come. I looked at my wife and at my son. I thought about the happy families. About how often I had looked at Michel and his mother — and how I had never tried to come between them; that, too, was a part of the happiness.

After she had caressed Michel's back and the back of his head — over the black cap — Claire raised her eyes and looked at me.

How much do you know? that look asked.

Everything, I looked back.

Almost everything, I corrected myself then, thinking about Claire's voice mail message to her son.

Claire took him by the shoulders and kissed his forehead.

"What are you doing here, sweetheart?"

she asked. "I thought you were meeting someone."

Michel's eyes sought mine. Claire, I knew there and then, knew nothing about the videos. She knew a great deal more than I had thought, but about the videos she knew nothing.

"He came to get some money," I said, keeping my eyes on Michel. Claire raised her eyebrows. "I borrowed some money from him. I was going to pay him back tonight, before we left for the restaurant, but I forgot."

Michel lowered his eyes and scraped his feet on the gravel. My wife stared at me, but said nothing. I felt around in my inside pocket.

"Fifty euros," I said; I pulled out the banknote and handed it to Michel.

"Thanks, Dad," he said, stuffing the money in his coat pocket.

Claire breathed a deep sigh, then took Michel's hand. "Weren't you going to . . ." She looked at me. "It would be better if we went back inside. They were wondering what was taking you so long."

We hugged our son. Claire kissed him three more times on his cheeks. Then we stood and watched as he cycled off along the path to the bridge. Halfway there it looked as though he were going to turn and wave, but he only raised one arm in the air.

After he had disappeared from view, through the bushes and across the canal, Claire asked: "How long have you known?"

I suppressed my initial urge to come back with "And what about you?" Instead, I said: "Ever since *Opsporing Verzocht.*"

She took my hand, exactly as she had done with Michel just now.

"Oh, honey," she said.

I turned slightly, so I could see her face.

"And you?" I asked.

Now my wife took my other hand as well. She looked at me and made a sorry attempt at a smile: it was a smile that, while knowing better, wanted to take us back in time.

"I want you to know that I was thinking of you first and foremost, in all of it, Paul," she said. "I didn't want . . . I thought maybe it would be too much for you. I was afraid . . . I was afraid it would make you go, all over again . . . well, you know."

"Since when?" I asked quietly. "When did you find out?"

Claire squeezed my fingers.

"On the night itself," she said. "The same night they were at the ATM machine."

I stared at her.

"Michel called me," Claire said. "It had

just happened. He wanted to know what they should do."

29

Back when I was still working, one day I stopped in the middle of a sentence about the Battle of Stalingrad and looked around the class.

All these heads, I thought. All these heads into which everything disappears.

"Hitler had his sights set on Stalingrad," I said. "Even though, strategically speaking, it would have been wiser for him to press straight on to Moscow. But for him it was all about the name of the town: Stalingrad, the city that bore the name of his great opponent, Joseph Stalin. That city had to be conquered first. Because of the psychological impact that victory would have on Stalin."

I paused and looked around the classroom again. Some of the students were writing down what I was telling them; others were looking at me. There were both interested and glassy gazes turned on me — more interested ones than glassy ones, I tried to tell myself, realizing at the same time that it no longer made much difference to me.

I thought about their lives, about all their lives, which would just go on.

"It's on the basis of irrational considerations like that that wars are won," I said. "Or lost."

Back when I was still working — it's still hard for me to say that phrase out loud. I could go on here and explain that once, in a distant past, I'd had other plans for my life, but I'm not going to do that. Those other plans really existed, but precisely what they involved is nobody's business. "Back when I was still working . . ." at least appeals to me more than "When I was still standing before a class . . ." or — the most horrible of all, the favorite phrase of the worst-of-the-worst, the former teachers who say of themselves that teaching is their blood — "Back when I was still in education . . ."

I would have preferred not to mention which subject I taught. That, too, is nobody's business. It becomes a label so quickly. Oh, he's a _____ teacher, people say. That explains a lot. But when you ask what it actually explains, they usually can't tell you. I teach history. Taught history. These days, not anymore. I stopped about ten years ago. Had to stop — although in my case, I still believe that both *stopped* and *had to stop* are equally far from the truth. At equal and opposite ends of it, indeed, but the distance between them and the truth is almost the same.

It started on the train, the train to Berlin. The beginning of the end, let's say: the start of (being forced into) stopping. Counting back, it seems the whole process took barely two or three months. Once it started, it went quickly. Like someone who is diagnosed with a malignant illness and is gone six weeks later.

In retrospect, what I feel most is pleasure and relief. My days before a class had lasted long enough. I sat by myself at the window of my otherwise empty compartment and looked outside. The only thing that rolled by for the first half hour were birch trees, but now we were moving through the out-skirts of some town. I looked at the houses and the flats, the houses with their little gardens that often ran all the way up to the rail embankment. In one of those gardens white sheets were hanging out to dry; in another there was a swing. It was November, and it was cold. There were no people in the gardens. "Maybe you should take a little vacation," Claire had said. "For a week or so." She had noticed something about me, she said: I reacted to everything too quickly and too irritatedly. It had to be the job, the school. "Sometimes I wonder how you keep it up," she said. "There's really no reason for you to feel guilty." Michel was still only three. She could handle things easily enough. He went to day care three days a week — she had those days all to herself.

I had thought about Rome and Barcelona, about palm trees and outdoor cafés, and finally decided on Berlin, mostly because I had never been there. At first I felt a certain cheerful excitement. I packed a small suitcase. I would take as little with me as possible — traveling light, I told myself. The excitement lasted until I got to the station, where the train to Berlin was waiting at the platform. The first part of the journey went smoothly. Without regret, I watched the housing blocks and industrial estates disappear. And when we got to the first cows, ditches, and power masts, my thoughts were still fixed mostly on what lay ahead. On what was to come. But then the cheerfulness made way for something else. I thought about Claire and Michel. About the distance between us, which was growing all the time. I saw my wife at the door of the day care center, the child's bicycle seat into which she lifted Michel, and then her hand sliding the key into the lock of our front door.

By the time the train crossed into German territory, I had already been to the buffet a few times for more beer. But it was too late. I had passed a point beyond which there was no return.

It was then that I saw the houses and gardens. People are everywhere, I thought. There are so many of them that they build their houses all the way up to the railroad tracks.

From my hotel room, I called Claire. I tried to make my voice sound normal.

"What's wrong?" Claire said right away. "Are you okay?"

"How's Michel?"

"Good. He made an elephant out of clay at the day care center. But maybe he should tell you himself. Michel, this is Daddy on the phone . . ."

No, I tried to say. No.

"Daddy . . ."

"Hi, pal. What's this I hear from Mama? Did you make an elephant?"

"Daddy?"

I had to say something. But nothing came out.

"Have you got a cold, Daddy?"

During the days that followed I did my

best to play the part of the interested tourist. I strolled past the remnants of the Wall. I ate in restaurants where the guidebook I'd brought with me said only ordinary Berliners ate. The evenings were the worst. I stood at the window of my hotel room and looked at the traffic and the thousands of little lights and the people who all seemed to be on their way to something.

There were two possibilities for me to choose from: I could stay there at the window and watch, or I could go out and join the other people. I could pretend I was on my way to something too.

"How was it?" Claire asked a week later as I pressed her to me again. I pressed harder than I'd been planning to. But, on the other hand, not hard enough.

A few days later, it started at school as well. At first I'd been able to tell myself that it had to do with being far away.

But something had happened, and that something I had now brought home with me.

"You might ask yourself how many people there would be if the Second World War had not taken place at all," I said as I wrote the figure 55,000,000 on the board. "If everyone had been able to just go on fucking. I want you to do the arithmetic for me, for the next time we meet."

I was aware that more students than usual were staring at me now, perhaps all of them: from the board to me and then back again. I grinned. I looked out the window. The school building had a central ventilation system. The windows didn't open. "I'm going for a breath of fresh air," I said, and walked out of the classroom.

30

I don't know whether some of the students had already complained at that point, whether parents brought it to the school board's attention, or whether that only happened later. Whatever the case, one day I was summoned to the principal's office.

The principal was the kind of man you rarely see these days: hair parted on the side, a brown herringbone suit.

"I've been approached with some complaints about the content of the history lessons," he said after having me sit down in the only chair across from his desk.

"By whom?"

The principal looked at me. On the wall behind his head hung a classroom map of the Netherlands, showing all thirteen provinces.

"That's not really relevant," he said. "The point is —"

"It is relevant. Did those complaints come

from parents or from the students themselves? Parents are always bitching about things that don't bother the students."

"Paul, what this is really about is something you said about victims. Please correct me if I I'm wrong. About victims of the Second World War."

I leaned back, or at least I tried to lean back, but it was a hard, straight-backed chair that didn't give.

"It has been said that you have expressed yourself in rather belittling terms about those victims," the principal said. "You supposedly said that they had only themselves to blame for being victims."

"I never put it that way. I only said that not all victims are automatically innocent victims."

The principal looked at a sheet of paper lying on his desk.

"It says here . . . ," he began, but then he shook his head, took off his glasses, and pinched the bridge of his nose between thumb and forefinger. "You must realize, Paul, that these are indeed parents who have complained. Parents always complain. Tell me something I don't know already about complaining parents. Usually it's about nothing. About whether their children can get apples in the school cafeteria. What is our policy with regard to gymnastics during menstruation? Trifles. Rarely about the content of the lessons. But this time, that's what it is. And that is not good for the school. It would be better for all of us if you would simply stick to the curriculum."

For the first time during our meeting, I felt a slight tingling at the back of my neck. "And in what way have I allegedly not stuck to the curriculum?" I asked calmly.

"It says here . . ." The principal fumbled anew at the paper lying on his desk. "But why don't you tell me yourself? What exactly did you say, Paul?"

"Nothing special. I let them do some simple arithmetic. In a group of one hundred people, how many assholes are there? How many fathers who humiliate their children? How many morons whose breath stinks like rotten meat but who refuse to do anything about it? How many hopeless cases who go on complaining all their lives about the nonexistent injustices they've had to suffer? Look around you, I said. How many of your classmates would you be pleased not to see return to their desks tomorrow morning? Think about that one member of your own family, that irritating uncle with his pointless horseshit stories at birthday parties, that ugly cousin who mistreats his cat.

Think about how relieved you would be —
and not only you, but virtually the entire
family — if that uncle or cousin would step
on a land mine or be hit by a five-hundred-
pounder dropped from a high altitude. If
that member of the family were to be wiped
off the face of the earth. And now think
about all those millions of victims of all the
wars there have been in the past — I never
specifically mentioned the Second World
War; I only used it as an example because
it's the one that most appeals to their
imaginations — and think about the thousands, perhaps tens of thousands of victims
who we need to have around like we need a
hole in the head. Even from a purely statisti-
cal standpoint, it's impossible that all those
victims were good people, whatever kind of
people that may be. The injustice is found
more in the fact that the assholes are also
put on the list of innocent victims. That
their names are also chiseled into the war
memorials."

I paused for a moment to catch my breath.
How well did I know this principal, anyway?
He had let me have my say without inter-
ruption, but what did that mean? Maybe he
had heard enough. Maybe this was all he
needed to give me a probationary warning.

"Paul . . . ," he began. He had put his

glasses back on, but he was not looking at me; he was looking at a point on his desktop. "Could I ask you a personal question, Paul?"

I didn't reply.

"Have you perhaps reached the end of your rope, Paul?" the principal asked. "When it comes to teaching, I mean? Please understand me — I am not blaming you for anything. It happens to all of us at times, sooner or later. That we don't feel like it anymore. That we start thinking about the senselessness of our profession."

I shrugged. "Oh, well . . . ," I said.

"I've been through it too. When I was standing before a class myself. It's a very nasty feeling. It knocks the blocks out from under everything. From under everything you've believed in. Is that the kind of thing you're going through now, Paul? Can you still believe in it?"

"I have always had the students in mind, first and foremost," I answered truthfully. "I've always tried to make the subject as interesting as possible for them. In doing that, I've always used myself as a measuring stick. I have never tried to woo them with wishy-washy, trendy stories. I've always thought of what I was like when I was in high school. What really interested me.

That's always been the bottom line for me."

The principal smiled and leaned back in his office chair. He can lean back, I thought. And I'm sitting here with a straight back.

"What I remember most about my own high school history classes are the ancient Egyptians, the Greeks and Romans," I said. "Alexander the Great, Cleopatra, Julius Caesar, Hannibal, the Trojan Horse, the elephants marching across the Alps, the sea battles, the gladiatorial contests, the chariot races, the spectacular murders and suicides, the eruption of Vesuvius. But on the other hand, also the beauty, the beauty of all those temples and arenas and amphitheaters, the frescoes, the baths, the mosaics. That's the kind of beauty that lasts forever. Those are the colors that make us prefer a holiday on the Mediterranean to Manchester or Bremen, even today. But then Christianity comes along, and it all begins to crumble and fall. In the end you're actually glad when the barbarians come and level the whole thing. Those are the things I remember, as clearly as though I learned about them yesterday. And what I also remember most is that, after that, for a long time, there was nothing. The Middle Ages, when you come right down to it, were a disgusting, backward time during which, with the exception of a few violent sieges, very little happened. And then Dutch history! The Eighty Years' War: I remember always hoping that the Spanish would finally win. There was a spark of hope when William of Orange was assassinated, but in the end, that club of religious fanatics succeeded in seizing the day anyway. And darkness settled in for good across the Low Countries. I also remember how, year after year, our history teacher dangled the prospect of the Second World War in front of our noses, like a fat sausage. 'I deal with World War Two in the sixth,' he said, but once you got to the sixth, he was still talking about William I and the Belgian secession. At best, he threw in a little bit of trench warfare to keep us interested. But, except for the mass destruction of human lives, the First World War was mostly boring. It had no zing, after a manner of speaking. There was no momentum. Later I was told that it's always like that. You never get to World War Two. You never get to the most interesting period in the last fifteen hundred years, even for the Netherlands, where, after the Romans decided it was not their kind of place, nothing truly interesting happened until May 1940. I mean, when they talk about Holland in other countries, who do they talk about?

About Rembrandt. About Vincent van Gogh. About painters. The only historical Dutch figure who ever had an international breakthrough, if you can put it that way, was Anne Frank."

For what seemed the umpteenth time, the principal began shuffling papers around on his desk and flipping through something that looked vaguely familiar to me. It was a folder, a folder with a clear cover, the kind of folder students use when they hand in their papers.

"Does the name _____ mean anything to you, Paul?" he asked.

He named one of the female students in my class. I'm not omitting the name here on purpose. I vowed at the time to forget it. And I succeeded.

I nodded.

"And do you remember what you said to her?"

"More or less," I said.

He closed the folder and laid it back on his desk.

"You give her a three," he said, "and when she asks why, you say —"

"That three was entirely fitting," I said. "It was complete garbage. Not the kind of thing I expect the students to hand in."

The principal smiled, but it was a watery

smile, a flaky smile, like curdled milk. "I have to admit that I am not particularly impressed either, but this is not about that. This is about —"

"In addition to the Second World War, I also deal with a large part of the history that came afterwards," I interrupted again. "Korea, Vietnam, Kuwait, the Mideast and Israel, the Six-Day War, the Yom Kippur War, the Palestinians. I deal with all of that during my classes. So then you can't expect to turn in a paper about the state of Israel in which people mostly pick oranges and dance in sandals around a campfire. Cheerful, happy people everywhere, and all that horseshit about the desert where flowers blossom again. I mean, people are shot and killed there every day. Buses are blown up. What's this all about?"

"She came in here crying, Paul."

"I'd cry too if I turned in garbage like that."

The principal looked at me. I saw something in his eyes that I hadn't seen there before: something neutral, or rather, something noncommittal, as noncommittal as his herringbone suit. He leaned back again, but farther back than the first time.

He's distancing himself, I thought. Not distancing himself — I corrected myself right away — he's saying good-bye.

"Paul, you simply can't say things like that to a fifteen-year-old girl," he said. A more neutral tone had come into his voice as well. He was not going to enter into a discussion with me. He was delivering his judgment. I knew for certain that if I had asked him at that moment why you couldn't say things like that, his reply would have been: "Because you can't."

For a brief moment, I thought about the girl. She had a sweet, but too-cheerful face. Cheerful for no good reason. A happy but sexless cheer was what it was, just as happy and sexless as the page and a half she had dedicated in her paper to the picking of oranges.

"Things like that may be something you shout from the stands at a soccer match," the principal went on, "but not at a high school. At least, not at our school, and certainly not as a teacher."

Exactly what I said to that girl doesn't matter here — let me be clear about that. It would only distract us from the real issue. It would add nothing. Sometimes things come out of your mouth that you regret later on. Or no, not regret. You say something so razor-sharp that the person you say it to carries it around with them for the rest of their life.

I thought about her cheerful face. When I said to her what I said, it broke down the middle. Like a vase. Or like a glass that shatters at a high-pitched note.

I looked at the principal and felt my hand curling into a fist. I couldn't help it. I had no desire to continue with the discussion. What's the phrase again . . . our positions had become irreconcilable. That was what was happening. A chasm was yawning. Sometimes talk comes to an end. I looked at the principal and imagined planting my fist right in the middle of that gray face of his. Just below the nose, the knuckles against that blank area between nostrils and upper lip. Teeth would break, blood would spurt from his nose, my position would be made clear. But I doubted whether that would help to resolve our differences. I wouldn't have to stop after that first punch, of course. I could rebuild that bland face in its entirety, but at best into something equally bland. My position at school would become untenable, as they put it, although that was the least of my worries at that moment. In all frankness, my position had been untenable for a long time. From the very first day that I walked through the front door of this school, one could have spoken of an untenable position. The rest was a temporary reprieve. All the hours that I had stood in front of classes here: they had never been anything but a reprieve.

The question was whether I should do the principal the favor of giving him a beating. Whether I should make him a victim. Someone for whom people would feel pity later on. I pictured the students crowding to the window as he was taken away in the ambulance. Yes, an ambulance would have to be called — I would not stop before the job was finished. In the end, the students would feel pity for him.

"Paul?" the principal said, shifting his weight in his chair. He could smell something. He smelled danger. He was looking for a stance in which to roll with the first blow as well as he could.

And if the ambulance were to drive away without the lights flashing? I thought to myself. I took a deep breath, then exhaled slowly. I had to decide quickly now — otherwise it would be too late. I could beat him to death. With my bare fists. It would be a dirty job, admittedly, but no dirtier than field-dressing a wild animal. Dressing a turkey, I corrected myself. He had a wife at home — I knew that — and some older children. Who knows, maybe I would be doing them a service. It was quite possible that they had grown tired of that bland face of his. At the funeral they would display their grief, but after that, in the entrance hall, relief would quickly gain the upper hand.

"Paul?"

I looked at the principal. I smiled.

"Could I ask you a personal question?" he asked. "I thought, perhaps there's something . . . I mean, I'm only asking. How are things at home, Paul? Is everything all right at home?"

At home. I kept smiling, but I was thinking about Michel the whole time. Michel was almost four. In the Netherlands, for beating to death a fellow human, you might receive eight years, I figured. It wasn't much. With a little good behavior, a little raking around the prison grounds, you would be out the gates within five. Michel would be nine by then.

"How are things with your wife . . . with Carla?"

Claire, I corrected the principal soundlessly. Her name is Claire.

"Wonderful," I said.

"And the kids? How are they?"

The kids. Even that was too much for this asshole to remember! It was impossible to remember everything about everyone, of course. That the French teacher lived with her girlfriend was an exception. Because it stood out. But all the others? The others did not stand out. They all had a husband or a wife and children. Or no children. Or only one child. Michel's bike still had training wheels. If I were in prison, I wouldn't get to see the moment when the training wheels were taken off. Only hear about it.

"Great," I said. "Sometimes it's amazing how quickly it all goes. How quickly they grow up."

The principal folded his hands and placed them on his desktop, ignorant of the fact that he had just crept through the eye of the needle.

For Michel. For Michel, I would keep my hands to myself.

"Paul. You may not like my saying this, I know, but I have to say it anyway. I think it would be good if you made an appointment with Van Dieren. With the school psychologist. And if you were to take a short break from teaching, just for a while. So you can recharge your batteries. I think you need it. We all need it from time to time."

I was remarkably calm. Calm and fatigued. There would be no violence. It was like a storm coming up. The café chairs are carried inside, the awnings are rolled up, but nothing happens. The storm passes over. And, at the same time, that's too bad. After all, we would all rather see the roofs ripped from the houses, the trees uprooted and tossed through the air; documentaries about tornados, hurricanes, and tsunamis have a soothing effect. Of course it's terrible — we've all been taught to say that we think it's terrible. But a world without disasters and violence — be it the violence of nature or that of muscle and blood — would be the truly unbearable thing.

The principal could go home later, undamaged. In the evening he would sit at the table with his wife and children. With his bland presence he would fill the chair that would otherwise have remained vacant. No one would be going to intensive care or to the funeral home, quite simply because it had just been decided that way.

Actually, I'd known from the very start. From the moment he started talking about home. How are things at home? It's another way of saying that they want to get rid of you, that they're going to dump you. It's nobody's business how things are at home. It's like "Did you enjoy your meal?" That's nobody's business either.

When I agreed without further ado to talk to the school psychologist, the principal looked genuinely surprised. Pleasantly surprised. No, I was not going to give him the slightest reason to push me aside without a struggle. I stood up, to indicate that, as far as I was concerned, our meeting was over.

At the door, I held out my hand. And he shook it. He shook the hand that could have added a new twist to his life — or ended it completely.

"I'm glad you're taking it so . . . ," he said; he didn't finish his sentence. "And please give my warmest regards to . . . to your wife," he said.

"To Carla," I said.

31

And so, a few days later, I went to the school psychologist. To Van Dieren. At home, I told the truth. I told Claire that I wanted to take things a bit easier for a while. I told her about the medication the psychologist had prescribed, by way of the family doctor. This was after a first appointment that had lasted barely thirty minutes.

"And, oh yeah," I said to Claire. "He advised me to wear sunglasses."

"Sunglasses?"

"He said too many things were getting to me and that it might help to reduce the stimuli."

I was keeping back only a small part of the truth, I reasoned. By keeping back only a small part, I could avoid having to tell a barefaced lie.

The psychologist had mentioned a name. A German-sounding name. It was the surname of the neurologist who'd had this particular disorder named after him.

"With therapy, I can influence it a little," Van Dieren had said, looking at me earnestly, "but you should see it primarily as a neurological matter. With the right medication, it can be kept under control quite effectively."

Then he had asked me whether, as far as I knew, there were other members of my family with a similar complaint or symptoms. I thought about my parents, then about my grandparents. I ran through the whole laundry list of uncles and aunts and cousins, trying to keep in mind what Van Dieren had said — namely, that the syndrome was often hard to detect. People tended to function normally; they were at most a little withdrawn, he said. In a social setting, they were either the ones with the biggest mouths, or they said nothing at all.

At last I shook my head. I couldn't think of anyone.

"But you asked about my family," I said. "Does that mean it's hereditary?"

"Sometimes, yes. Sometimes, no. We always try to take family histories into account. Do you have children?"

It took a moment for the full implications to sink in. Until that point, I had been thinking only about where my genes had come from. Now, for the first time, I thought about Michel.

"Mr. Lohman?"

"Just a moment."

I thought about my son, who was almost four. About the floor of his bedroom, littered with toy cars. For the first time in my life I thought about the way he played with those cars. The next moment I wondered whether, from now on, I would ever be able to see it any differently.

And what about the day care center? Hadn't they noticed anything at the day care center? I racked my brains, trying to remember whether anything had ever been said, a passing remark about Michel withdrawing from the group or displaying other aberrant behavior — but I couldn't come up with anything.

"Is it taking you so long to figure out whether you have children?" the psychologist asked with a smile.

"No," I said. "It's just that . . ."

"Maybe you're thinking about having them."

To this day, I'm sure I didn't even blink when I answered.

"That's right," I said. "Would you advise against it? In my case?"

Van Dieren leaned his elbows on the desk

and folded his hands beneath his chin. "No. That is to say: these days, it's quite possible to identify defects like that before birth. With a pregnancy test or amniocentesis. Of course, you have to be aware of what you're getting into. Terminating a pregnancy is no trifling matter."

A number of things flashed through my mind then. One by one, I held them up to the light. I could only deal with them one by one. I hadn't lied when I answered the psychologist's question by saying that we were thinking about having children. At most, I had omitted to say that we already had one. It had been a very trying birth. The first few years after Michel was born, Claire had refused to even consider getting pregnant again, but lately it had come up more often. We both realized that we would have to decide soon. Otherwise, the difference in age between Michel and a little brother or sister would be too great — if it wasn't already.

"So a test like that could show whether a child has inherited this disorder?" I asked. My mouth was drier than it had been a few minutes earlier, I noticed, and I had to moisten my lips with the tip of my tongue before I could talk normally.

"Well, I should probably correct myself

259

there. What I just said was that the illness could be identified even in the amniotic fluid, but it's not quite like that. At best, it's the other way around. The amniocentesis can show that something's not right, but precisely what it is is something only further testing can tell us."

It had already become an illness, I noted. We had started with a defect and then, by way of a disorder and a syndrome, ended up with an illness.

"But in any case, it's reason enough for an abortion," I said. "Even without further testing?"

"Listen. With Down's syndrome, for example, or what they call spina bifida, we can see clear signs in the amniotic fluid. In those cases, we always advise the parents to terminate the pregnancy. With this illness, though, we find ourselves in a gray area. But we always warn the parents. In actual practice, most people decide not to run the risk."

Van Dieren had started using the word *we*. As though he represented the entire medical profession. But he was only a plain old psychologist. And a school psychologist at that. That was about as low on the totem pole as you could get.

Had Claire ever had an amniotic fluid

test? The stupid thing was, I didn't know. I had gone along with her almost every time. To the first ultrasound. To the first prenatal exercise class — only the first one, thank God — Claire had found it even more ridiculous than I did that the husband was expected to pant and puff along. To the first visit to the midwife, which was also immediately the last visit. "I don't want any midwives pawing me!" she had said.

But Claire had also gone to the hospital alone a few times. There was no sense in my missing half a day's work for a routine visit to her gynecologist at the hospital, she had said.

I was about to ask Van Dieren whether all pregnant women were given an amniotic fluid test, or only a particular high-risk group, but gulped back the question right away.

"Were there amniotic fluid tests thirty or forty years ago?" I asked instead.

The school psychologist thought about it for a moment. "I don't believe so. No, now that you mention it. In fact, I'm a hundred percent sure. That was definitely not something they did back then, no."

We looked at each other. At that moment, I was also a hundred percent sure that Van Dieren and I were thinking the same thing.

261

But he didn't say it. He probably didn't dare to say it, so I said it for him.

"In other words, the inadequate state of medical science forty years ago is the only reason I'm sitting here across from you today?" I said. "That I'm here at all," I added. It was a superfluous thing to add, but I felt like hearing it from my own mouth.

Van Dieren nodded slowly. A smile of amusement appeared on his face.

"If you put it that way," he said. "Had this test been available back then, it's not entirely unimaginable that your parents would have decided to be safe rather than sorry."

32

I took the pills. For the first few days, nothing happened. But I'd been told that beforehand, that nothing would happen, that the effects would become noticeable only after a couple of weeks. Still, it struck me that Claire had started looking at me differently from the very beginning. "How are you feeling?" she asked, several times a day. "Fine," was my stock answer. And it was actually true. I felt quite fine — I relished the change. Above all, I relished the fact that I didn't have to get up in front of the classroom every day: all those faces looking at me, a full hour long, and then other faces that came in for the next hour, and on and on, one hour after the next. If you've never stood in front of a class, you don't know what it's like.

After a little less than a week, earlier than predicted, the medication began to take effect. I hadn't expected it to be like that. I had been dreading it — I especially dreaded the thought that it would kick in without my noticing. Personality change, that was my biggest fear, that my personality would be affected, that I would become, though more bearable to those around me, lost to myself. I had read the information leaflets, and they included absolutely alarming side effects. "Nausea," "dry skin," and a "decreased appetite" were things you could live with, but they also talked about "feelings of fear," "hyperventilation," and "memory loss." "This is really potent stuff," I told Claire. "I'm going to take it — I don't have any choice — but I want you to promise that you'll warn me if it goes wrong. If I start forgetting things or acting weird, you have to tell me. Then I'll stop."

But my fears proved unfounded. It was on a Sunday afternoon, about five days after I had gulped down the first pills. I was lying on the couch in the living room with the big, fat Saturday newspaper on my lap. Through the sliding glass doors I looked out at the garden, where it had just started to rain. It was one of those days of fluffy white clouds and patches of blue in between. The wind was blowing hard. I should mention right away that for the last few months, my own house, my own living room, and along with it, above all, my own presence in that house and in that living room had often frightened me. The fear was directly connected to the existence of so many other people in similar houses and living rooms. Especially in the evening, after dark, when most people were "at home," this fear would quickly take over. From where I lay on the couch I could see, through the bushes and trees, the light from windows across the street. I rarely saw actual people, but those lit windows betrayed their presence — just as my own lit window betrayed my presence. I don't want to give the wrong impression: I wasn't afraid of people themselves, of people as a species. I don't suffer from panic attacks in big crowds, and I'm also not the antisocial guest at parties, the loner no one wants to talk to, whose body language itself announces nothing more loudly than his desire to be left alone. No, it's something else. It had to do with the provisional status of all those people in their living rooms, in their houses, their housing blocks, their neatly laid-out neighborhoods of streets, each of which directly leads to another, each square connected by streets to the next square.

That was how I sometimes lay on the couch in our living room in the evening and thought about things. Something in me whispered that I needed to stop thinking, that I should above all not go too far with thinking. But that never worked. I always thought things through to the end, to their most extreme consequence. At this exact moment, I thought, there are people everywhere, lying on couches in living rooms like this one. Later on, they will go to bed. They'll toss and turn a bit, or say something nice to each other, or remain stubbornly silent because they've just had an argument and neither of them wants to be the first to admit he was wrong. Then the light goes out. I thought about time — the passing of time, to be precise — how vast, how endless, how long and dark and empty one hour can be. Anyone who thinks like that has no need to think about the infinity of space. I thought about the sheer quantity of people, their numbers, not even in terms of overpopulation, or pollution, or whether in the future there would be enough for everyone to eat, but strictly about the quantity itself. About whether three million or six billion served any given purpose. Once I had arrived at this point, the first feelings of discomfort would appear. It isn't that there are too many people, not per se, I would think to myself, but there are an awful lot of them. I thought about the students in my classroom. They all had to do something: they had to make a start in life; they had to go through life. Even though a single hour can be so long. They had to find jobs and form couples. Children would come, and those children too would sit through history classes at school, although no longer taught by me. From a certain vantage point, you could see only the presence of people, not the people themselves anymore. That was when I would start to panic. From the outside, you wouldn't have noticed much of anything, except that the newspaper was still lying unread on my lap. "Do you want a beer?" Claire would ask, coming into the room just then with a glass of red wine in her hand. Now I had to say "okay," without the tone of my voice giving cause for concern. I was afraid my voice would sound like that of someone who has just woken up, who just got out of bed and hasn't spoken yet. Or simply a strange voice, not completely recognizable as my own, a scary voice. Claire would raise her eyebrows and ask, "Is something wrong?" And of course I would deny it. I would shake my head, but much too vehemently, which would give me away, as I, in a strange, scary, squeaky voice that didn't sound at all like my own, would say: "No, everything's fine. What could be wrong?"

And then? Then Claire would sit down beside me on the couch. She would take my hand — she might also lay a hand on my forehead, the way you do with a child when you're checking for a temperature. And here it comes. I knew that the door to normal was wide open now: Claire would ask again whether there was really nothing wrong, and I would shake my head again (less vehemently this time). She would go on looking worried at first but would soon put aside her concern: I was reacting normally, after all. My voice had stopped squeaking, and I was answering her questions calmly. No, I had only been sort of lost in thought. About what? I don't even remember anymore. Come on, do you know how long you've been sitting here with that newspaper on your lap? An hour and a half, maybe two! I was thinking about the garden, that maybe we should build a little shed back there. Paul . . . Hmm? No one thinks about the garden for an hour and a half. No, of course not. I mean, I was thinking about the garden for the last fifteen minutes or so. But what about before that?

On that Sunday afternoon, though, a week after my appointment with the school psychologist, I looked at the garden for the first time in a long time without thinking about anything. I heard Claire in the kitchen. She was singing quietly along to something on the radio, a song I didn't know but in which the words "roses by day" kept coming back.

"What are you laughing about?" she said when she came into the room a little later with two mugs of coffee.

"Oh, just laughing," I said.

"What do you mean, just laughing? You should see yourself. You look like one of those born-again Christians. One big lump of happiness."

I looked at her. I felt warm, but in a pleasant way, the warmth of a down quilt. "I was just thinking . . . ," I said, but stopped quickly. I'd been planning to start in about a second child. We hadn't touched on the subject for the last few months. I thought about the difference in age, which in the best case would be almost five years. It was now or never. Still, there was a voice that told me that this was not the time — in a few days, perhaps, but not on this Sunday afternoon when the medication had started doing its work.

"I was thinking that maybe we should build a little shed in the back garden," I said.

33

Looking back on it, that Sunday was the high point as well. The novelty of living a life without guarded thoughts quickly wore off. Life became more constant, more muted, like a party where you can see everyone talking and gesturing but can't hear what anyone in particular is saying. No more peaks and troughs. Something was missing. You sometimes hear about people who have lost their sense of smell and taste: for those people, a plate of the most delicious food means nothing at all. That was how I looked at life sometimes, as a warm meal that was growing cold. I knew I had to eat, or else I would die, but I had lost my appetite.

A few weeks later, I made a final attempt to regain the euphoria of that first Sunday afternoon. Michel had just gone to bed. Claire and I were lying together on the couch, watching a program about convicts on death row in the United States. We have a wide couch; with a little maneuvering we could both fit on it. Because we were lying next to each other, I didn't have to look her in the eye.

"I was just thinking," I said. "If we were to have another child now, Michel would be five by the time it's born."

"I was thinking the same thing, just recently," Claire said. "It really isn't a good idea. We should just be happy with what we have."

I felt my wife's warmth — my arm around her shoulders may have pulled her closer for a moment. I thought about my talk with the school psychologist.

Did you ever actually have an amniotic fluid test?

I could ask that, as casually as possible. One disadvantage was that I couldn't see her eyes at the moment I asked. A disadvantage, and an advantage.

Then I thought about our happiness. About our happy family. Our happy family that should be happy with what it had.

"Shall we go somewhere next weekend?" I said. "Hire a bungalow or something? You know, just the three of us?"

34

And then? Then Claire became ill. Claire, who was never ill, at least never had more than a runny nose, who in any case never spent the day in bed with flu, ended up in the hospital. From one day to the next. There was nothing that could have prepared us for her hospitalization — there had been no time to, as they say, make arrangements. In the morning, she said, she had felt a little "wobbly," but she had gone out anyway, she had kissed me good-bye, on the lips, then climbed onto her bike. That afternoon I saw her again, but now with a whole series of drips in her arm and a monitor beeping at the head of her bed. She tried to smile, but it was clearly an effort. A surgeon standing in the corridor gestured to me to come over. He needed to talk to me alone.

I'm not going to say what was wrong with Claire, not here. I consider that a private matter. It's nobody's business what kind of illnesses you've had — in any case it's up to her if she wants to talk about it, and not up to me. Let's just say it wasn't a life-threatening illness, at least not at that stage. That's a word that was used a few times by friends and family and acquaintances and colleagues when they called. "Is it life threatening?" they asked. They said it slightly sotto voce, but you could hear the thirst for sensation right through it: when people get a chance to come close to death without having it touch them personally, they never miss the opportunity. What I also remember well is the urge I felt to answer that question in the affirmative. "Yes, it's life threatening." I wanted to hear the silence that would drop at the other end after an answer like that.

So without going into detail about Claire's illness, I just want to report here what the surgeon said to me in the corridor, after he told me about the coming operation. "No, it's not peanuts," he said, having allowed a little pause for me to deal with the news. "Your whole life changes from one day to the next. But we do everything we can." The last phrase was said in an almost cheerful tone, a tone that clashed with the expression on his face.

And after that? After that, everything went

wrong. Or rather, everything that could go wrong did go wrong. A second operation followed the first, then a third. More and more monitors were clustered around her bed. Tubes emerged from her body and went back into it at other places. Tubes and monitors that were supposed to keep her alive, but after that first day the surgeon dropped his cheerful tone. He still kept saying that they were doing everything they could, but by then Claire had lost more than forty pounds. She could no longer even raise herself up to lean against the pillows.

I was glad that Michel didn't see her like that. At first I had acted chipper and suggested that we go together to see her at visiting hours, but he acted as though he hadn't heard me. On the day itself, the day his mother had gone out the door but not come back in the evening, I had emphasized the festive aspect, the uniqueness of the situation, like sleeping over at a friend's house or a field trip. We went out to eat together at the café-restaurant for regular people. Spareribs with fries was his favorite meal back then, and I did my best to explain to him what had happened. I explained it to him and talked around it at the same time. I omitted things, mostly my own fears. After dinner, we rented a movie at the video shop.

He was allowed to stay up longer than normal, even though he had to go to school the next day (he was no longer at the day care center by then; he was in first grade at elementary school). "Is Mama coming later?" he asked when I kissed him good-night. "I'll leave the door open a crack," I answered. "I'm going to watch TV — that way you can hear me."

I didn't call anyone that first evening. Claire had made me promise not to. "No reason to make a fuss," she'd said. "Maybe it will all turn out to be nothing and I can come home in a couple of days." I had already talked to the surgeon in the corridor by that time. "Okay," I said. "No reason for a fuss."

The next afternoon, after school, Michel didn't ask about his mother. He asked me to take the training wheels off his bike. I had done that once a few months earlier, but then, after a few lurching attempts, he had ended up cycling into the low fence around the park. "Are you sure?" I asked. It was a lovely day in May, and he went riding off, without wobbling even once, all the way to the corner and then back. When he passed me, he let go of the handlebars and raised his hands in the air.

"They want to operate tomorrow already,"

Claire told me that evening. "But what are they going to do, exactly? Did they tell you anything?"

"Did I tell you that Michel had me take the training wheels off his bike today?" I said.

Claire closed her eyes for a moment. Her head was resting deep among the pillows, as though it were heavier than usual. "How's he doing?" she asked quietly. "Does he miss me terribly?"

"He's so anxious to come and see you," I lied. "But I think it would be better to wait a little bit."

I'm not going to mention the name of the hospital where Claire was. It was fairly close to our home. I could get there by bike, or by car if the weather was bad — either way, it never took me more than ten minutes. During visiting hours, Michel stayed with the woman next door, who had children as well; sometimes our babysitter came over, a fifteen-year-old girl who lived around the corner. I don't feel like going into detail about everything that went wrong at the hospital. I would only like to urgently advise those who attach any value to life — their own, or that of their family and loved ones — to never let themselves be admitted there. That, by the same token, is my dilemma: it's nobody's business which hospital Claire was in, but at the same time I want to warn everyone to stay as far away from it as possible.

"How are you coping?" Claire asked one afternoon — I think it was after the second or third operation. Her voice was so weak that I had to put my ear almost to her lips. "Don't you need any help?"

At the word *help,* a muscle or a nerve under my left eye began to twitch. No, I didn't want any help. I could manage quite well by myself, or perhaps I should say I amazed myself, above all, with how well I was able to manage. Michel got to school on time, his teeth brushed and his clothes clean. More or less clean. I was less critical of a few spots on his trousers than Claire would have been, but then, I was his father. I never tried to be "both father and mother" to him, the way some half-assed, homemade-sweater-wearing head of a single-parent household put it once in some bullshit program I saw on afternoon TV. I was busy, but busy in a good way. The last thing I needed was for people, with or without the best of intentions, to take work off my hands so that I would have more time for other things. I was grateful to have every moment accounted for. Sometimes I

277

would sit in the kitchen with a beer in the evening, after having kissed Michel good-night. The dishwasher was zooming and bubbling, the newspaper lay unread on the table before me, and then suddenly I would feel uplifted. I don't know how else to put it. It was a feeling of lightness — above all, extreme lightness. Had someone pursed their lips and blown at me right then, I would undoubtedly have gone floating off, up to the ceiling, like a down feather from a pillow. Yes, that was it: weightlessness. I'm deliberately not using words like *happiness,* or even *satisfaction.*

I sometimes heard the parents of Michel's playmates sigh about how, after a busy day, they really needed "a moment to them-selves." The children were in bed at last, and then came the magic moment, and not a minute earlier. I've always thought that was strange, because for me that moment began much earlier. When Michel came home from school, for example, and every-thing was as it should be. My own voice, above all, asking him what he wanted on his sandwich, also sounded as it should have. The larder was full — I had done all the shopping that morning. I took care of myself as well: I looked in the mirror before leav-ing the house. I made sure my clothes were clean, that I had shaved, that my hair didn't look like the hair of someone who never looks in the mirror. The people in the supermarket would have noticed nothing unusual. I was no divorced father reeking of alcohol, no father who couldn't handle things.

I clearly remember the goal I set for myself: I wanted to keep up the appearance of normalcy. As far as possible, everything had to remain the same for Michel as long as his mother wasn't around. A hot meal every day, for a start. But also in other aspects of our temporary single-parent family, there shouldn't be too many visible changes. Normally, it wasn't my habit to shave every day — I didn't mind walking around with stubble. Claire had never made a big deal out of that either, but during those weeks, I shaved every morning. I felt that my son had a right to sit at the table with a clean-smelling, freshly shaven father. A freshly shaven and clean-smelling father would not prompt him to think the wrong things, would in any case not cause him to doubt the temporary character of our single-parent family. No, on the outside there was nothing for anyone to notice about me. I remained one pillar of a trinity. Another pillar was lying only temporarily (temporarily! temporarily! temporarily!) in the hospital. I was the pilot of a three-engine aircraft, one of whose engines had stalled. There is no reason to panic. This is not a crash landing. The pilot has thousands of flight hours behind him. He will land the plane safely on the ground.

35

One evening, Serge and Babette showed up. Claire was going to be operated on again the next day. I remember it well. That evening I had made macaroni, macaroni *alla carbonara* — to be honest, the only dish I have ever mastered down to the smallest detail. Along with the spareribs from the café-restaurant for regular people, it was Michel's favorite dish, which was why I made it every day during the weeks that Claire was in the hospital.

I was just about to put the food on the table when the bell rang. Serge and Babette didn't ask to come in — before I knew it, they were already in the living room. I saw how Babette in particular looked around the room, then the whole house. During those weeks, we didn't eat in the kitchen, the way we usually did. I had set up trays in the living room, in front of the TV. Babette looked at the trays and cutlery and then at the television that was already on, because the weekly sports news was going to start in a few minutes. Then she looked at me, with a special look — I don't know how else to describe it.

That special look, as I can still recall, made me feel as though I had something to explain. I mumbled something about the festive aspect of the meals we took together. There were, after all, occasions on which I did depart from the normal run of things. The household didn't have to be a carbon copy of the way Claire ran it, as long as there were no visible traces of decline. I believe that in explaining this to Babette, I used the phrase "male household," and even "holiday feel."

That was pretty stupid. Looking back on it now, I could kick myself. I didn't owe anyone an explanation. But by then Babette had climbed the stairs and was standing in the doorway to Michel's room. Michel was sitting on the floor amid his toys. He was in the process of lining up hundreds of dominoes, in imitation of World Domino Day, but when he saw his aunt, he jumped up and leapt into her outstretched arms.

A little too enthusiastically, if you ask me. He was very fond of his aunt, it's true, but the way he wrapped both arms around her thighs, making it look like he would never let go, still created the impression that he missed having a woman around the house. A mother. Babette cuddled him and ran her fingers through his hair. Meanwhile, she looked around the room, and I looked with her.

The space on the floor was not fully occupied by dominoes. There were toys everywhere. Toys had been slung all over the room, perhaps that's more like it. There was almost no place to put a foot down. To say that Michel's room was a mess would be an understatement, I saw myself, now that I looked at it through Babette's eyes. There was the explosion of toys, of course, but that wasn't all. The two chairs, the couch, and Michel's bed were all covered in clothing, both clean and dirty clothing, and on his little desk and on the stool beside his (unmade) bed were plates with crumbs and half-empty glasses of milk and soda pop. Worst of all, perhaps, was the apple core that wasn't on a plate at all, but lying on an Ajax soccer jersey with the name Kluivert on it. The apple core, like all apple cores exposed for more than a few minutes to sunlight and air, was a dark brown. I remembered having given Michel an apple and a glass of soda pop that very afternoon, but now you couldn't tell that the apple core had only been there for a couple of hours. Like all apple cores, it looked as though it had been lying on top of that jersey for days, rotting away.

I also recalled having said to Michel that morning that later in the day we would clean up his room together. But for a variety of reasons, or rather, due to the comforting thought that there was plenty of time to clean up later on, it hadn't happened.

As she stood there, still holding my son and running one hand affectionately over his back, I looked at Babette's eyes, and again I saw that special look. I'll clean it up! I felt like screaming at her. If you had come by tomorrow, you could have eaten off the floor in this room. But I didn't. I only looked at her and shrugged. It's a bit of a mess, my shoulders said, but who cares? There are more important things to think about at the moment than a messy or tidy room.

Again, that need to explain! I didn't want to explain — no explanations were needed, I told myself. They had dropped in without calling first. Let's turn this around, I thought to myself. Let's turn this thing around and imagine what would happen if I suddenly showed up at my brother and sister-in-law's door — while Babette was shaving her legs, for example, or while Serge was clipping his toenails. Then I would also see something that was essentially private, that normally wasn't meant for the eyes of outsiders. I shouldn't have let them in, I thought then. I should have said it was a bad moment.

On the way downstairs, after Babette had promised Michel that later, when he was finished, she would come back and watch the dominoes fall, and after I had told him that dinner was almost ready, that we were going to eat in a minute, we walked past the bathroom and the bedroom, Claire's and my bedroom. Babette glanced at each of them quickly. She barely tried to disguise those glances, particularly at the overflowing laundry basket and the unmade bed strewn with newspapers. This time she didn't look at me, though — and that was perhaps even more painful, more humiliating, than the special look. I had been very clear in saying to Michel, and only to Michel, that we were going to eat in a minute. I wanted to broadcast the unambiguous signal that my brother and his wife would not be invited to eat with us. They had come at a bad moment, and it was high time for them to leave.

Downstairs, in the living room, Serge was standing in front of the television with his hands in his pockets; the weekly sports news had already begun. More than anything else — more than the brazen way my brother stood there, hands in his pockets, his feet planted squarely on the carpet, as though it were his living room and not mine; more than my sister-in-law's special looks at Michel's room, at our room, at the laundry basket — it was the footage on the sports news, of a group of soccer players running laps around a sunny field, that told me now that my plan for the evening was about to fall to pieces — no, that it had already fallen to pieces. My evening together with Michel in front of the TV, our plates of macaroni *alla carbonara* on our laps, a normal evening — without his mother, of course, without my wife — but a festive evening nonetheless.

"Serge . . ." Babette had walked over to my brother and laid her hand on his shoulder.

"Yeah," Serge said. He turned and looked at me without taking his hands out of his pockets. "Paul . . . ," he began. He stopped and looked helplessly at his wife.

Babette breathed a deep sigh. Then she took my hand and held it between her

286

lovely, her long and elegant, fingers. She no longer had that special look in her eyes. Her gaze was friendly now, but resolute, as though I were no longer the initiator of the total chaos here in the house, but myself an overflowing laundry basket or unmade bed, a laundry basket that she, in no time, would empty into the washing machine, a bed she would make in the twinkling of an eye, neater than it had ever been before: a bed in a hotel, in the royal suite.

"Paul," she said. "We know how hard this is for you. You and Michel. With Claire in the hospital and all. Of course, we all hope for the best, but at this point no one knows how long this could take. And that's why we thought that, for you, but also for Michel, it might be a good idea for him to come stay with us for a while."

I felt something, a white-hot rage, an ice-cold wave of panic. Whatever it was, it was probably written all over my face, because Babette squeezed my hand gently and said: "Take it easy, Paul. We're only here to help."

"That's right," Serge said. He took a step forward — for a moment it looked as though he was going to take hold of my other arm, or lay a hand on my shoulder, but decided against it.

"You have enough on your mind with

Claire," Babette said with a smile, as she started running a finger over the back of my hand. "If Michel could come with us for a little while, you'd be able to relax. And it would be a break for Michel, too. He puts up a brave front. A child may not say some things out loud, but they really do notice everything."

I took a few deep breaths. The most important thing now was not to let my voice waver.

"I'd love to be able to invite the two of you to eat with us," I said, "but I'm afraid I wasn't counting on visitors."

Babette's finger came to a halt on the back of my hand. The smile remained suspended on her face, but it was as though it had been disconnected from the emotion behind it — if there ever had been any emotion behind it. "We weren't planning on eating with you, Paul," she said. "We just thought, with Claire being operated on tomorrow and all, that it would be best for Michel to come with us tonight . . ."

"I was just about to sit down to dinner with my son," I said. "Your visit has come at a bad moment. So I'd like to ask the two of you to just leave now."

"Paul . . ." Babette squeezed my hand. The smile had vanished now, replaced by something more entreating, a facial expression that didn't suit her at all.

"Paul," my brother echoed. "I'm sure you realize that these aren't the most ideal conditions for a child of four."

I yanked my hand out of Babette's grasp. "What did you say?" I asked. My voice didn't waver at all. It sounded calm — too calm, probably.

"Paul!" Babette sounded alarmed. Maybe she saw something I couldn't see myself. Maybe she considered me capable of doing something rash, of doing something to Serge, but I would never have given him the satisfaction. True, the cold wave of panic had definitively given way to white-hot rage, but the fist I would have loved to plant squarely right in his noble face, so full of concern for me and my son, would have been decisive proof that I could no longer control my emotions. And a person who can't control his emotions is not the most suitable person to run a (temporary) single-parent family. Within the last minute, I had heard my own first name repeated — how often? — six times. It's my experience that when people go on repeating your first name, they want something from you, and it's usually not something you want to give.

"Serge is only trying to say that maybe it's

all a bit too much for you, Paul." Seven times. "We, of all people, know that you're doing your very best to make things seem as normal as possible for Michel. But it's not normal. The situation isn't normal. You need to be with Claire, and with your son. In a situation like that, you can't expect anyone to run a normal household." Her arm was raised, her hands and fingers pointed flutteringly upstairs: at the strewn toys, the laundry basket, and the messy bed covered in newspapers. "Right now, for Michel, his father is the most important thing he has. His mother is ill. He mustn't get the impression that his father can't handle things anymore."

I was just about to start cleaning up around the house, I wanted to say. If you two had come an hour later . . . But I didn't say it. I wasn't going to be put on the defensive. Michel and I clean up around the house when we damn well feel like it.

"I really do have to ask the two of you to leave now," I said. "Michel and I were going to eat fifteen minutes ago. I attach a lot of importance to regularity in such things. In this situation," I added.

Babette sighed. For a moment, I thought she was going to say "Paul . . ." again, but she looked from me to Serge, and then back at me. From the television came the theme tune that announced the end of the weekly sports news, and suddenly I was overcome by a deep sadness. My brother and sister-in-law had come by at a bad moment, to stick their noses into the way I ran my household, but now something had happened that could never be undone. It seems like nonsense — it *is* nonsense — but the simple conclusion that my son and I would not watch the sports news that evening almost brought tears to my eyes. I thought about Claire in her room in the hospital. For the last few days, thankfully, she'd had a room to herself. Before that, she had shared a room with some flatulent old cow who blew great rumbling farts. All through visiting hours, the two of us did our best to pretend not to hear, but after a few days Claire had gotten so sick of it that every time the woman farted, she began spraying aerosol deodorant around in the air. It made you feel like laughing and crying, all at the same time, but after visiting hours that day, I went to the head nurse and insisted that Claire be given a room of her own. The new room looked out onto a side wing of the hospital. When it was dark and the lights went on, you could see the patients in that wing lying in their beds, wriggling up against their pillows to start in on the evening meal. We had agreed that tonight, the night before the operation, I would not come to visit but would stay at home with Michel. Everything as normal as possible. But now I thought about Claire, about my wife, alone in her room, about darkness falling and the view of the lit windows and the other patients, and I wondered whether we had done the right thing. Maybe I should have called our babysitter so that this evening, on this of all evenings, I could be with my wife.

I resolved to call her as soon as I could, later on. Later on, after Serge and Babette had left and Michel had gone to bed. It really was time for them to buzz off, so that Michel and I could finally start our dinner together, our evening, which was now completely ruined anyway.

And then, suddenly, a new thought dawned. A nightmarish thought. A thought from which you awaken in a sweat: the quilt is lying on the floor, the pillow is soaked with your own perspiration, your heart is pounding — but there's light coming through the bedroom window. It didn't really happen. It was all just a dream.

"Did the two of you visit Claire today, by any chance?" I asked. I had adopted a friendly and nonchalant, a cheerful tone. Whatever the cost, I had to keep them from seeing the kind of shape I was in.

Serge and Babette looked at me. The expressions on both their faces told me that my question had come as a surprise. But that didn't mean anything — maybe they were surprised by the sudden mood swing. A few moments before, after all, I had been ordering them to leave.

"No," Babette said. "I mean . . ." Her eyes sought my brother's for support. "I talked to her, though, this afternoon."

So it really had happened. The unthinkable had actually happened. It was not a dream. The idea of taking Michel away from here had come from my own wife. She had talked to Babette on the phone that afternoon, and the idea had come up then. Maybe it hadn't been Claire herself — maybe Babette had brought up the idea — but Claire, weakened perhaps by her condition, just to put an end to the harping, had agreed. Without talking to me about it first.

In that case, I'm worse off than I figured, I thought. If my wife thinks it's a good idea to make important decisions about our son without consulting me, I've probably given her reason to think so.

I should have picked up Michel's room, I

thought. I should have emptied the laundry basket, the washing machine should have been running when Serge and Babette rang the bell, I should have put the newspapers on the bed into plastic bags, and the plastic bags should have been lined up in the hall, beside the front door, as though I were just about to bring them out to the garbage can.

But it was too late for that. I realized that it would probably have been too late no matter what. Serge and Babette had come by with a plan in mind; even if Michel and I had been sitting at the table in three-piece suits, with a damask tablecloth and sterling silver cutlery, they would have come up with some other excuse to take my son away from me.

And did the two of you, this afternoon, happen to talk about Michel? I didn't actually pose the question — I left it hanging in the air, as it were. The silence I let fall gave Babette the chance to fill in the missing pieces.

"Why doesn't Michel ever go with you to the hospital?" Babette asked.

"What?" I said.

"Why doesn't Michel ever go to visit his mother? How long has Claire been in there already? That's not normal, a son who doesn't want to see his mother."

"Claire and I have talked about that. She was the one who didn't want him to, at first. She didn't want Michel to see her like that."

"That was at first. But later. Later there must have been a moment, right? What I'm saying is that Claire herself doesn't understand anymore. She thinks her child has already forgotten her."

"Don't be ridiculous. Of course Michel hasn't forgotten his mother. He's . . ." I was going to say "He's always talking about her," but that simply wasn't true. "He just doesn't want to see her. He doesn't want to go to the hospital. I ask him often enough. 'Shall we go to the hospital tomorrow and see Mama?' I say. And then he starts looking doubtful. 'Maybe . . . ,' he says, and when I ask him again, the next day, he shakes his head. 'Maybe tomorrow,' he says. I mean, I can't force him, can I? No, that's not it: I don't *want* to force him. Not in this situation. I'm not going to drag him to the hospital against his will. It seems to me that that would be the wrong memory for him to have later on. I'm sure he has his reasons. He's four. Maybe he knows for himself the best way to deal with all this. If he wants to repress the fact that his mother is in the hospital, at this moment, then let him. That's what I figure. It seems very grown up to me. Grown-up people repress every-thing too."

Babette sniffed a few times and raised her eyebrows.

"Isn't that . . . ?" she said. And at the same moment I smelled it too. As soon as I spun around and ran for the kitchen, I could see the smoke hanging in the hallway.

"Goddamn it!" As I turned off the gas under the macaroni and opened the door to the garden, I felt tears coming to my eyes. "Goddamn it! Goddamn it! Goddamn it!" I waved my arms, but the smoke only drifted around the kitchen without going away.

With moist eyes, I stared into the pan. I picked up the wooden spoon from the counter and tried to stir the hard, black goo.

"Paul . . ."

The two of them were standing in the doorway, Serge with one foot in the kitchen, Babette with her hand on his shoulder.

"Aw, look at that!" I screamed. "Look at that, would you!"

I smacked the wooden spoon down on the counter. I was fighting against more tears, but it wasn't really working.

"Paul . . ." My brother had put his other foot in the kitchen now. I saw a hand held out and ducked to one side.

"Paul," he said. "It all makes a lot of

sense. First your job, and now Claire. There's no reason for you not to admit that to yourself."

The way I remember it, there was an audible hiss when I grabbed the glowing handles of the pan and the skin on my fingers began to burn. I felt no pain, at least not at that point.

Babette screamed. Serge tried to duck, but the bottom edge of the pan hit him square in the face. He staggered back and, when I hit him the second time, he sort of fell against Babette. There was a cracking sound, and blood now as well: it spattered across the white tiles on the kitchen wall and the little jars in the spice rack beside the oven.

"Daddy."

By then Serge was sprawled on the kitchen floor, the area around his mouth and nose a mushy, bloody mess. I was already poised, pan in the air, ready to bring it down again against the mushiest, bloodiest part of his face.

Michel was standing in the doorway. He wasn't looking at his uncle on the floor, but at me.

"Michel," I said. I tried to smile. I let the pan drop. "Michel," I said again.

■ ■ ■ ■

DESSERT

■ ■ ■ ■

36

"The blackberries are from our own garden," said the manager. "The parfait is made from homemade chocolate, and these are shaved almonds, mixed with grated walnuts."

His little finger pointed to a few irregularities in the brown sauce, a sauce that in my opinion was much too thin — in any case thinner than what one thought of as a "parfait" — and had leaked down between the blackberries to the bottom of the bowl.

I saw the way Babette looked at the bowl. At first only in disappointment — a disappointment that gave way over the course of the manager's explanation to unadulterated disgust.

"I don't want this," she said when he had finished.

"Excuse me?" the manager said.

"I don't want this. Please take it back."

I thought for a moment that she was going to push the bowl away, but instead she leaned far back in her chair, as though to establish the greatest possible distance between her and the washed-out dessert.

"But this is what you ordered."

For the first time since the manager had put the desserts down in front of us, she raised her head and looked at him. "I know this is what I ordered. But I don't want it anymore. I want you to take it away."

Serge began to fidget with his napkin. He pressed one corner of it against the corner of his lips and wiped off a nonexistent something. Meanwhile, he tried to catch his wife's eye. Serge himself had chosen the *dame blanche.* Perhaps Babette's behavior embarrassed him; more likely, however, was that he couldn't stand another delay. He had to eat his dessert now. My brother always chose the most ordinary desserts on the menu. Vanilla ice cream, crepes with syrup, and that was about it. I sometimes thought it had to do with his blood sugar level, the same blood sugar level that left him high and dry in the middle of nowhere at the most inopportune moments. But it also had to do with his lack of imagination; as far as that went, the *dame blanche* was on the same level as the tournedos. In fact, I had been surprised to see such a straightforward dessert on the menu in this place.

"These are the tastiest blackberries you'll ever taste," the manager said.

Christ, man, take the bowl and fuck off with it! I said silently. That was another thing. At any normal place — or one should actually say, at any restaurant worth its salt anywhere in Europe, with the exception of Holland — waiters and managers didn't even try to argue, following the motto: "Customer not satisfied? Back to the kitchen!" Of course, you had difficult customers everywhere, spoiled scum who wanted a blow-by-blow description of every dish on the menu, unbothered by any actual knowledge of food. "What's the difference between tagliatelle and spaghetti?" they'll ask serenely. When it came to people like that, a waiter had every right to slam his fist right into their inquisitive, spoiled mouths, knuckles hard against the front teeth, breaking them off close to the root. They should change the law, so that restaurant personnel could claim this as self-defense. Usually, though, it was the other way around. People were afraid to say anything. They excused themselves a thousand times over, even if they were only asking for the salt. Dark-brown green beans that tasted of licorice, stewed meat stuck together with rubbery nerves and chunks of cartilage, a cheese sandwich with stale bread and green spots on the cheese — without a word, the Dutch diner grinds it all to a pulp between his teeth and swallows it down. And when the waiter comes by to ask if they are enjoying their meal, they run their tongues over the fibers and mold stuck between their teeth and nod.

We had returned to our earlier seating arrangement, Babette to my left, across from Serge, and Claire right across from me. All I had to do was raise my eyes from my plate to look at her. Claire looked back and waggled her eyebrows.

"Oh, it doesn't really matter," Serge said. "I can handle those blackberries as well." He rubbed his stomach and grinned, first at the manager and then at his wife.

There was a full second of silence. A second during which I let my gaze descend to my plate. For the moment, it seemed wise to look at no one, and so I looked at my plate: at the three wedges of cheese, to be exact, that were still lying there untouched. The manager's pinky had hovered over each of the three pieces in turn; I had listened to the names that went with them without letting any of it register. The plate was no more than half the size of those on which the appetizers and main dishes had been served, yet again it was the emptiness that was most striking. The three little wedges had been arranged so they pointed at each other, probably to make the whole thing look like more than it really was.

I had ordered cheese because I don't like sweet desserts. I never have, even as a child, but as I stared at the plate — mostly at the empty part of it — I was suddenly overcome by the kind of heavy fatigue I had been trying to put off all evening.

What I would have liked best was to go home. With Claire, or maybe even on my own. Yes, I would have paid a king's ransom to be able to collapse on the couch at home. I can think better in a horizontal position. I would be able to think over this evening's events, to dot the i's and cross the t's, as they say.

"You keep out of it!" Babette said to Serge. "Maybe we should get Tonio to come over, if it's so hard to order another dessert."

Tonio, I took it, was the man in the white turtleneck, the restaurant owner who had greeted them personally at the entrance, because he was so pleased to have people like the Lohmans among his clientele.

"That won't be necessary," the manager

305

said quickly. "I can talk to Tonio myself, and I'm sure the kitchen will be able to offer you an alternative dessert."

"Darling . . . ," Serge said, but apparently had no idea of what to say next, because all he did was grin at the floor manager again and make a helpless gesture with both hands in the air, palms face up, as if to say "Women? Go figure."

"What's that stupid grin all about?" Babette asked.

Serge lowered his hands. There was something pleading in the way he looked at Babette. "Darling . . . ," he said again.

Michel too had always disliked sweet desserts, I realized. As a child, when waiters tried to win him over by offering him ice cream or a lollipop, he had always shaken his head resolutely. We never tried to influence him; we would have let him have any dessert he liked, so you couldn't blame it on his upbringing. It was hereditary. Yes, that was the only word for it. If heredity existed, if anything was hereditary, then it had to be our shared aversion to sweet desserts.

At long last, the manager took the bowl of blackberries from the table. "I'll be right back," he mumbled, and hurried off.

"Christ, what an asshole!" Babette said.

She wiped her hand angrily across the tablecloth, across the spot where her dessert had just been, as though trying to wipe away any traces the bowl of blackberries might have left there.

"Babette, please," Serge begged, but there was genuine irritation in his voice now as well.

"Did you see the look on his face?" Babette said, reaching across the table to touch Claire's hand. "Did you see how quickly he backed down when he heard his boss's name? His master, ha ha!"

Claire laughed too, but not wholeheartedly, I saw.

"Babette!" Serge butted in. "Please! I think you're way out of line. I mean, we come here a lot . . . we've never —"

"Oh, is that what you're afraid of?" Babette interrupted him. "That next time you suddenly won't get a table?"

Serge looked at me, but I looked away quickly. What did my brother know about heredity? All right, maybe when it came to his own children: his own flesh and blood. But what about Beau? When did you simply have to admit that something had apparently been inherited from someone else? From the biological parents who had remained behind in Africa? To what extent

307

could Serge, for his part, distance himself from the actions of his adopted son?

"I'm not afraid of anything," Serge said. "It just appalls me when you go after someone in that patronizing tone of voice. That's precisely the kind of people we've never wanted to be. That man is only doing his job."

"Who started with the patronizing tone?" Babette said. "Huh? Who started it?" Her voice had gone up a few decibels. I looked around — at the neighboring tables, all heads were turned in our direction. This was, of course, extremely interesting, a woman raising her voice at the table of our future prime minister.

Serge also seemed aware of the looming danger. He leaned across the table. "Babette, please," he said quietly. "Let's stop. Let's talk about this later."

In all domestic arguments — as in all fist-fights and armed conflicts, for that matter — there comes a moment when both, or one, of the parties can step back and prevent the situation from deteriorating any further. This was that moment. I wondered briefly what it was I was hoping for. As family and table companions, it was our role to intervene, to speak words that would put things into perspective and so allow the parties to

308

be reconciled.

But did I feel like doing that, to be frank? Did we feel like doing that? I looked at Claire, and at the same moment Claire looked at me. Playing around her lips was something outsiders would not have recognized as a smile, but which was in fact a smile. It was to be found in a quivering at the corners of her mouth, invisible to the naked eye. I knew that invisible quiver well. And I knew what it meant: Claire, too, felt absolutely no urge to referee. No more than I did. We were not going to do anything to intervene. On the contrary, we would do everything in our power to enable things to escalate even further. Because that suited us best at this moment.

I winked at my wife. And she winked back.

"Babette, please . . ." It wasn't Serge this time. It was Babette herself. She was imitating him, in an exaggeratedly affected tone, as though he were a sniveling child whining for ice cream. He's got no reason to whine, I thought to myself, looking at the *dame blanche* on the table in front of him. He's already got his ice cream. I almost burst out laughing. Claire must have read it on my face, because she shook her head as she winked at me again. Don't start laughing now! her eyes said. That will ruin everything.

Then we'll be the ones to blame and the row will blow over.

"You're such a coward!" Babette screamed. "You should be supporting me instead of thinking about your own image, about what it might look like. What other people might think about the fact that your wife finds her dessert too disgusting for words. What your little friend might think of you. Tonio! *Tony* or *Anton* is probably too common for him! It probably sounds too much like collard greens or split-pea soup!" She threw her napkin on the table — too forcefully, because it hit her wineglass, which fell over. "I never want to come to this place again!" Babette said. She had stopped screaming, but her voice still carried at least four tables away. People had put down their knives and forks. Their stares had already become less veiled. It would have been almost impossible for them not to stare. "I want to go home," Babette said, a bit more quietly now, already almost back to normal volume.

"Babette," Claire said, holding out her hand. "Sweetheart . . ."

Claire's timing was perfect. I grinned — in admiration of my wife. Red wine had spread across the tablecloth; most of it was seeping in Serge's direction. My brother got

310

up from his chair. I thought at first that he was afraid of having wine dribble onto his trousers, but he pushed back his chair and stood up.

"I'm sick and tired of this," he said.

All three of us looked at him. He had taken his napkin from his lap and laid it on the table. I saw that the ice cream in his *dame blanche* was beginning to melt — a thin trickle of vanilla had run over the top of the glass (the vase? the goblet? — what did you call that with a *dame blanche*?) and reached its base. "I'm leaving for a moment," he said. "I'm going outside."

He took a step to one side, away from our table, then a step back. "I'm sorry," he said, looking first at Claire and then at me. "I'm sorry this had to happen. I hope that when I come back we can talk calmly about the things we need to talk about."

I had actually expected Babette to start screaming again. Something like "That's right, walk away! Just walk away! Take the easy way out!" But she said nothing — which, to be honest, I felt was too bad. It would have made the scandal more complete: a famous politician leaving the restaurant with his head bowed, while his wife shouts after him that he is an asshole, or a coward. Even if it never made the newspapers, the story would spread like wildfire, from mouth to mouth, dozens, hundreds — who knows, maybe even thousands — of potential voters would find out that regular-guy Serge Lohman also had very regular marital problems. Like everyone else. Like us.

You might even wonder whether the fight between husband and wife, if it leaked out, would actually cost him votes, I realized now, or whether it would in fact attract more voters. A domestic quarrel might make him more human — his unhappy marriage would bring him closer to the electorate. I looked at the *dame blanche*. A second rivulet of ice cream had now passed the base of the glass and spilled onto the tablecloth.

"The globe really is warming up," I said, pointing at my brother's dessert; the best thing, I thought, was to say something lighthearted. "You see? It's not just fashionable cant. It's really true."

"Paul . . ."

Claire looked at me and rolled her eyes in Babette's direction. Following my wife's gaze, I saw that Babette had started crying. Almost noiselessly at first — all you saw was the shaking of her back and shoulders — but soon enough the first sobs could be heard.

People at a few tables had stopped eating again. A man in a red shirt leaned over to an older woman (his mother?) and whispered something: Don't look now, but that woman is crying — it had to be something like that — that's Serge Lohman's wife . . .

Meanwhile, Serge still hadn't left; he was standing there with his hands on the back of the chair, as though, with his wife crying like this, he couldn't decide whether to suit the action to the word.

"Serge," Claire said without looking at him — without even raising her head, "sit down."

"Paul." Claire had taken my hand. She tugged on it, and it took a moment before I realized what she was saying: she wanted me to get up so we could change places and she could sit beside Babette.

We stood up at the same time. While we were shuffling past each other, Claire grabbed my hand again; her fingers wrapped firmly around my wrist and she gave it a little yank. Our faces were no more than a few inches apart. I'm not much taller than my wife. All I would have had to do was bow my head in order to bury my face in her hair — something I felt more of a need to do at that moment than anything else.

"We've got a problem," Claire murmured.

I said nothing, only nodded faintly.

"With your brother," Claire said.

I waited to see if she would say anything else, but she seemed to feel that we had been standing beside the table long enough. She edged past me and sat down in my chair, beside the weeping Babette.

"How are things here?"

I turned around and looked into the face of the man in the white turtleneck. Tonio! Serge had slid back his chair and was still busy seating himself again, so the restaurant owner had probably decided to address me first. Whatever the case, it was not merely the difference in our heights — he was a whole head shorter than me — that made me feel he was groveling. He stood slightly bent over, his hands clasped in front of him, head turned to one side, which left him looking at me obliquely and from below: lower than necessary.

"I heard there were problems with the choice of desserts," he said. "We'd like to offer you an alternative dessert of your choice."

"The dessert of the house?" I asked.

"Excuse me?"

The restaurateur was almost bald. The few gray hairs left around his ears had been coiffed with care. His slightly too-tanned head stuck out of the white collar like a tortoise from its shell.

It had occurred to me earlier, when Serge and Babette came in, that he reminded me of something or someone, and now I suddenly knew what it was. Years ago, a few doors down from us, there had lived a man with this same servile air. He was perhaps even smaller than "Tonio," and he had no wife. One evening, Michel, who was about eight at the time, had come home with a pile of LPs and asked whether we still had a turntable somewhere.

"Where did you get the records?" I asked.

"From Mr. Breedveld," Michel had said. "He's got at least five hundred of them, man! And I get to keep these."

It took a moment before I connected the name Breedveld to the little single man living a few doors down. They went to his house all the time, Michel told me, a whole bunch of little boys from the neighborhood, to listen to Mr. Breedveld's old albums.

I remember quite well how my temples began pounding, first in fear, then in rage. Trying to keep my voice as normal as possible, I asked Michel what Mr. Breedveld did while the boys were listening to records.

"Oh, you know. We sit on the couch. He always has peanuts and chips and cola."

315

That evening, after dark, I rang Mr. Breedveld's bell. I didn't ask whether I could come in — I pushed him aside and walked right through to his living room. The curtains, I noted, were already drawn.

Mr. Breedveld moved away a few weeks later. The final picture in my mind from that time is of the neighborhood children rummaging through boxes of shattered LPs, to see whether there were any left intact. Mr. Breedveld had put the boxes out on the curb in front of his house the day before he moved.

I looked at "Tonio" and clenched the arm of the chair with one hand.

"Get the fuck out of here, you pervert!" I said. "Fuck off, before things really get out of hand."

37

Serge cleared his throat, placed his elbows on either side of his *dame blanche,* and formed a tent with his fingers.

"We all know by now what happened," he said. "All four of us are familiar with the facts." He looked at Claire, then at Babette, who had stopped crying but was still pressing a corner of her napkin to her cheek — just below her eye, behind the tinted lens of her glasses. "Paul?" He turned his head and looked at me: his look was one of concern, but I wondered whether it was the concern of the man or the concern of the politician Serge Lohman.

"Yes, what is it?" I said.

"I take it you are also aware of all the facts?"

All the facts. I couldn't help smiling: then I looked at Claire, and wiped the smile off my face. "Yes, of course," I said. "Although it depends on what you mean by facts."

317

"I'll get to that later. What matters is how we deal with this. How we bring it all out into the open."

At first I wasn't sure I'd heard him correctly. I looked back at Claire. We've got a problem: that's what she'd said. This is the problem, her eyes were saying now.

"Wait a minute," I said.

"Paul." Serge laid his hand on my forearm. "Give me a chance to finish. Then it will be your turn. When I'm done."

The diners at the neighboring tables had gone back to their dining, but things were restless around the open kitchen. I saw three waitresses standing around "Tonio" and the manager. They didn't look once in our direction, but I would have bet my cheese platter that they were talking about us — about me, I corrected myself.

"Babette and I spoke with Rick this afternoon," Serge said. "Our impression is that Rick is suffering badly from all this. He thinks it's terrible, what the two of them did. It keeps him awake at night, quite literally. He looks distraught. It's affecting his academic achievements."

I wanted to say something but restrained myself. It was something in Serge's tone: as though, even at this early stage, he was trying to compare his son favorably to ours.

318

Rick couldn't sleep. Rick looked distraught. Rick thought it was terrible. It felt as though Claire and I had to defend Michel — but what were we supposed to say? That Michel thought it was terrible too? That he slept even less than Rick?

It simply wasn't true, I realized. Michel had other things on his mind besides the incinerated homeless woman in the ATM cubicle. And what was all this moaning about academic achievements? It was too disgusting for words, if you thought about it.

If Claire said something, I would side with her, I decided. If Claire said that it was inappropriate, in view of what had happened, to be talking about academic achievements, I'd chime in and say that we wanted to leave Michel's schoolwork out of this.

Was Michel's schoolwork being affected? I asked myself the next instant. I didn't have that impression. As far as that went, he had his feet more firmly on the ground than his cousin.

"What's more, from the very start I have tried to see this separately from my own political future," Serge went on. "Which is not to say that I've never thought about that."

From the looks of things, Babette had started crying again. Noiselessly. I got the sneaky feeling that I was present at something at which I would rather not be present. It made me think of Bill and Hillary Clinton. Of Oprah Winfrey.

Was that the way it would go? Was this the dress rehearsal for the press conference at which Serge Lohman would announce that the boy on camera in *Opsporing Verzocht* was his son, but that he hoped nonetheless to retain the trust the voters had shown in him? He couldn't be that naïve, could he?

"To me, the most important thing is Rick's future," Serge said. "Of course, it's very possible that this whole thing will never be solved. But could you live with that? Can Rick live with that? Can we live with that?" He looked at Claire first, then at me. "Can the two of you live with that?" he asked. "I can't," he added then, without waiting for us to answer. "I can just see myself, standing on the palace stairs with the queen and the cabinet ministers. Knowing that, at any moment, at any old press conference, a journalist might raise his finger and ask: 'Mr. Lohman, is there any truth to the rumor that your son was involved in the murder of a homeless woman?' "

"Murder?" Claire cried out. "So it's

murder already, is it? Where do you get that from all of a sudden?"

A brief silence fell; the word *murder* must have been audible four tables away. Serge looked over his shoulder, then back at Claire.

"I'm sorry," she said. "That was too loud. But that's not the point. To call it 'murder' — I find that taking things a step too far. What am I saying? Ten steps too far!"

I looked at my wife in admiration. Anger made her prettier. Especially her eyes — it was a look that put men to shame. Other men.

"So what would you call it, Claire?" Serge had picked up his dessert spoon and was stirring it around in his melted ice cream. It was one of those spoons with a very long handle, but he still managed to get ice and whipped cream on his fingers.

"An accident," Claire said. "An unfortunate series of events. No one in his right mind would even begin to claim that they went out that evening to murder a homeless woman!"

"But that's what the security camera shows. That's what all of Holland saw. I mean, so don't call it murder, call it manslaughter as far as I'm concerned, but that woman never raises a finger against them.

That woman gets a lamp and a chair and finally a gas can thrown in her face."

"What was she doing in that ATM cubicle?"

"That doesn't matter, does it? There are homeless people everywhere. Unfortunately. They sleep wherever they can keep a bit warm. It was probably warm and dry in there."

"But she was lying in the way, Serge. I mean, she could have gone and slept in the hall at your house. It's probably warm and dry there, too."

"Let's try to stick to the point," Babette said. "I really don't think that —"

"This *is* the point, sweetheart." Claire had put her hand on Babette's forearm. "I hope you'll forgive me, but when I hear Serge talking like this, it sounds like we're dealing with some poor little bird here, a fledgling that has fallen out of its nest. What we're talking about is a full-grown person. A grown-up woman who, in complete possession of her senses, goes to sleep in an ATM cubicle. Don't misunderstand me: I'm only trying to put myself in someone else's shoes. Not the homeless woman's, but Michel and Rick's. They're not drunk. They're not on drugs. They just want to withdraw some money. But someone is lying in the ATM cubicle, stinking to high heaven. So isn't your first reaction: oh gecch, fuck off, would you?

"But they could have gone somewhere else for their money, right?"

"Somewhere else?" Claire started laughing. "Somewhere else? Yes, of course. You can always go out of your way to avoid things. I mean, what would you do, Serge? You open the front door of your house and you have to step over a sleeping vagrant. What would you do? Would you just turn around and go back inside? Or suppose someone was standing there pissing against your door. Would you just close the door? Would you pack up and move to another house?"

"Claire . . . ," Babette said.

"Okay, all right," Serge said. "I see what you're getting at. That wasn't what I was trying to say. Of course we shouldn't walk away from problems or difficult situations. But you can, you have to, try to find solutions to problems. To . . ." Here he hesitated for a moment. ". . . take the life of a homeless person doesn't bring you any closer to the solution."

"Jesus, Serge!" Claire said. "I'm not talking about a solution to the problem of the homeless. I'm talking about one homeless

323

person. And more than that one homeless person, I think we should be talking about Rick and Michel. I'm not going to deny what happened. I'm not trying to say there was nothing wrong with it. But we have to keep it in perspective. It's an incident. An incident that can have a major impact on our children's lives, on their future."

Serge sighed and rested his hands on the table, on either side of his dessert; he was trying to make eye contact with Babette, I saw, but she had her purse in her lap and was looking for something — or pretending to.

"Exactly," he said. "That future. That's precisely what I wanted to talk about. Don't get me wrong, Claire. I'm just as concerned about our boys' futures as you are. The only thing is, I don't believe they can live with it, with a secret like that. In the long run, it's going to tear them apart. Rick, in any case, is being torn apart already." He sighed again. "It's tearing me apart."

Once again, I had the feeling I was witnessing something that only obliquely had anything to do with reality. At least with our reality, the reality of two couples — two brothers and their wives — who had gone out to dinner together to talk about their children's problems.

"I've made up my own mind about my son's future," Serge said. "Later, when this is all behind us, I want him to be able to go on with his life. Let me emphasize that I've made this decision on my own. My wife . . . Babette . . ." Babette had fished a pack of Marlboro Lights from her purse, an unopened pack, and was now tearing off the cellophane wrapper. "Babette doesn't agree with me. But my mind is made up. She only heard about this this afternoon."

He took a deep breath. Then he looked at us in turn. Only then did I notice the moist glistening in his eyes.

"In the best interests of my child, and also in the best interests of this country, I'm going to withdraw my candidacy," he said.

Babette had put a cigarette between her lips, but now she removed it. She looked at Claire and me.

"Dear Claire," she said. "Dear Paul . . . the two of you have to say something. Please tell him he can't do this. Tell him he's out of his mind."

38

"You can't do that," Claire said.

"He can't, can he?" Babette said. "You see, Serge? What do you think, Paul? Don't you think it's a ridiculous idea? There's no reason to do that, is there?"

To me, personally, it seemed like an excellent idea for my brother to put an end to his political career, right here and now. It would be the best thing for everyone: for all of us, for the country — the country would be spared a four-year Serge Lohman administration: four costly years. I thought about the unthinkable, about things I had mostly been able to suppress: Serge Lohman standing beside the queen on the steps of the royal palace, posing for the official photo with his newly formed cabinet; with George Bush in an easy chair in front of a fireplace; with Putin on a boat on the Volga . . . "After the conclusion of the European summit, Prime Minister Lohman raised a toast to success with the French president . . ." First of all, it was the sense of vicarious embarrassment, the unbearable thought that government leaders all around the world would become acquainted with my brother's vacuous presence. How, even in the White House and at the Élysée Palace, he would wolf down his tournedos in three bites because he had to eat *now*. The meaningful looks the government leaders would exchange. "He's from Holland," they would say — or perhaps only think to themselves, which was even worse. That sense of vicarious shame was a constant. Our being ashamed of our prime ministers was the only feeling that created a seamless connection between one Dutch administration and the next.

"Maybe he should take some time to think through it carefully again," I said to Babette with a shrug. The most terrible image of all was that of Serge sitting at our dinner table at home, somewhere in the — until recently — near future, but a future that was now thankfully fading fast: telling stories about his meetings with the world's rulers. They would be lame stories, stories brimming over with platitudes. Claire and I would be able to see through them. But Michel? Whether he liked it or not, my son would be fascinated by the anecdotes, the corners of the veil that my brother would lift to his own honor and glory, the behind-the-scenes views of international affairs with which he would justify his presence at our table. "What are you griping about, Paul? Your son finds it interesting — you can see that, can't you?"

My son. Michel. I had thought about a future, without stopping to ask myself if there would be one.

"Think it through carefully?" Babette said. "That's exactly it. If only he would stop sometimes and think things through!"

"That's not what I mean," Claire said. "I mean that Serge isn't free to simply decide this on his own."

"I'm his wife!" Babette said, and she began sobbing again.

"That's not what I mean either, Babette," Claire said, looking at Serge. "I mean that all of us have a stake in this. We're all in this together. All four of us."

"That's why I wanted us to meet," Serge said. "So we could talk together about how we're going to do it."

"How we're going to do what?" Claire said.

"How we're going to bring it out into the open. In a way that will give our children a fair chance."

"But you're not giving them a chance, Serge. What you're planning to bring out into the open is that you're withdrawing from politics. That you don't want to be the prime minister anymore. Because you can't live with it, that's what you said."

"Can you live with it?"

"It's not about whether I can live with it. It's about Michel. Michel has to be able to live with it."

"And can he?"

"Serge, don't be obtuse. You make a decision. With that decision, you also decide about your son's future. That's up to you. Although I wonder whether you realize what kind of damage you're going to cause. But your decision will also destroy the future of my son."

My son. Claire had said "my son." She could have glanced over at me then, for support, even if only for a knowing look, then recouped and said "our son" — but she didn't. She didn't even look my way. She kept her eyes fixed on Serge.

"Oh, come on, Claire," my brother said. "That future has already been ruined. Whatever happens. That has nothing more to do now with what I decide or don't decide."

"No, Serge. That future will only be ruined if you give in to your urge to play the noble politician. Just because you can't live with something, you assume that that applies to my son as well. Maybe you'll be able to make it up to Rick — I hope for your sake that you can explain to your son what you're about to do to his life — but please leave Michel out of it."

"How can I leave Michel out of it, Claire? How am I supposed to do that? Explain that to me first. I mean, they were both there, if I remember correctly. Or are you trying to deny that, too?" He fell silent for a moment, as though shocked by his own uncompleted thought. "Is that what you're trying to do?" he asked.

"Serge, try to be realistic. There is nothing happening. No one has been arrested. There isn't even any suspicion. We're the only ones who know what happened. It's just not enough to justify sacrificing the future of two fifteen-year-old boys. And I'm not even talking now about your own future. You have to do whatever you think you have to do. But you can't go dragging other people into it. Especially not your own child. Let alone mine. You present it as an act of pure self-sacrifice: Serge Lohman, the ambitious politician, our next prime minister, gives up his political career because he can't live with a secret like this. In fact, he doesn't mean a secret, he means a scandal. It all seems entirely noble, but in fact it's purely egocentric."

"Claire," Babette said.

"Wait a minute, wait a minute," Serge said, silencing his wife with a gesture. "Let me finish, I'm not done yet." He turned to Claire again. "Is it egocentric to give your son a fair chance? Is it egocentric of a father to give up his own future for his son's future? You have to at least explain to me what's egocentric about that."

"And what does a future like that consist of? What is he supposed to do with a future in which his father puts him up on trial? How will his father explain to him that it was his own doing that put him behind bars?"

"But that's maybe only for a couple of years. That's all you get for manslaughter in this country. I'm not denying that it will be hard, but after a couple of years they will have served their sentences and can try to carefully pick up their lives again and move on. I mean, what else do you propose, Claire?"

"Nothing."

"Nothing." Serge repeated the word as a

neutral conclusion, not a question.

"Things like this blow over. You can see it happening already. People say it's a disgrace. But in the end, they want to get on with their own lives. In two or three months, no one will be talking about it anymore."

"I'm referring to something else, Claire. I . . . we notice that it's starting to tear Rick apart. People may forget it, but he won't."

"But we can help them with that, Serge. With that forgetting. I'm only saying that you shouldn't rush decisions like this. In a few months, maybe even a few weeks, everything may have changed. We can discuss it calmly then. We. The four of us. With Rick. With Michel."

With Beau, I felt like adding, but held myself back.

"I'm afraid that's not on," Serge said.

In the silence that followed, the only thing you could hear was Babette's quiet sobbing. "Tomorrow there is going to be a press conference, where I'll announce that I'm stepping down," Serge said. "Tomorrow at noon. It's going to be broadcast live. The twelve o'clock news is going to lead with it." He looked at his watch. "Oh, is it already that late?" he said, seemingly indifferent to whether this sounded natural or not. "I have to . . . I've got another appointment," he

332

said. "In a little bit. In half an hour."

"An appointment?" Claire said. "But we have to — Who are you meeting?"

"The director wants to confirm the location for my press conference and run through a few things beforehand. It didn't seem to me like a good idea to do something like this in The Hague, a press conference like this. That's never really been my kind of thing. So I was thinking of someplace less formal . . ."

"Where?" Claire said. "Not here, I hope?"

"No. You know that café that serves meals across the street, where you took us a few months ago? We ate there too. The . . ." Here he pretended to be searching for the name of the café; then he named it. "When I was trying to think of a suitable place, it suddenly came into my mind. An ordinary café. Ordinary people. I can be myself there, more than in some frigid press center. I suggested to Paul that we have a beer there tonight before coming here, but he didn't feel like it."

39

"Could I interest you in coffee?"

The manager had popped up out of no-where beside our table. He had his hands tucked behind his back and was leaning over slightly. His eyes were caught for a moment by Serge's collapsed *dame blanche.* Then he looked at each of us inquiringly, in turn.

I might have been mistaken, but I thought I noted a certain briskness in the manager's movements and facial expression. That's how things often go in restaurants like this: as soon as you've finished your meal and there is no longer any real chance of your ordering another bottle of wine, you might as well get lost.

Even if you were going to be the new prime minister in seven months' time, I thought. There was a time to come and a time to go.

Serge checked his watch again.

"Well, I think . . ." He looked first at

Babette, then at Claire. "Why don't we order a cup of coffee at the café?" he said.

Ex, I corrected myself. Ex–prime minister. Or no . . . what did you call someone who had never been prime minister, but decided not to run anyway? Ex-candidate?

The prefix *ex*, in any case, didn't sound good. Ex-footballers and ex-cyclists know what that's like. It was doubtful whether my brother, after tomorrow's press conference, would still be able to reserve a table at this restaurant. On the same day. It seemed more likely that an ex-candidate would be put on the waiting list for three months, at the very least.

"Then would you bring us the check?" Serge said. Maybe I'd missed something, but I couldn't remember his having waited to see whether Babette and Claire also thought it was a better idea to move to the café.

"I'd like coffee," I said. "An espresso," I added. "And something to go with it." I thought about it for a moment. I'd been moderate throughout the evening — I just didn't know right away what I felt like drinking.

"I'll have an espresso as well," Claire said. "And a grappa."

My wife. The thought gave me a warm

feeling. I wished I was sitting beside her and could touch her now. "A grappa for me too," I said.

"And you, sir?" The manager seemed a bit confused at first and looked at my brother. But Serge shook his head. "Just the check," he said. "My wife and I . . . we have to . . ." He glanced over at his wife — a panicky glance, I could see that even from this angle. It wouldn't have surprised me if Babette had then ordered an espresso as well.

But Babette had stopped blubbering. She dabbed at her nose with the tip of her napkin. "Nothing for me, thank you," she said without looking at the manager.

"So that will be two espressos and two grappas," he said. "Which grappa would you like? We have seven kinds, from old wood ripened to young —"

"The ordinary one," Claire interrupted him. "The clear one."

The manager gave a bow barely visible to the naked eye. "A young grappa for the lady," he said. "And what would you like, sir?"

"The same," I said.

"And the check," Serge repeated.

After the manager had hurried away, Babette turned to me — with an attempt at a smile. "And you, Paul? We haven't heard from you at all. What do you think?"

"I think it's ridiculous that Serge has picked our café for this," I said.

The smile, or at least the attempt at one, disappeared from Babette's face.

"Paul, please," Serge said. He looked at Claire.

"Yeah, I think it's ridiculous," I said. "We took the two of you to that café. It's a place where Claire and I go all the time, for the daily special. You can't just walk in there and hold a press conference."

"Paul," Serge said. "I don't know whether you realize how serious —"

"Let him finish," Babette said.

"I was finished," I said. "Anyone who doesn't understand something like that, I can't explain it to him."

"We thought it was a nice café too," Babette said. "We have only pleasant memories of that evening."

"Spareribs!" Serge said.

I waited to see if anything else was coming, but they were silent. "Precisely," I said. "Pleasant memories. What kind of memories will Claire and I have after this?"

"Paul, don't be silly," Serge said. "We're talking about our children's futures here. To say nothing of my own future."

"But he's right," Claire said.

"Oh no, please," Serge said.

"No, no *pleases*," Claire said. "What it's about is the casual way you appropriate everything that's ours. That's what Paul is saying. You talk about our children's futures. But you're not really interested in them, Serge. You've co-opted that future. Just as casually as you co-opt a café as a backdrop to your press conference. Only because that will make it seem more authentic. It doesn't even occur to you to ask what we think about it."

"What are you talking about?!" Babette said. "You talk about that press conference as though it's going to go ahead. I was expecting something more from the two of you. I'd hoped you'd at least try to talk him out of this craziness. Especially from you, Claire. After what you said to me in the garden."

"Is that what this is all about?" Serge said. "About your café? I didn't realize it was *your* café. I thought it was a public establishment, open to one and all. Please forgive me."

"It's our son," Claire said. "And yes, it's also our café. Maybe we don't have any control over how it's used, but that's the way it feels. But Paul's right when he says that you can't explain something like that.

338

You either understand it, or you don't."

Serge pulled his cell phone from his pocket and looked at the screen. "Excuse me. I have to take this." He held the phone to his ear, slid back his chair, and began rising to his feet. "Hello, Serge Lohman here . . . Hello."

"Holy fuck!" Babette threw her napkin down on the table. "Holy fuck," she said again.

Serge had moved a few steps away from our table. He was bent over at the waist, plugging his other ear with two fingers. "No, it's not that," I was able to make out. "It's more complicated than that." Then he walked off past the other tables, heading for the toilets or the front entrance.

Claire took her cell phone from her bag. "I need to check with Michel," she said, looking at me. "What time is it? I don't want to wake him up."

I never wear a watch. Ever since they put me on nonactive, I've tried to live by the position of the sun, the rotation of the earth, the intensity of the daylight.

Claire knew that I had stopped wearing a watch.

"I'm not sure," I said. I felt something, a tingling at the back of my neck. It was because of the way my wife kept looking at me — kept staring at me, that was more like it — that I got the feeling I was being drawn into something, even though at that point I hadn't the faintest idea what.

It was better than being drawn into nothing, I thought. It was better than "Your father doesn't know about any of this."

Claire looked over.

"What is it?" Babette asked.

"Do you know what time it is?" Claire asked.

Babette pulled her cell phone out of her purse and looked at the screen. Then she said the time. She didn't put her phone back — she put it on the table in front of her. She didn't say to Claire: But you can see what time it is on your own phone, can't you?

"The poor darling has been home alone all evening," Claire said. "He's almost sixteen . . . He tries to act grown up, but still . . ."

"Some things, though, they're not too young for," Babette said.

Claire was silent for a moment. She ran the tip of her tongue across her lower lip: she always does that when she's getting angry. "Sometimes I think that's precisely where we're mistaken," she said. "Maybe we don't take that seriously enough, Ba-

340

bette. How young they are. To the outside world they're suddenly adults, because they did something that we, as adults, consider a crime. But I feel that they've responded to it more like children. That's exactly what I was trying to tell Serge. That we don't have the right to take away their childhood, simply because, according to our norms, as adults, it's a crime you should have to pay for, for the rest of your life."

Babette sighed deeply. "I'm afraid you're right, Claire. There's something gone, something . . . his spontaneity. He was always so . . . well, you two know what Rick was like. But that Rick isn't there anymore. For the last few weeks he's just stayed in his room. At the table, he barely says a word. It's something about the way he looks, something miserable, as though he's worrying all the time. He never used to do that, worry."

"But it's really important how you deal with that. How the two of you deal with that. I mean, maybe he's so worried because he thinks that's what you expect him to be."

Babette remained silent. She laid a hand on the table, fingers flat, and pushed her cell phone half an inch away from her. "I don't know, Claire. His father . . . I think his father expects him to worry more than I

341

do, although it might not be completely fair for me to say that. But Rick often has a hard enough time as it is, because of who his father is. At school. With friendships. I mean, he's only fifteen — he's still very much the son-of. But alongside that he's also the son of someone whose face everyone sees all the time on TV. He wonders about his friendships, sometimes. He thinks people are nice to him because of his famous father. Or the other way around: that teachers sometimes treat him unfairly because they have a problem with that. I remember it so clearly . . . when he went to secondary school, he said to me: 'Mama, it's like I get to start all over again!' He was so happy. But after a week, everyone at school already knew who he was."

"And soon the whole school will know something else too. If it's up to Serge."

"That's what I keep telling him. That Rick has already suffered so much for who his father is, more than can be good for him. And now Serge wants to drag him into this mess. He'll never get over that."

I thought about Beau, about the adopted African son who could do no wrong in Babette's eyes.

"With Michel we've noticed that — what you call spontaneity — well, he's still got that. Of course, he doesn't have a famous father, but still . . . It doesn't bother him so much. Sometimes I even worry about that, because it doesn't seem to have sunk in, what this could all mean for his future. In that way he really does react more like a child. A carefree child, not a worried adult, old before his time. That was the real dilemma for Paul and me. How we could make him aware of his responsibility without, at the same time, damaging his childish innocence."

I looked at my wife. For Paul and me . . . How long ago was it that Claire and I still thought the other one didn't know a thing? An hour ago? Fifty minutes? I looked at Serge's untouched *dame blanche:* technically, just as with the rings of a tree or carbon-14, it had to be possible to measure the passage of time by the melting of vanilla ice cream.

I looked into Claire's eyes, the eyes of the woman who represented happiness to me. Without my wife I would have been nowhere; you hear sentimental men say that sometimes — "helpless" is what they often call themselves. And indeed, all they mean is that their wives have been there to clean up after them all their lives and have kept bringing them cups of coffee at every hour of the day. I wouldn't go that far: without Claire I wouldn't have been nowhere, but I would have been somewhere else.

"Claire and I keep telling ourselves that Michel needs to be able to go on with his life. We don't want to talk him into a guilt complex. I mean, in some ways he is guilty of something, but that isn't to say that a homeless person who lies down in the way in an ATM cubicle should suddenly become innocence itself. That's the verdict you'd get soon enough if you left it up to the prevailing sense of justice around here. And that's what you hear around you all the time too: what's become of our wayward youth, never a word about wayward vagrants and homeless people who conk out wherever they feel like. No, they want to set an example, just you wait and see; indirectly, the judges are worried about their own children. Who they maybe can't control any longer either. We don't want to hand Michel over to some lynch mob that's only out for blood, the same lynch mob that's crying out to reinstate the death penalty. Michel is too precious to us for that, for us to offer him up to that kind of gut reaction. What's more, he himself is too intelligent for that. He stands head and shoulders above that."

Throughout my little speech, Claire kept

her eyes on me. The look and the smile she gave me now were part of our happiness. It was a happiness that could survive a lot, that outsiders couldn't come between so easily.

"Oh, I almost forgot!" she said, holding up her cell phone now. "I was going to call Michel. What time did you say it was again?" she asked Babette as she punched the first key — but she kept her eyes on me as she said it.

Once again, Babette checked the screen on her cell phone and told Claire the time.

I'm not going to say exactly what time it was. Exact times can turn on you later.

"Hi, sweetheart!" Claire said. "How are you doing? You're not too bored, are you?"

I looked at my wife's face. There was always something about that face, her eyes, that began to shine when she talked to our son on the phone. No, she was smiling and talking cheerfully — but she wasn't shining.

"Okay, we're just going to drink our coffee. We'll be home in about an hour. So you have time to clean up your own mess. What did you have for dinner . . . ?"

She listened, nodded, said yes and no a few times and then, after a final "Bye, dearest, love you," she hung up.

Looking back on it, I don't know if it was

because of her face that didn't shine, or whether it was because she hadn't referred even once to our having seen our son in the restaurant garden, that I was suddenly certain that we had just witnessed a fine bit of acting.

But for whom was the act intended? For me? That didn't seem likely. For Babette? But to what end? On two occasions, Claire had asked Babette emphatically to tell her what time it was — as though to make sure Babette wouldn't forget later on.

Your father doesn't know about any of this.

And suddenly his father knew.

"The espressos were for . . . ?" It was one of the serving-girls-in-black. She was carrying a silver tray with two cups of espresso and two weensy little glasses of grappa.

And it was while she was putting down the cups and glasses in front of us that my wife pursed her lips, as if for a kiss.

She looked at me — and then kissed the air between us.

DIGESTIF

40

It wasn't so long ago that Michel had written an essay about capital punishment. An essay for history class. It was prompted by a documentary about murderers who served their sentence, returned to society, and often, within almost no time, committed another murder. Advocates and opponents of the death penalty were given their say. There was an interview with an American psychiatrist who argued that some people should never be set free again. "We have to accept that there are real monsters out there," the psychiatrist said. "Monsters who should never, under any condition, be released."

A few days later, I had seen the first few pages of Michel's essay lying on his desk. As a cover illustration he had downloaded a picture from the Internet, a photograph of the hospital bed on which, in some American states, the lethal injection was administered.

"If I can help with anything . . . ," I'd said; and a few more days later he had shown me his first rough draft.

"What I really need to know from you," he said, "is whether I can do this."

"Do what?" I asked.

"I don't know. Sometimes I think things . . . Then I don't know whether you're really allowed to think things like that."

I read the rough draft — and I was impressed. For a fifteen-year-old, Michel had a refreshing way of looking at any number of aspects of crime and punishment. He had thought through several moral dilemmas to their most extreme consequences. I understood what he meant about things you might not be allowed to think.

"Very good," I said, handing it back to him. "And I wouldn't worry if I were you. You're allowed to think whatever you like. There's no reason to put on the brakes at this point. You've written it all down very clearly. Let the others try to poke holes in it first, if they can."

From then on he let me read the subsequent versions as well. We discussed the moral dilemmas. I have fond memories of that period: only fond memories.

Less than a week after he had turned in his essay, I was called into the principal's office. Or at least I received a telephone invitation to come in, on a given day, at a certain time, and talk about my son, Michel. On the phone, I asked the principal whether there was anything special I should know. Even though I suspected that it was about his essay on capital punishment, I wanted to hear it from the man's own mouth — but he brushed the question aside: "There are a few things I'd like to talk to you about, but not on the phone," he said.

On the afternoon in question I reported to his office. The principal invited me to sit down in a chair across from his desk.

"I want to talk to you about Michel," he started in right away. I crossed my legs, fought back the urge to say, "Of course, who else?" and assumed the pose of a careful listener.

On the wall behind him was a gigantic poster for an aid organization — I can't remember whether it was Oxfam Novib or UNICEF. You saw a parched, seemingly barren field. At the bottom left was a child dressed in rags, holding up his skinny little hand.

The poster put me even more on my guard. The principal was probably against

351

global warming and injustice in general. Perhaps he didn't eat the flesh of mammals and was anti-American or, in any case, anti-Bush: the latter stance gave people carte blanche not to think about anything anymore. Anyone who was against Bush had his heart in the right place and could behave like a boorish asshole toward anyone around him.

"Until now, we have always been quite pleased with Michel," the principal said. I smelled something peculiar. It wasn't what you'd call a sweaty smell, more like the odor of garbage that's been separated for collection — or, to be precise, the separated garbage that usually ends up in the green compostables container. I couldn't escape the impression that the odor was coming from the principal himself. Maybe he didn't use deodorant, in order to spare the ozone layer, or else his wife washed his clothes in environmentally friendly detergent; as everyone knows, detergents like that turn white clothes gray after a while — clean is one thing they will never be again.

"But recently, he wrote an essay for his history class that we find rather alarming," the principal went on. "Or at least, it caught the eye of our history teacher, Mr. Halsema, who then came to me with the paper in

352

question."

"About capital punishment," I said, just to put an end to this beating around the bush.

The principal looked at me for a moment. His eyes had something dull about them, expressionless, the bored look of a mediocre intelligence that wrongly supposes it has "seen it all before." "Indeed," he said. He picked up something from his desk and began leafing through it. "Capital punishment," I saw in familiar white letters against a black background, and below that the picture of the hospital bed.

"It's mostly these passages," the principal said. "Here: '. . . given the inhumanity involved in capital punishment as practiced by the state, one might wonder whether, for some offenders, it wouldn't be better if they — at a much earlier stage —' "

"You don't have to read it out loud — I know what it says."

The look on the principal's face said that he was not accustomed to being interrupted. "Indeed," he said again. "So, you're familiar with the contents?"

"Not only that. I helped my son here and there. Little bits of advice, but of course he wrote the lion's share of it himself."

"But apparently you didn't see any need

to advise him concerning the section about what I will refer to as 'taking the law into one's own hands'?"

"No. But I protest against the phrase 'taking the law into one's own hands.' "

"So what would you call it? This is clearly about applying the death penalty before a trial has taken place."

"But it's also about the inhumanity of capital punishment. The cold, clinical capital punishment carried out by the state. With a hypodermic needle, or the electric chair. About all those grisly details of the last meal that the condemned man is allowed to choose for himself. Your favorite dish, one last time, whether that's caviar with champagne or a Double Whopper from Burger King."

The dilemma I was faced with was one every parent faces sooner or later: you want to defend your child, of course; you stand up for your child, but you mustn't do it all too vehemently, and above all not too eloquently — you mustn't drive anyone into a corner. The educators, the teachers, will let you have your say, but afterwards they'll take revenge on your child. You may come up with better arguments — it's not too hard to come up with better arguments than the educators, the teachers — but in the end, your child is going to pay for it. Their frustration at being shown up is something they'll take out on the student.

"We all see it that way," the principal said. "Normal people with healthy minds see capital punishment as inhuman. That's not what I'm talking about. Michel has presented that extremely well. I'm only talking about the section in which he tries to justify the liquidation of suspects, accidentally or otherwise, before they have had their day in court."

"I consider myself normal and healthy. And I also consider capital punishment to be inhuman. But unfortunately, we also share this world with inhuman humans. Should those inhuman humans be allowed, after deducting a few years for good behavior, to reenter society? I think that's what Michel is talking about."

"So then you should simply be allowed to shoot them or — how does he put it?" He leafed through the essay again. " 'Throw them out the window'? The tenth-floor window of police headquarters, I believe. That is, to say the least, hardly the way things go under the rule of law."

"No, but now you're taking it out of context. This is about the worst kind of human beings. Michel is talking about men who rape children, who hold them prisoner for years. And there are other factors that play a role as well. During a trial, all that filth has to be dredged up again in the name of a 'fair legal process.' But who's actually waiting for that to happen? Those children's parents? That's the crucial point you're sort of skipping over now. No, civilized people don't throw other people out the window. And they also don't let a pistol go off by accident on the way from a police station to a jail. But we're not talking here about civilized people. These are people everyone would be relieved not to have around anymore."

"Yes, that was it. Shooting a suspect in the head, supposedly by accident. In the back of the police van — now I remember." The principal put the paper back down on his desk. "Was that one of your 'little bits of advice,' Mr. Lohman? Or did your son come up with that all by himself?"

Something about his tone of voice made the hair stand up on the back of my neck. At the same time, I felt a tingling in my fingertips, or to put it more precisely: my fingertips went numb. I was on my guard. I wanted to give Michel all due credit for his essay — he was, in any case, more intelligent than the moronic heap of compost sitting across the desk from me — but on the other hand, I needed to protect him from being harassed in the future. They could suspend him, it occurred to me. They could kick him out of school. Michel felt at home here — this was where his friends were.

"I have to admit that he may have let himself be somewhat swayed by my own opinions on such matters," I said. "I have rather outspoken ideas of my own about what should happen to those suspected of certain crimes. Consciously or unconsciously, perhaps, I may have sort of pressed those ideas on him."

The principal looked at me inquisitively, insofar as you can call a subintelligent look inquisitive. "But you just said that your son wrote the lion's share of it himself."

"That's right. By 'lion's share,' I mostly meant the passages in which state-implemented capital punishment is referred to as inhuman."

When faced with lower intelligences, the most effective strategy in my opinion is to tell a barefaced lie: with a lie, you give the pinheads a chance to retreat without losing face. And what's more: did I really remember anymore which parts of the essay had been my idea and which had been Michel's?

I could recall a conversation, a conversation at the dinner table, about a murderer on probationary release, a murderer who had been out only a few days and who had most probably already killed someone else. "They should never let someone like that go again," Michel had said. "Never let him go, or never put him back in prison?" I'd asked. Michel was fifteen: we talked to him about everything; he was interested in everything — the war in Iraq, terrorism, the Middle East. At school they hardly dealt with all that, he claimed — they just talked around it. "What do you mean by 'never put him back in prison'?" he asked. "Well, just that," I said. "Exactly what I said."

I looked at the principal. This gob of slime, who believed in global warming and the total eradication of all war and injustice, probably also subscribed to the belief that you could cure rapists and serial killers. That, after they'd had years of gabbing with a psychiatrist, you could allow them to take their first, shaky steps back into the real world.

The principal, who so far had been leaning back slightly in his chair, now leaned forward and placed both forearms — palms down, fingers spread — on his desk.

"If I'm not mistaken, you once worked in

teaching yourself?" he said.

The little hairs on the back of my neck and my tingling fingers had not betrayed me: when the lower intelligences are about to lose an argument, they grasp at other straws in order to justify themselves.

"I taught for a few years, yes," I said.

"That was at _____, wasn't it?" He mentioned the name of the school, a name that still produced mixed feelings in me, like the name of a disease of which you have been officially cured, but which you know could turn up any moment again in some other part of the body.

"Yes," I said.

"And you were placed on nonactive."

"Not exactly. I was the one who suggested that I take it a bit easier for a while. That I would come back later, when everything had calmed down a little."

The principal cleared his throat and looked at a piece of paper that was lying in front of him. "But, in fact, you didn't go back. In fact, you've been unemployed for twelve years."

"On nonactive. I could go back to work tomorrow, somewhere else."

"According to my information, though, the information _____ sent me, that depends on a psychiatric report. Whether or not you can go back to work. That decision, in other words, is not up to you."

Again, the name of that school! I felt the muscles beneath my left eye start to twitch. It was nothing, but others might interpret it as a tic. That's why I acted as though I had something in my eye: I rubbed it with my fingers, but the twitching only seemed to get worse.

"Oh, that doesn't really mean much," I said. "I assure you, I don't need a psychiatrist's signature in order to practice my profession."

The principal looked at the piece of paper again. "That's not what it says here . . . here it says . . ."

"Could I look at what you've got there in front of your face?" My voice was sharp, commanding, and left no room for misunderstanding. Still, the principal didn't do what I said right away.

"If you would let me finish," he said. "A few weeks ago I happened to run into a former colleague who works at _____ these days. I don't remember exactly how it came up . . . we were talking, I believe, about the pressure on teachers in general. About burnouts and nervous collapses. He mentioned a name that sounded familiar to me. I didn't know why at first, but then I thought of Michel. And then you."

"I've never had a burnout. That's just a trendy term. And I've absolutely never suffered a nervous collapse."

Now it was the principal's turn to blink, I saw. And even though it wasn't what you would have called a tic, not by any stretch of the imagination, still it was a sign of sudden weakness. Or, in fact: of fear. I wasn't aware of it myself, but perhaps there was something about my voice — I had spoken those last few sentences quite slowly, more slowly than before, in any case — something that made the warning lights start to flash in the principal's mind.

"But I didn't say that you'd had a burnout," he said.

He drummed with his fingers on the desk. And he blinked his eyes again! Yes, something had changed. The pedantic tone in which he'd tried to sell me his wishy-washy theories about capital punishment had disappeared as well.

I could smell it clearly now, above the odor of compost: fear. The way a dog can smell when someone is afraid, I detected a vague, sourish smell that hadn't been there before.

I believe that was the moment when I

started to get up from my chair. I don't remember exactly — there's a blank in there somewhere, a gap in time. I don't remember whether anything else was said. Whatever the case: suddenly I was on my feet. I had stood up from my chair and was looking down at the principal.

What happened after that had everything to do with the difference in elevation, with the fact that the principal was still sitting and I was looking down on him. Towering over him — that might be more like it. It's sort of an unwritten law, the way water runs to the lowest level or, to employ a canine analogy, the fact that the principal was at a disadvantage in his chair, that he found himself, as it were, in a position of submissive vulnerability. Dogs do the same thing: For years they let their owners feed and pet them. They're as gentle as lambs — they are really lovely animals. But then one day the owner suddenly loses his balance. He trips and falls. Within seconds, the dogs are on him. They sink their teeth into his neck and bite him to death — sometimes they even tear him completely to pieces after that. It's instinct: That which falls is weak. That which lies on the ground is prey.

"I insist that you show me that," I said, purely for the sake of formality, pointing at the piece of paper that was lying in front of the principal, and which he now covered with both hands. Purely a formality, because it was too late now to put anything right.

"Mr. Lohman," he said. Then I punched him squarely in the nose. Right away there was blood, lots of blood: it sprayed from his nostrils and spattered across his shirt and the desktop, and then on the fingers with which he pawed at his nose.

By that time I had come around the desk and hit him in the face again, lower down this time. His teeth hurt my knuckles as they broke off. He screamed. He shouted something unintelligible, but I had already pulled him up out of his chair. Undoubtedly, people would be alarmed by the principal's scream. Within thirty seconds the door to his office would fly open, but in thirty seconds you can do a lot of damage — thirty seconds seemed like enough to me.

"You dirty, filthy, stinking pig," I said, before simultaneously planting a fist in his face and a knee in his gut. But then I made a mistake. I hadn't thought it was possible that the principal would have any strength left. I thought I could calmly take him apart before the teachers burst in and put an end to the performance.

With great speed, he swung up his head

and butted me on the chin, then wrapped his arms around my calves and pulled, causing me to lose my balance and fall over backwards. "Fucking shit!" I yelled. The principal ran, not to the door, but to the window. He had it open before I could get to my feet. "Help!" he screamed out the window. "Help!"

But I was already on him. I grabbed him by the hair and pulled his head back, then brought it down hard on the windowsill. "We're not done yet!" I shouted in his ear.

There were a lot of people in the schoolyard, most of them students; it must have been lunch break. They all looked up — at us.

I picked the boy in the black cap out of the crowd almost immediately. There was something comforting, something reassuring, about seeing a familiar face amid all those other faces. He was standing in a little group, off to one side, close to the steps that led to the front entrance, along with a couple of girls and a boy on a scooter. The boy in the black Nike cap had a pair of headphones slung around his neck.

I waved. I remember that clearly. I waved to Michel, and I tried to smile. The wave and the smile were meant to show that, from out there, it probably looked worse than it was. That I'd had an argument with the principal about his, Michel's, essay, but that in the meantime everything had come closer to being sorted out.

41

"That was the prime minister," Serge said; he sat down and put his cell phone back in his pocket. "He wanted to know what the press conference was going to be about tomorrow."

Any one of the three of us could have asked at that point: "Well? What did you tell him?" But no one at the table spoke a word. Sometimes people allow silences like that to fall — when they don't feel like saying the obvious. If Serge had told a joke, a joke that started with a question (Why can't two Chinamen go to the barber at the same time?), a comparable silence would probably have ensued.

My brother looked at his *dame blanche,* which, probably out of courtesy, still had not been removed. "I told him that I didn't want to tell him anything about it, not yet, not this evening. He hoped it was nothing serious. Like me withdrawing from the race.

Those were his exact words: 'It would bitterly disappoint me, on both our behalves, were you to throw the towel in the ring at this point, seven months before the elections.' " Serge made an attempt to imitate the prime minister's accent, but so poorly that it seemed more like a crudely drawn version, a political cartoon badly traced, rather than the cartoon itself. "I told him the truth, that I'm still talking to my family. That I'm keeping a number of options open."

When the prime minister was only newly elected, the jokes had never stopped: about his appearance, his wooden way of speaking in public, his numerous — often literal — slipups. Since then, however, a process of habituation had taken place. You got used to it, like a stain on the wallpaper. A stain that seemed simply to belong there, and which could only surprise you by one day not being there at all.

"Oh, that's interesting," Claire said. "So you're keeping your options open. I thought it was all cut and dried for you. For all of us."

Serge tried to make eye contact with his wife, but she acted as though she were more interested in the cell phone on the table in front of her. "Yes, I'm keeping my options open," he said with a sigh. I want us to do this together. As . . . as a family."

"The way we've always done things," I said. I thought about the scorched macaroni *alla carbonara,* the pan I'd smashed in his face when he tried to take my son away, but apparently Serge's memory was not as keen as mine, because a warm smile actually appeared on his face.

"Yes," he said — he looked at his watch — "I have to . . . we really have to go now. Babette . . . What's taking so long with that check?"

Babette got up.

"Yes, let's go," she said; she turned to Claire. "Are the two of you coming?"

Claire held up her half-full glass of grappa. "Go ahead, both of you. We'll be there in a bit."

Serge held out his hand to his wife. I thought Babette was going to ignore him, but she didn't. She even offered Serge her arm.

"We can . . . ," he said. He was smiling, yes, almost beaming as he took his wife by the elbow. "We'll talk more about this later. We can have another at the café, and then we'll talk about it some more."

"That's fine, Serge," Claire said. "Just run along, the two of you. Paul and I will finish our grappa — then we'll be there."

"The check," Serge said. He patted his coat pockets, as though searching for a wallet or a credit card.

"Don't worry about it," Claire said. "It's taken care of."

And then they actually left. I watched as they walked toward the exit, my brother holding his wife by the arm. Only a few guests looked up or turned their heads as they passed. A process of habituation seemed to be taking place here as well; if you stayed in one place long enough, you became a face like all the rest.

As they passed the open kitchen, the man in the white turtleneck hurried up to them: Tonio — the name in his passport had to be Anton. Serge and Babette stopped. Hands were shaken. Waitresses came rushing over with their coats.

"Are they gone yet?" Claire asked.

"Almost," I said.

My wife knocked back the rest of her grappa. She laid her hand on mine.

"You have to do something," she said, applying a little pressure with her fingers.

"You're right," I said. "We have to stop him."

Claire took my hand now.

"*You* have to stop him," she said.

369

I looked at her.

"Me?" I said, even though I could feel something coming: something to which I might not be able to say no.

"You have to do something to him," Claire said.

I just stared at her.

"Something that will keep him from holding that press conference tomorrow," Claire said.

It was at precisely that moment, from somewhere close by, that a cell phone began to beep. First only a few quiet beeps, which grew louder and merged into a tune.

Claire looked at me questioningly. And I looked back. We both shook our heads at the same time.

Babette's phone was lying half hidden under her napkin. Automatically, I looked toward the exit first: Serge and Babette were gone. I put out my hand, but Claire was too quick for me.

She slid open the phone's cover and looked at the screen. Then she slid it closed. The peeping stopped.

"Beau," she said.

42

"His mother's too busy to talk to him right now," Claire said, putting the cell phone back where it had been. She even tucked it under the napkin.

I didn't reply. I waited. I waited to see what my wife was going to say.

Claire breathed a deep sigh. "Do you know that he . . ." She didn't finish her sentence. "Oh, Paul," she said. "Paul . . ." She tossed her head and shook back her hair. I saw a wetness in her eyes, something glistening, tears not of sorrow or despair, but of rage.

"Do you know that he what . . . ?" I said. Claire knew nothing about the videos, I'd been telling myself all evening. I still hoped I was right.

"Beau is blackmailing them," Claire said.

I felt a cold stab in my chest. I rubbed my hands over my cheeks, so that if I blushed it wouldn't give me away.

"Oh yeah?" I said. "What do you mean?"

Claire sighed again. She clenched her fists and drummed them on the tabletop.

"Oh, Paul," she said. "I wanted so badly to keep you out of this. I didn't want it to happen . . . for you to get upset. But now everything has changed. It's too late anyway."

"What do you mean, he's blackmailing them? Beau? With what?"

From under the napkin came a beep. A single beep this time. A little blue light was now flashing on and off on the side of Babette's cell phone: it looked as if Beau had left a message.

"He was there. At least, that's what he claims. He says he was planning to go home, but then he changed his mind and decided to go back. That's when he saw them. As they came out of that bank cubicle. He says."

The coldness in my chest was gone. I felt something new, a feeling almost like happiness. I had to be careful not to start grinning.

"And now he wants money. Oh, the hypocritical little prick! I always did . . . You did too, right? You thought he was horrid, you said one time. I remember that clearly."

"But does he have proof? Can he prove

372

that he saw them? Can he prove that Michel and Rick threw that gas can?"

That last question I asked only to reassure myself once and for all: the final check. Inside my head, a door had opened. A crack. And through that crack, light was shining. Warm light. Behind the door was the room with the happy family.

"No, he has no proof," Claire said. "But maybe he doesn't need it. If Beau were to go to the police and point to Michel and Rick as the culprits . . . The pictures from that security camera are awfully vague, but if they can compare them to real people . . . I don't know."

Your father doesn't know about any of this. You two have to do it tonight.

"Michel wasn't there, was he?" I said. "When you called him just now. When you kept asking Babette what time it was."

A smile appeared on Claire's face. She took my hand again and squeezed it.

"I called him. You all heard me get him on the line. I talked to him — Babette is the impartial witness who heard me talking to my son at a fixed point in time. They can check my phone's memory to see that that call was made and how long it lasted. All we have to do is erase the answering machine on the phone at home when we get back."

I looked at my wife. There must have been admiration in my look. I didn't even have to fake it. I really did admire her.

"And now he's with Beau," I said.

She nodded. "And with Rick. Not at Beau's house. They agreed to meet somewhere. Somewhere outside."

"And what are they going to talk to Beau about? Are they going to try to change his mind?"

My wife now laid her other hand on mine as well.

"Paul," she said. "I already told you that I wanted to keep you out of this. But we can't go back now. You and me. It's about our son's future. I told Michel that he should try to talk reason to Beau. And that if that didn't work, he should do whatever seemed best. I told him that I don't need to know what that is. He's going to turn sixteen next week. He doesn't have to wait for his mother to tell him everything. He's old and wise enough to decide for himself."

I stared at her. There may still have been admiration in my look, but it was a different type of admiration from a few minutes earlier.

"Whatever the case, it's better if you and I

374

can say that Michel was at home all evening," Claire said. "And if Babette can confirm that."

43

I called the manager over.

"We're still waiting for the check," I said.

"Mr. Lohman took care of it, sir."

It could have been my imagination, but it seemed as though he relished being able to say that to me. Something about his eyes, as though he were laughing at me only with his eyes.

Claire rummaged through her bag, pulled out her cell phone, looked at it, and put it back.

"It's too damn much, isn't it?" I said when the manager had left. "He claims our café. Our son. And now this. And the worst thing about it is, it doesn't mean anything. That he can pick up a check doesn't mean a goddamn thing."

Claire took my right hand, then my left.

"You only have to hurt him," she said. "He's not going to hold a press conference with a damaged face. Or a broken arm in a sling. That's too much to explain, all at the same time. Even for Serge."

I looked into my wife's eyes. She had just asked me to break my brother's arm. Or damage his face. And all that out of love, love for our son. For Michel. I had to think about that mother, years ago in Germany, who had shot and killed her child's murderer in the courtroom. That's the kind of mother Claire was.

"I haven't taken my medication," I said.

"Yes." Claire didn't seem surprised. She ran one fingertip gently across the back of my hand.

"I mean, not for a long time. It's been months."

It was true: shortly after that episode of *Opsporing Verzocht,* I had stopped. I had the feeling that I would be of less use to my son when my emotions were blunted, day in and day out. My emotions and my reflexes. If I wanted to help Michel to the fullest of my ability, I first had to recover my old self.

"I know," Claire said.

I looked at her.

"Maybe you think other people don't notice," Claire said. "Well, I mean other people . . . Your own wife — your own wife notices right away. There were things . . . that were different. The way you looked at me, the way you smiled at me. And then there was that time when you couldn't find your passport. Do you remember? When you started kicking your desk drawers? From then on, I began paying attention. You took your medication with you when you went out and threw it away somewhere. Didn't you? I took your trousers out of the wash one time — the pocket had turned completely blue! Pills you'd forgotten to throw away."

Claire had to laugh — she laughed only briefly, then looked serious again.

"And you didn't say anything," I said.

"At first I thought: what's he up to? But, suddenly, I saw my old Paul again. And then I knew: I wanted my old Paul back. Including the Paul who kicks his own desk drawers to bits. And that other time, when that scooter cut you off on the road. When you took off after it . . . ."

And that time you battered Michel's principal into the hospital, I thought Claire would say then. But she didn't. She said something else.

"That was the Paul I loved . . . that I love. That's the Paul I love. More than anything or anyone else in the world."

I saw something glistening in the corners

of her eyes. My own eyes were smarting now as well.

"You, and Michel of course," my wife said. "You and Michel I both love just as much. Together, you two are what make me the happiest."

"Yeah," I said. My voice sounded hoarse — it had a little squeak in it. I cleared my throat.

"Yeah," I said again.

We sat across from each other in silence like that for a while, my wife's hands still clasping mine.

"What did you say to Babette?" I asked.

"What do you mean?"

"In the garden. When the two of you went for a walk. Babette looked so happy when she saw me. 'Dear, sweet Paul' she called me. What did you say to her?"

Claire took a deep breath. "I told her you would do something. That you would do something to make sure that press conference didn't go ahead."

"And Babette thought that was okay?"

"She wants Serge to win the election. But what hurt Babette most was that he only told her about it in the car on the way over here. So that she wouldn't have enough time to talk him out of his nonsense."

"But here at the table, just now, she said —"

"Babette is smart, Paul. It wouldn't do for Serge to suspect anything later on. When Babette becomes the First Lady, maybe she'll hand out soup at a shelter for the homeless. But there is one homeless person about whom she cares as little as you or I do."

I pulled my hands away. That is to say, I pulled my hands from my wife's hands and clasped her hands in mine.

"It's not a good idea," I said.

"Paul . . ."

"No, listen. I'm me. I am who I am. I haven't been taking my pills. Right now, you and I are the only people who know that. But things like that get found out. They'll dig around, and they'll find out. The school psychologist, my being on nonactive, and then that principal at Michel's school . . . it would all be out on the table, like an open book. To say nothing of my brother. My brother will be the first to say that something like that, coming from me, doesn't surprise him at all. Maybe he won't say it out loud, but his little brother has done things to him before. His little brother who suffers from a syndrome he needs medication for. Pills, which he then flushes down the toilet."

Claire said nothing.

"He won't let anything I do change his plans, Claire. It would send the wrong signal."

I waited a moment. I tried not to blink.

"It would send the wrong signal if I did it," I said.

44

About five minutes after Claire left, I heard another beep coming from under Babette's napkin.

We'd both stood up at the same moment. My wife and I. I put my arms around her and held her against me. I buried my face in her hair. Very slowly, without making a sound, I breathed in through my nose.

Then I sat down again. I watched my wife go, until she disappeared from sight somewhere around the lectern.

I picked up Babette's phone, opened the cover, and looked at the screen.

2 new messages

I pressed Display. The first was a text message from Beau. It contained only one word. One word, without a capital and without a full stop: "mama."

I pressed Delete.

The second message said there was a voice mail message in her In-box.

Babette used a different carrier. I didn't know which number I needed to use for voice mail. On a hunch, I looked in Contacts, and under the *V* I found Voice Mail. I couldn't suppress a smile.

After the voice mail lady's announcement that there was one new message, I heard Beau's voice.

I listened. As I listened, I closed my eyes briefly once, then opened them again. I closed the cover. I didn't put Babette's cell phone back on the table, but stuck it in my pocket.

"Your son doesn't like restaurants like this?"

I was so startled that I sat bolt upright in my chair.

"Oh, excuse me," the manager said. "I didn't mean to frighten you. But I saw you talking to your son in the garden. At least, I assume it was your son."

At first, for a moment, I had no idea what he was talking about. But then, right away, I knew.

The smoking man. The man smoking outside the restaurant. The manager had seen Michel and me this evening, in the garden.

I felt no panic — to be honest, I felt absolutely nothing.

Only then did I see that the manager was holding a saucer, a saucer containing the bill.

"Mr. Lohman forgot to take the check with him," he said. "So I thought I'd give it to you. Perhaps you'll see him again before long."

"Yes," I said.

"I saw you standing there like that with your son," the manager said. "There was something in your posture. In both of your postures, I should say, something identical. Something you'd only see in a father and son, I thought."

I looked down at the saucer, the saucer with the check on it. What was he waiting for? Why didn't he go away, instead of hanging around here, blathering about people's postures?

"Yes," I said again. It was not meant as a confirmation of the manager's assumptions, only as a polite way to fill the silence. I had nothing else to say to him anyway.

"I have a son too," the manager said. "He's only five. But still, sometimes I'm surprised by how much he looks like me. How he does certain things exactly the way I do. Little gestures. I often touch my hair,

384

for example, twist it between my fingers when I'm bored, or worried about something . . . I . . . I also have a daughter. She's three — she's the spitting image of her mother. In everything."

I took the check from the saucer and looked at the total. I won't go into all the things you could do with a sum of money like that, or about how many days a normal person would have to work to earn it — if they weren't forced by the tortoise in the white turtleneck to spend weeks washing dishes in the open kitchen. And I won't mention the figure itself, the kind of sum that would make you burst out laughing. Which was precisely what I did.

"I hope you had an enjoyable evening," the manager said — but still he didn't go away. He brushed the edge of the empty saucer with his fingertips, slid it a few inches across the tablecloth, picked it up, and put it back down.

45

"Claire?"

For the second time that evening I opened the door of the ladies' room and called her name. But there was no answer. From somewhere outside I heard the sound of a police siren. "Claire?" I called again. I took a few steps forward, until I was past the vase of white daffodils, and noted that all the cubicles were empty. I heard the second siren as I walked past the cloakroom and the lectern to the exit, and then outside. Through the trees I could now see the flashing lights in front of the regular-people café.

A normal reaction would have been for me to walk faster, to start running — but I didn't. True, I felt something dark and heavy at the place where my heart should have been, but the heaviness was a calm heaviness. The dark feeling in my chest, too, had everything to do with a sense of inevitability.

My wife, I thought.

Again I felt a powerful urge to start running. To arrive at the café out of breath — where I would almost certainly not be allowed in.

My wife! I'd pant. My wife is in there!

And it was precisely that scene projected on my mind's eye that made me slow down. I reached the gravel path that led to the bridge. By the time I got there, I was no longer walking slowly in any natural sense — I could tell that by the sound my soles made on the gravel, by the pauses between my steps — I was walking in slow motion.

I put my hand on the balustrade and stopped. The flashing lights were reflected in the dark surface beneath my feet. Through the opening between the trees on the far side I now had a clear view of the café. Pulled up onto the curb, in front of the outdoor tables, were three police Volkswagens and an ambulance.

One ambulance. Not two.

It was pleasant to feel such calm, to be able to see all these things in this way — almost independently of each other — and to draw my own conclusions. I felt the way I had felt before at moments of crisis (Claire's hospitalization; Serge and Babette's failed attempt to take away my son;

the footage from the security camera): I had felt, and I felt again now, that from within my calmness I could take action. Promptly and efficiently.

I looked back toward the restaurant entrance, where a few waitresses had now gathered, apparently drawn by the sirens and flashing lights. I thought I also saw the manager there — at least I saw a man in a suit lighting a cigarette.

They probably couldn't see me from there, I thought for a moment, but then realized that a few hours ago I had actually seen Michel come cycling across this very bridge.

I had to move on. I couldn't stand still any longer. I couldn't run the risk of having one of the waitresses testify that she had seen a man on the bridge. "So weird. He was just standing there. Do you think that might be important?"

I took Babette's cell phone out of my pocket and held it above the water. At the sound of the splash, a duck came swimming up. Then I stepped away from the railing and began moving. No longer in slow motion, but at the most normal pace I could: not too slowly, not too fast. On the far side of the bridge, I crossed the bicycle path, looked to the left, and walked on to the tram stop. Some spectators had already gathered, not really a crowd at this hour, no more than twenty onlookers. To the left of the café was an alley. I made for the alley.

I had barely reached the curb when the café's swinging doors flew open, quite literally flew open with two loud bangs. A stretcher came out, a stretcher on wheels, pushed and pulled at each end by two paramedics. One of the paramedics at the back was holding up a plastic IV bag. Behind him came Babette. She wasn't wearing her glasses anymore and was pressing a handkerchief to her eyes.

The head of the person on the stretcher was the only thing sticking out from beneath the green sheet. I'd known it the whole time, in fact, but still I breathed a sigh of relief. The head was covered with compresses and gauze. Blood-stained compresses and gauze.

The paramedics pushed the stretcher through the liftback of the ambulance, which was already open and waiting. Two of them climbed in front, the other two in the back, along with Babette. The door closed and the ambulance raced away from the curb and turned right, toward the center of town.

The siren came on, which was a good sign.

Or not . . . it depended on how you looked at it.

I didn't have much time to think about the immediate future, though, because the swinging doors opened again.

Claire walked out between two uniformed officers. She wasn't handcuffed — in fact they weren't even holding her. She looked around — she searched the faces in the little crowd, looking for that one familiar face.

Then she found it.

I looked at her and she looked at me. I took a step forward, or at least my body betrayed the fact that I wanted to take a step forward.

It was at that moment that Claire shook her head.

Don't, she was saying. She was almost at one of the patrol cars already; the back door was being held open by a third policeman. I looked around quickly to see if anyone in the crowd might have noticed whom Claire had shaken her head at, but no one had eyes for anything but the woman being led to the patrol car.

When she arrived at the cruiser, Claire stopped for a moment. She searched for and found my eyes again. She made a movement with her head: to an outsider it might have looked as though she were simply ducking in order not to collide with the door, but to me Claire's head was unmistakably pointing in a given direction.

To something just behind her and to one side, to the alley, the shortest way to our house.

Home, my wife had said. Go home.

I didn't wait for the police car to drive away. I turned around and walked off.

46

What kind of tip are you supposed to leave at a restaurant where the bill makes you burst out laughing? I could remember our talking about that before, quite often, not only with Serge and Babette, but also with other friends with whom we'd eaten in Dutch restaurants. Let's say that after a dinner with four people you are asked to pay four hundred euros — mind you, I'm not saying our dinner cost four hundred euros — and you count on giving a tip of ten to fifteen percent. The logical consequence is that you'd be expected to leave behind a sum of no less than forty and no more than sixty euros.

A sixty-euro tip — I can't help it, it makes me giggle. I had to be careful at times like that: if I wasn't careful, it would make me burst out laughing all over again. A rather nervous laugh, like laughing at a funeral, or in a church, where you're supposed to be silent.

But our friends never laughed. "These people have to live off their tips, don't they?" a good friend said once during a meal at a comparable restaurant.

On the morning of our dinner, I had withdrawn five hundred euros from a cash machine. I had sworn to pay the entire bill, including the tip. I would do it quickly — I would lay the ten fifty-euro notes on the saucer before my brother had time to produce his credit card.

At the end of the evening, when I laid the remaining four hundred and fifty euros on the saucer anyway, the manager thought at first that I had misunderstood. He was about to say something. Who knows, maybe he was going to say that a one hundred percent tip was really too much of a good thing, but I beat him to the punch.

"This is for you," I said. "If you promise me that you never saw me with my son in the garden. Never. Not now. Not in a week's time. And not a year from now either."

Serge lost the election. At first there had been some voter sympathy for the candidate with the battered face. A glass of white wine — a glass of white wine broken off just above the stem, I should really say — leaves peculiar wounds. The way they heal is particularly peculiar, leaving lots of excrescences and blank patches where the old face never comes back. Over the first two months, they operated on him three times. After the final operation, he wore a beard for a while. Looking back on it now, I think the beard marked the turning point. There he stood, at the street market, at the construction site, outside the factory gates, handing out flyers in his windbreaker — with a beard.

Serge Lohman began to plummet in the polls. What had seemed like a done deal only a few months earlier now became a free fall. One month before the elections, Serge shaved off his beard. It was a final act of desperation. The voters saw the scarred face. But they also saw the empty areas. It's amazing, and in some sense unfair, what a damaged face can do to a person. You look at the blank patches and can't help wondering what used to be there.

The beard, though, was definitely the coup de grâce. Or rather: first the beard, then the shaving it off. When it was already too late. Serge Lohman doesn't know what he wants — that was the voters' conclusion — and they cast their votes for what they already knew. For the stain on the wallpaper.

Serge, of course, never pressed charges. To press charges against his sister-in-law, his brother's wife . . . that would indeed have given the wrong signal.

"I think he understands now," Claire said a few weeks afterwards at the café. "He said it himself: he wanted to solve this as a family. I think he understands now that some things simply have to stay within the family."

Whatever the case, Serge and Babette had other things on their minds. Things like the disappearance of their adopted son, Beau. They made a real effort. An ad campaign in newspapers and magazines, posters all over the country, and an appearance on the TV show *Missing.*

During the TV program, they played back the message Beau had left on his mother's voice mail before he went missing. Babette's cell phone was never recovered, but the message had been saved, although it had now taken on a different portent from the evening of our dinner.

"Mama, whatever happens . . . I just want you to know that I love you . . ."

You could say they moved heaven and earth in order to find Beau, but there were doubts as well. One of the opinion weeklies was the first to suggest that Beau might have grown tired of his adoptive parents, that he had returned to his native country. "Often, during 'the difficult years,' " the magazine wrote, "adopted children go looking for their natural parents. Or at least become curious about the place where they were born."

A newspaper dedicated a full-page article to the case, in which the question was publicly raised for the first time of whether biological parents would put more effort into looking for their child than adoptive parents did. Examples were given of adoptive parents with troubled children who finally distanced themselves from those children. The problems that accompanied the raising of such children were often due to a combination of factors. The inability to find a niche in a foreign culture was mentioned as the primary one, followed by the biological aspects: the "flaws" that those children had inherited from their natural parents. And, in the case of adoption at a more advanced age, the things that might have happened to the child before being absorbed into the new family.

I thought about that time in France, the party in my brother's garden. When the French farmers caught Beau stealing one of their chickens and Serge said that his children would never do something like that. *His* children, he had said, without drawing any distinction.

I was reminded again of an animal shelter. There too you have no idea what has happened to a dog or cat before you take it home with you, whether it has perhaps been beaten or locked up for days in a darkened cellar. It doesn't matter much in that case. If the dog or cat turns out to be unmanageable, you take it back.

At the end of the article, the writer wondered whether biological parents would tend to be less likely to distance themselves from an unmanageable or otherwise troubled child.

I knew the answer, but I gave the article to Claire to read first.

"What do you think?" I asked when she had finished. We were sitting at our little kitchen table, over the remains of breakfast. Sunlight was falling on our garden and on the kitchen counter. Michel had gone to soccer practice.

"I've often wondered whether Beau would have tried to blackmail his brother and cousin if he had really been a part of their family," Claire said. "Of course, natural brothers and sisters fight sometimes . . . sometimes they even refuse to see each

397

other anymore. But still . . . when it comes right down to it, in matters of life or death, then they're still there for each other."

Claire started laughing.

"What is it?" I asked.

"No, I just suddenly heard myself talking," she said, still laughing. "About brothers and sisters. And listen who I'm talking to!"

"Yeah," I said. I was laughing now too.

Then, for a little while, we said nothing. We only looked at each other now and then. As man and woman. As two parts of a happy family, I thought. Of course things had happened, but lately I had been reminded more often of a shipwreck. A happy family can survive a shipwreck. I'm not trying to say that the family will be happier afterwards, but in any case not unhappier.

Claire and I. Claire and Michel and I. We shared something. Something that hadn't been there before. All right, we didn't all share the same thing, but maybe that's not necessary. You don't have to know everything about each other. Secrets didn't get in the way of happiness.

I thought about that night, after our dinner. I had been alone in the house for a while before Michel got home. In our living room there is an antique wooden chest of drawers in which Claire keeps her things. Even as I opened the first drawer, I had the feeling I was going to do something that I would regret later.

I couldn't help thinking about when Claire had been in the hospital. At one point they had performed an internal examination on her while I was there. I sat in a chair beside her bed and held her hand. The doctor invited me over to look at the monitor while they put something into my wife — a tube, a catheter, a camera. I only looked for a moment before averting my eyes. It wasn't that the images were too much for me, or that I was afraid of fainting — no, it was something else. I don't have the right, I thought.

I was already on the point of stopping my search when I found what I was looking for. The top drawer contained a few old pairs of sunglasses, barrettes, and earrings she no longer wore. But the next drawer down was full of papers: a membership card for the tennis club, an insurance policy for her bicycle, an expired parking permit, and a window envelope with the name of a hospital in the lower left-hand corner.

The name of the hospital where Claire had been operated on, but also the hospital where Michel had been born.

"Amniotic fluid test" was printed across the top of the sheet of paper that I pulled from the envelope. Right below that were two little boxes, one with "boy," the other "girl."

The box with "boy" had been checked.

Claire had known that we were going to have a boy — that was the first thing that came into my mind. But she had never told me. What's more, we had gone on coming up with girls' names until the day before she went into labor. There was never any question about a boy's name: that had been "Michel" years before Claire even got pregnant. But in the event of a girl, we were still wavering between "Laura" and "Julia."

There was a whole column of handwritten figures on the form. A few times I also saw the word "good."

Close to the bottom, under the heading "details," was a box of about two by four inches. That box was completely filled by the same, almost illegible hand that had written the figures and checked the box that said "boy."

I started to read. And stopped again right away.

This time it wasn't that I felt I didn't have the right. No, it was something else. Do I need to know this? I thought. Do I want to know this? Will it make us happier as a family?

Beneath the box with the handwritten account were two smaller boxes. "Decision physician/hospital" was printed beside one of them, and "Decision parents" beside the other.

The box with "Decision parents" had been checked.

Decision parents. It didn't say "Decision parent" or "Decision mother." It said "Decision parents."

Those are the two words I will carry with me from now on, I thought as I folded the form back into the envelope and tucked it under the expired parking permit.

"Decision parents," I said to myself out loud as I closed the drawer.

After he was born, everyone, including Claire's parents and other members of her immediate family, said that Michel was the spitting image of me. "A copy!" the visitors to the recovery room cried out as soon as Michel was lifted from his cot.

Claire had to laugh about it too. The resemblance was too strong to deny. Later things changed slightly. As he grew older, you could, with a healthy effort and a dose of goodwill, also detect some of his mother's features. His eyes in particular, and something in that little space between nose and upper lip.

A copy. After I closed the drawer, I went and listened to the answering machine.

"Hi, sweetheart!" I heard my wife's voice say. "How are you doing? You're not too bored, are you?" In the silence that followed then I could clearly hear the sounds of the restaurant: the murmur of human beings, a plate being piled onto another plate. "Okay, we're just going to drink our coffee. We'll be home in about an hour. So you have time to clean up your own mess. What did you have for dinner . . . ?"

Again, silence. "Yes . . ." Silence. "No . . ." Silence. "That's right."

I was familiar with the menu on our home phone. If you pressed the three, the message would be erased. My thumb was already resting on the three.

"Bye, dearest, love you."

I pressed it.

Half an hour later, Michel came home. He kissed me on the cheek and asked where Mama was. I told him she'd be home a little later, that I would explain it all soon. The knuckles of Michel's left hand were barked, I noticed. He was left-handed, just like me, and on the back was a rivulet of dried blood. Only then did I look at him from head to toe. I saw blood on his left eyebrow as well. There was dried mud on his coat and even more mud on his white tennis shoes.

I asked him how it had gone.

And he told me. He told me that "Men in Black III" had been taken down from You-Tube.

We were still standing in the hallway. At a certain point, halfway through his story, Michel stopped and looked at me.

"Dad!" he said.

"What? What is it?"

"Now you're doing it again!"

"What?"

"You're laughing! You did that then, too, the first time I told you about the cash machine. You remember? Up in my room? When I told you about the desk lamp, you started laughing, and when I got to the gas can, you were still laughing."

He looked at me. I looked back. I looked into my son's eyes.

"And now you're laughing again," he said. "You want me to go on? Are you sure you want to hear everything?"

I didn't say anything. I just looked.

Then Michel took a step forward. He threw his arms around me and hugged.

"Dear old Dad," he said.

ABOUT THE AUTHOR

Herman Koch is the author of seven novels and three collections of short stories. *The Dinner,* his sixth novel, has been published in twenty-five countries, and was the winner of the Publieksprijs Prize in 2009. He currently lives in Amsterdam.